Daniel Raybould dropped out of music college and started writing stories at the age of seventeen, after only having become interested in reading less than a year before. He quickly became very passionate about writing, and by the age of nineteen he had finished his first story. Though he felt it was quite rough around the edges, but at the time he was unsure how to solve this problem, he decided to send it to a publishers. They accepted. Since the age of seventeen he has become passionate about all arts.

To Jesus, Bob, Brod and Bobbit.

Daniel Raybould

THE VOICE OF HIGH HOPE AND WIND

AUSTIN MACAULEY PUBLISHERS™

LONDON ★ CAMBRIDGE ★ NEW YORK ★ SHARJAH

A CIP catalogue record for this title is available from the British Library.

ISBN 9781528988315 (Paperback)
ISBN 9781528988322 (ePub e-book)

www.austinmacauley.com

First Published (2021)
Austin Macauley Publishers Ltd
25 Canada Square
Canary Wharf
London
E14 5LQ

Part 1
Volume 1
Planet Suberailn

Chapter 1
Hippopokerypopotamus?
Present Days

Ranglu and Fellei were in Swoolah, a unique tavern that they liked. They were sitting beside each other alone in a cosy four-person booth, their feet up on the metal table beside their almost finished drinks. A flute player and a lute player played a fun tune, on a raised semi-circle stage. The flutist wore a long, thin and dramatic dark-red coat that reached his pointed, upward curving black boots. The lute player wore a dark-green long coat. He had dark skin and big, bright-blue eyes. A single tentacle rose out the right side of his head. The other musician was tanned with wholly black eyes. He had slicked back black hair.

The song they played danced away in the back of the lovers' heads, as they talked about nothing. "Much shit," as they would say.

"Interesting how the leather is red, isn't it?" Fellei remarked looking at the single chair which curved around the dimly lit booth.

Ranglu nodded. "Yes."

"No red animals…that you can make leather from," she explained.

"I understood why it was interesting."

Fellei nodded, her dark eyebrows furrowed.

"Do you think someone would notice if we suddenly burst into flames?" asked the dark-blonde, shorthaired, tanned young man.

"Did we die?" the brown-haired, tanned young woman questioned.

"It's likely."

"And how did we die?"

"Someone shot us."

"So the flames didn't kill us?"

Ranglu shook his head in reply.

"Who shot us?"

"Twenty dwarves."

"Every one of them?"

The nineteen-year-old man nodded. "Real blood bath."

The nineteen-year-old woman made a disgruntled face. "So the fire happened before the dwarven army attacked us?" she asked.

"Correct."

"I think someone would probably notice."

"Interesting words."

"Absolutely fascinating scenario you conjured up just then," she complimented.

He nodded.

Suddenly, all the lights went out and the music tumbled to a stop. Some friendly, some sarcastic, some rude, some curious and some nervous shouts, mumbles, questions and chatterings filled Swoolah. Then only moments later, the power came back on and all seemed to swiftly return to normal.

"Probably ninja dwarves," Ranglu mused.

"Most definitely." Fellei smiled. "Crafty bastards."

The young man laughed a little at this.

"I like it when the power goes out," Fellei decided. "Keeps the adrenaline pumping. It's like jumping off a cliff when you have nothing to stop you from smashing into the ground far below."

"I would imagine the feelings created by such events are identical," Ranglu agreed.

"And so the sun set on a fresh eve."

"And so it did…"

The inn was very large, the big circular bar sat in the middle of it. It wasn't too busy tonight. It was pleasant. Beings of varying kinds had drinks, ate food and talked, laughed, argued and expelled wind as the evening rolled on.

Later on that evening – it would technically be morning very soon – after much more of the same kind of chatter, the two lovers left the tavern and began the walk home in the deep-violet tinted darkness of night. The single, deep-violet moon – that often glowed a little paler – was watching from above, surrounded by bright, beautiful stars.

Where they were now – not far away from the tavern, Swoolah – the ground was rocky and sandy, and a cliff face rose on their left. They were walking on a path, heading neither up nor down at this point, as far as they could tell.

"Your mother will not be pleased by those dirty boots of yours," Fellei commented, looking down at her partner's black, scuffed, dirty and sandy boots.

"At least I have a mother," he returned.

She laughed out loud. "Good lord man," said she, a tiny bit surprised. Ranglu was chuckling away.

"She was probably very ugly," he added and began laughing again. "If your face is anything to go by." He met Fellei's eyes which were trying not to smile. Her mouth was moving but nothing was coming out.

"Oh dear," said Ranglu, shaking his head. "What a night, eh?" The young woman still couldn't think of anything to say. The green-eyed man made a line with his mouth.

"You're mud," she mumbled, giving up on thinking of anything better. He smiled, took her hand and bit it. They both chuckled for a few moments. A man wearing a hooded cloak passed them on their right – beyond him was a drop that was a little treacherous to traverse but not for those like Fellei and Ranglu who had traversed up and down it many times – they both shivered unintentionally.

"He had a real bad...aroma," Fellei quietly said moments later.

"Indeed."

"Do you—" she began slowly.

"I don't know. Felt pretty...dark though," the young man interrupted, knowing what she was going to ask.

She nodded. "Anyway, it's probably best I don't let any such thoughts linger in my head. Probably nothing. And nothing we could do anyway."

"Indeed, young lady," he replied brightly. "Let us not...linger like...vermin but venture forth...like the...mighty snail."

"I reckon you just shot straight out of your mother's womb and smacked into a wall head first."

Ranglu chuckled. "That's a funny image."

He began to sing.

A womb and a dragon once met.
What an interesting show it was.
One had legs. The other had none.
Oh what an interesting show it was...

A short while later, the two came to a stop and looked down the drop to a village named, Hushn. Then they began to make their way down a manmade path which there were a few of upon the rocky hill. The moon was bright enough for them to be able to see clearly enough without any torches or anything of the sort. And soon, they were entering the village, made of uniquely designed homes and a pleasant atmosphere. There were now some warm hanging lamps lighting their path, as they weaved their way to Ranglu's home.

They walked up to a large, round, wooden door. Ranglu took out a large, rusty iron key from his pocket, put it in the large keyhole and twisted. A deep click sounded. Then he twisted the large, hanging, horse hoof shaped iron handle and entered with Fellei close behind him. They both immediately halted. The square room was glowing ever so slightly violet but also the tiniest bit red. A dark, rectangular, wood table sat in the middle of the room as it usually did but on top of that table was something unusual. A small stone that was longer than it was wide and pointed at its ends. The stone was dimly, faintly glowing, but in the darkness of the room, it was obvious. Ranglu's father, Falsen, entered the room. His shocked expression quickly disappeared when he realised who was in his house.

"Shut the door, son. I don't want any Moon Worshipers seeing this."

Ranglu did so, then asked, "And what is this?"

"This is a Moon Stone I believe. I found it." He grinned, looking a little mad with scruffy, brown hair and wide, brown eyes.

Ranglu looked around the large, stonewalled room. The curtains were closed over the one window in this room, the window located relatively close to the front door. "Why's it also glowing red?" he asked. "I thought they just glowed the colour of the moon?"

"Red Moon," answered Fellei. The young man looked at her questioningly. "Tomorrow there's going to be a Red Moon."

"Oh," he said. "Well, don't look at me like I'm dumb. How would I know?"

"You are dumb, son," said Falsen.

"You're dumb," he returned.

"Good one."

"So the stone somehow is...I don't know...anticipating the Red Moon? That's probably not the right way to put it but you know what I mean," Fellei asked, walking closer.

"Something like that," replied the older, skinny but strong man. "I'm honestly not sure at all how it all works but I plan on figuring it out."

"I assume Mother's asleep?" asked Ranglu.

"Indeed, Rang," she said, "yes, that's very lovely, dear. Good bye now."

"It's because she doesn't love you."

The older man laughed. "Neither of us loves you."

"That's debatable."

"It's fact."

"What discoveries have you made so far?" the son asked, moving and leaning in close to the stone.

"Zilch, my son."

"Very good."

"I've just been staring at it for a while. Hoping something might happen."

The young man looked to Fellei and met her eyes. "Can you do some hippopokerypopotamus?"

She smiled. "Like?"

"I don't know. Anything. Just to see if it reacts in any way."

"Okydoky." Her black boots moved unsurely upon the stone floor as she thought.

"Of course…you know…do something…gentle," advised Falsen.

Fellei pulled out a simple, elegant wooden chair and took a seat at the table. She closed her eyes and began to empty her mind yet concentrate at the same time. Concentrate on interlocking with what she called the Spirit. People of different religions or no religion at all called it different things and thought of it differently but she knew the Spirit to be the spirit which flowed through, inside and outside of everything that is not dark. This was a different thing to the energy that scientists talked about. This was Spirit, something that not all believed was real. She began to call upon it silently, calmly in her head. "Spirit come." She started to feel an unexplainable sensation. As Ranglu watched, the stone began to ever so slightly lift off the table. Fellei was reaching out to the stone through the Spirit, with the Spirit. Eyes still closed, the colour red started to fill her vision. It got brighter and brighter. The stone rose higher. Then suddenly, she could see beings dressed in deep-violet cloaks, their hoods shadowing their bowing faces. The moon was full and red, shining upon the gathered crowd of beings. Other men appeared. Loud, mouthy, ignorant folk. They began shouting and shoving at the hooded beings. At first, they were ignored but then, one hooded one retaliated. The cloaked being placed their hand upon one of the men's chest. It looked as if pure blackness then burst out of the being's palm, sending the man flying backwards, his back struck into an innocent girl who looked to be around thirteen years of age. She had red hair, blue eyes and dark skin. The girl fell, and her head struck the rocky ground hard.

Fellei jolted from out of her state. She had been still before, only her face moving, showing small emotions. The stone dropped violently. After she had been questioned, she told them what had happened.

Fellei and Ranglu exited the room through an empty arched doorway and entered the circular kitchen which also had a grey stone floor. Then they turned and went through another empty doorway and down a curving staircase. At the end of the staircase was a door which led into Ranglu's bedroom. It was a large room filled with much stuff. There were bits of machinery and technology both old and new, strange looking objects he had found and collected over the years, stones, parts, a weapon or two and so on. Needless to say, he liked his room. Fortunately, Fellei liked it also for she too was a collector. Though her hoard looked slightly different to Ranglu's, for she had looked for, found and collected objects of more ancient kinds over the years. Ancient things were her main interest. She got this from both her mother, now sadly deceased, and her father who themselves, in a way, were rare and ancient beings – not in age. This meant Fellei too was a rare and ancient being. Recently, she had been discovering more and more about all of this.

Ranglu tossed a metal ball to Fellei and after she had dropped her unique, sheathed sword and he had dropped his sheathed Lightpistol to the ground, they turned the lights off and flopped onto the double bed which had a beautiful wooden headboard with pictures of mountains engraved into its wood, a path running up the middle of them. The beds end posters were feathers. The young woman then put the metal ball to her lips. She breathed a word softly upon it and threw it into the air. It sounded as if it burst in the pitch black. At first, there was nothing but then it was as if stars began to appear and there was no longer a roof above, not far away, but a dark sky above, very far away. More stars and galaxies appeared the longer they looked…

"So cheesy," Fellei mumbled.

"Mmm," Ranglu agreed.

They soon fell into a deep sleep.

Chapter 2
You...know...

Fellei woke. Her eyes opened and filling her vision was Ranglu's face.

"Disgusting," she muttered to herself. Slowly, she sat up and leant her back against the headboard. She pulled her pillow up behind her, so it was comfier. "Stira," she said out loud. The stars above disappeared. The metal ball dropped onto the bed. The normal ceiling was above now. Fellei flicked the light switch located on the wall beside the bed. The young lady closed her eyes for a long moment, then opened them again. After looking at her palms, she slapped herself and then chuckled quietly. "Boy!" she shouted suddenly. Ranglu stirred and opened his eyes. He looked up at her. She was looking ahead.

"Good mmm," he mumbled, not aware that she was the reason he was awake.

"Good mmm," the young woman replied.

Ranglu looked down at his body and legs. "Oh good," he said.

Fellei nodded. "No sleep undressing."

"Always a fear," he told her.

"I imagine it is quite frightful."

There was a knock at the door. Both of them looked to the golden handle, shaped like a roaring dragon.

"Yes, wench?" Ranglu called.

His father entered, scruffy headed. "Would you like to journey with me? To a door shaped large rock I found with a hole in it?"

"What?" asked his son.

"I found a rock with a hole in it shaped like a door."

"The hole is shaped like a door," said Fellei like it was a statement.

"No," said Ranglu. "Sssshhhhh."

"The hole is not a rock," added his father.

"What?"

"There's a hole in a rock."

"And the rock is shaped like a door."

"Yeah."

"Good god."

"Well, you're both already dressed so come on," Falsen said.

"Now?" questioned Ranglu, his head still on his pillow.

"Why not."

"Let thy children eat first."

"Okay. Hurry up," said Falsen.

"You got it, you son of a bitch."

His father left.

"I feel quite nasty," Fellei stated. She was in the clothes she wore all of yesterday and she hadn't stayed clean or sweat free.

"You are nasty." He got out of bed and left the room shutting the door behind him. Fellei looked at the door for a couple of seconds, frowned and then followed him out.

"You have good sex?" asked Ranglu's mother – Unela – as he entered the circular kitchen. His eyes went wide. He said nothing. Fellei appeared behind him. She walked past, slapping him on the back of the head. He frowned at his mother who was still keeping eye contact.

"Sex was great," said Fellei out of the blue. Ranglu looked at her, eyes wide again.

"You both look quite dishevelled, my little ones," the mother commented, moving on. The young man scratched his head still standing on the same spot. Fellei and Unela now had their backs to him. "Yes. I don't feel pretty," the young woman replied, pouring herself some water from the tap. She swiftly downed the glass of water.

Ranglu's mouth opened, then closed again.

His father entered. "Ready?"

"No, Father, you toe. My mother just asked me, how was sex?" He put on a voice.

"Oh, that's a different kind of question, dear," the father said looking at his wife. Fellei nearly spat out the water she was drinking more of. She snorted and began to laugh. Ranglu tried not to smile. The other two were smiling.

"Eat some food please," Falsen told them in a mellow fashion. "Be speedy."

This is what they did. They whipped up some grub, ate it, then left the kitchen, walked down the curving steps but not all the way to the bottom where Ranglu's bedroom was. Not even halfway. Just down a small number of steps and then they stepped to the left, through a door, into a bathroom. There they washed their faces with water, brushed their teeth and that was it. They left the house having barely looked at themselves in the mirror and hopped in a four-seater vehicle which was dark-green and black. It had a pointed dark green nose, a wide, neither thin nor chunky green-and-black striped middle and a dark green, big back end. It didn't look too heavy though. It looked quite light.

The three sat in the three black front seats, side by side, one seat remained behind in the middle. The father started it up and the vehicle's wheels disappeared into the body and the Hoat – this is what they called the vehicles. Hoat was short for hovering boat – began to hover above the sandy ground. In one direction were more houses, in another were more houses and the hill Fellei and Ranglu had climbed down the night before. In the opposite were more houses and then a drop down. But Falsen drove in the remaining direction where there were few houses, no hills, no drops, just flat, rocky and sandy ground which opened up more and more the further they went.

Ranglu sniffed Fellei's shoulder as the wind – which their speed was mostly creating – blew against them. He scrunched his nose. The young lady looked at him and frowned. She sniffed his shoulder and mimicked fainting, falling limp against him. Ranglu's father wasn't noticing their antics. He was looking out ahead, the wind in a way making his hair look slightly more orderly. The sun was shining; the sky was blue with a good few white clouds drifting around. The father drifted right and headed for the rock walls and rising land over there.

They slowed when they reached these sand-coloured rocks that made a sort of small wall. Above and behind them were more rocks and above and behind them were more. Though it was all very much, easily climbable. Falsen stopped the Hoat, took the quite-big key out of the keyhole and put it in a large button-up pocket in his grey trousers. He hopped out without saying anything and the other two followed him. They clambered up the rocks quietly, enjoying themselves, looking for a rock that looked like a door and had a hole in it.

Ranglu started chuckling to himself as they clambered. "Is this literally just a rock with a hole in it, Father?" he questioned. Falsen looked at him and raised his eyebrows.

"Who bloody knows, son?"

Ranglu bobbed his head and carried on.

"It should be somewhere…" Falsen mumbled. "There." He pointed.

The two young ones looked. They could see a rock the size and shape of a door with what might have been a hole a little above and to the right of its centre.

"And there it is!" exclaimed Ranglu.

"And there it is," Fellei agreed.

They walked over a bed of some sharp, some more easy to traverse rocks. Falsen nearly twisted his ankle a couple of times but he was fine. And finally, they reached the rock.

"Now," said the father, looking at the two of them. "Put your arm through the hole."

"Ladies first," said Ranglu. "Actually no," he said stepping forward. "I don't want you getting…hurt."

Fellei's mouth turtled – the ends of her lips curved downwards. "Oh…that's sweet."

Ranglu walked up to the rock and stuck his hand through. Falsen gestured for Fellei to look around the back of the door. She did so. Her eyes widened.

"What?" questioned the young man.

"Nothing," answered the girl. "Your hands just disappeared."

"What?" he repeated, moving to look around the door, his arm going further through the hole. "Oh…" There was no sign of his arm or hand anywhere. Something different than air touched his hand. He whipped it out of the hole, banging it in the process. "Ow," he said.

"What happened?" asked Falsen, looking at him with wide eyes.

"Something touched my hand."

Fellei frowned and stuck her arm through the other side. The two men stared at her with raised eyebrows. She was still for a moment. Then her hand came darting back out. Falsen was next to give it a go.

A little, furry, pitch black being with large – disproportionate to the rest of him – white and black eyes watched as another hand appeared through the hole in the dark tree trunk. The forest around him was deep green and deep blue. Running water and the sound of creatures calling sounded throughout this forest. Angelfole was its name. It was never bright there; it was never truly dark either. The light was always the same deep, enchanting blue and green. The little being named Nimb reached out a furry paw and touched the hand. The hand didn't disappear this time. It just retracted a little in a sudden fashion which made Nimb jump again. The little creature hopped forward and went to sniff the hand. The hand stayed for a moment, then disappeared through the hole in the trunk.

Falsen shivered and made strange noises. "That's creepy, son!" he exclaimed.

Ranglu laughed. "I know!"

"Well, what do we do?" Falsen questioned.

"I don't know," he answered, raising his hands in the air.

Fellei gave it another go.

A hand came through and started wriggling around. Nimb hit it with a furry black topped, and a white palmed paw – the palm similar to a cat's palm in appearance – his two eye lids blinking horizontally, meeting in the middle. The hand went still. Nimb's eyes got smaller, he bent down, watching, getting ready to pounce. He pounced and embraced the hand, latching on.

A shocked expression showed on Fellei's face. She ripped her hand out and began shaking it around. Nimb held on for dear life. Fellei made a sudden, risky decision and stopped flailing about. They all stared at the black furry thing that was attached to her. It was small. Fellei knelt down and put her hand to the ground. She pushed at the thing. It wouldn't budge. She started to worry again, pushing harder. Falsen took out his Lightpistol. Suddenly, Nimb's head shot up and he looked at Fellei. He stayed very still as did she. Very slowly, he let go and began to back away on the rocks.

Ranglu raised his eyebrows at the thing when it looked at him. The mostly black and a little white creature looked back at the young woman and then stopped. He frowned. He cautiously walked over and slowly placed a paw on her arm. She was still kneeling. After a moment, he began to purr. Seconds later, he was leant up against her skin. His fur felt soft and lovely. It seemed he was going to sleep. They all watched it silently. Fellei slowly scooped it up and held it in her two hands. It had curled up into an impressively small ball.

"It's a Boob," she told them.

"What?" Ranglu replied.

"It's a Boob I think. I've read about them. They're basically a toy teddy bear. They don't eat, and they have no teeth or claws. They couldn't really hurt a fly. Nobody really knows anything else about them as far as I know."

"Well, we've discovered where they come from," said Ranglu. He looked the door up and down. Then he put his arm through the hole. The back of his hand touched something, and he whipped it back out, making uncomfortable noises.

"Do we put it back through the hole?" asked Fellei.

"That's probably right," Falsen agreed. Fellei nodded and stepped closer to the rock, reaching out to put the creature through. Seeing how tightly it could curl up, she knew getting it through wouldn't be a problem. But as Nimb got close to the hole, his head sprung up and he leapt onto the top of Fellei's head. She stood very still. "Nimb," he said. His voice was sweet and childlike. "Nimb," he repeated. "Nimb…no…Nimb…you…language…feel…language…stay …you."

"I'm not certain," Ranglu began. "But the little fellow might want to stay with you."

Nimb looked at Rang and slowly nodded. "Stay…you…" he touched Fellei's face as he said, "you."

"You…feel…you…feel…you…are…you…know…feel…stay…"

"Okay," said Fellei softly. She held her hands up for him to climb on too. He did. Slowly, she reached her hands towards the hole again. Nimb jumped back onto her head. He jumped down onto her shoulder and said, "Stay," quietly in her ear.

"Okay," she replied. She looked to Ranglu and his father and raised her eyebrows. "What do we do?"

"Ummm…"

No one was sure of what to do. They ended up driving back to Ranglu and Falsen's home. They parked the Hoat up outside the house beside Fellei's and Ranglu's Hoats and then entered. They took a seat at the table and placed Nimb on top. Ranglu fetched him a bowl of water. He started drinking, a small white tongue flicking from his mouth. He seemed happy.

Ranglu's mother was standing at the end of the table watching this rather cute new creature.

"The eyes are a little creepy," she commented.

"They're awesome," Ranglu replied.

"So it is called a Boob? And you think its name is Nimb?" Nimb looked up at her as she said this and smiled his tiny smile that could hardly be seen.

"Oh," she said, surprised. "Nimb," she repeated. The creature bobbed its head.

"I…Nimb."

She leant closer and poked a finger out towards him. As it approached, Nimb watched it suspiciously and then slapped it suddenly. The mother brought her hand back and exhaled in amusement. "Lord, you're sweet."

"It has a very cool tongue," Falsen commented.

Ranglu and Fellei nodded in agreement.

"So it seemed to attach itself to you, Fellei? As in, it seemed to really like you?" the mother asked curiously.

"It did," she replied, looking up to her from her chair.

"Any ideas why? Apart from the fact you are of course a lovely woman."

"Debatable," interjected Ranglu.

Fellei frowned. "I don't know why. It was saying something about me feeling and knowing."

"I wonder if it urinates," Falsen wondered out loud.

"And how," Ranglu added.

"Maybe it doesn't," said Fellei. "Somehow someone figured out that they don't need to eat. So if that is actually true, then maybe they have some strange insides that mean he doesn't go to the loo...I hope he doesn't go to the loo. It would make things easier."

"Toilet?" asked Ranglu, leaning down to the mostly black and a little white being. Nimb looked at him. "Wee?" Ranglu gestured. "Urinate?"

Nimb hopped into the bowl of water and then hopped back out. He looked down to the area beneath his legs. He gestured at his lower area, looking at Ranglu.

"That's right," said Falsen exhaling in disbelief and amusement. Ranglu nodded, unable not to grin. Then Nimb shook his head. He gestured at his lower area again and shook his head.

"You...do...not...urinate," Ranglu went through the actions. Nimb shook his fluffy head. "No...urinate."

"What a fascinating being," commented Falsen. "He's intelligent. He must be insanely intelligent unless someone has taught him Awne in the past" – Awne was the name of the language Falsen and the rest of them spoke. It was called Awne here anyway, not everywhere – Nimb looked at them all, still dripping.

"What is it little one?" asked the dar-blonde haired, Unela.

"History," he answered. "History...change...forever...future..."

Fellei's eyebrows furrowed. Nimb wandered over to her and put both of his paws on her hand. "History...change...forever...future...feel."

Chapter 3
True Hope

After washing and getting changed into a pair of grey trousers and a creamy white shirt, Ranglu walked through the kitchen area, through the dining area and through a door on the opposite wall to the front door. He walked through his mother and father's bedroom and then reached the biggest room in the house, the workshop. He closed the circular door behind him.

Nimb and Falsen looked up to him. The Boob was standing in the middle of a large, metal desk that had a lot of stuff neatly laid out on it. He was in the middle of all the stuff, where Falsen had made an empty area for him to stand in. Falsen was sitting on a chair, facing him.

"He can't hold tools. He doesn't really have big enough hands or any fingers…"

"I could have told you that," Ranglu replied.

"I know but you never know. He might have been able to grow fingers or something, maybe."

Nimb pressed a paw to the handle of a screwdriver. Falsen made a line with his mouth. "Sorry, chum."

The creature looked to Ranglu and began walking over his way, clambering over things. "Be careful," the young one said, reaching his hands down towards the creature. Nimb happily stepped onto the hands, then the young man brought him up and the creature got onto his shoulder. Nimb looked towards the large object that was sitting in the middle of the room.

He lifted a paw and asked, "What?"

"Oh, do you want to be a pilot?" asked Ranglu with a smile, walking over to the object and pulling the cover off. "It's a ship. A spaceship. It can just about fit two people. I'm sure you could squeeze in also."

The creature hopped onto the clear, slanted top and looked in. He then hopped onto the dirty white body which was quite thin, width wise. One dirty white wing came out of either side. The body widened out at the back.

Ranglu pressed hard on a small segment – that currently responded only to the touch of flesh – on the dirty white nose area beneath the clear, slanted top. The top opened. It would be guesswork finding the segment unless you knew where it was. He then pulled the top up further and looked to Nimb, gesturing at the front black chair. Nimb jumped in excitedly and stared, seemingly in awe at all the things that were in front of him. He would have been hard to spot if it wasn't for the white on his coat and in his eyes. He jumped onto the black steering wheel which had two sides going vertically up and down. Then a middle area between the two sides – the two sides grew taller and went lower than the middle area. He looked over all the switches and buttons and looked to Ranglu. He gestured at the chair... "S...sit..." Ranglu smiled and got in. Falsen was watching, intrigued. The young man grabbed the steering wheel and smiled at the creature. Nimb patted the middle of the wheel with his paw.

"History...change...forever...future..." he told him. Falsen's eyebrows furrowed, as did his son's. Before Ranglu could ask his question, the creature put his paw to his own mouth. "Ssshh," he said. Then he smiled, opening his dark mouth.

"Future...look...feel...know...a...voice...of...high...hope...and...wind...in... your...sails. In...her...sails...in...her...sails." He put a paw to his mouth again. "Ssshh." He smiled. "Red...moon...look..."

"Red moon?" Ranglu asked. "Look tonight?"

The creature just furrowed its invisible eyebrows in reply.

"We'll have to try and teach you to be a little less cryptic," Ranglu said with a smile. The creature didn't say anything, his attention had been lost. He jumped onto the young man's head and then into the back seat. After padding around for a moment, he hopped onto the chair's shoulder and then onto the ship's body. Ranglu got out and closed the slanted top.

"Name?" asked the creature, jumping up and down. The young man looked to his father. "It doesn't really have one," said Falsen, talking about the ship. Ranglu thought for many seconds.

"Tatter," he thought out loud.

"Because it's tattered looking? That's very imaginative, Ranglu."

"Tattermoath," he tried again.

"Sure."

"Cool. I like that. Tattermoath. Its name is Tattermoath," he told Nimb. The creature grinned and jumped up and down.

"He's proud of you," said Falsen. Ranglu laughed. "Hop on," he told Nimb, gesturing. He said it again when the creature was looking his way. To his surprise, Nimb made his way to his shoulder and the young man covered the ship back up. He took the Boob back to the desk and it jumped back on and looked between the two men. The door opened behind and to the side of Ranglu. Fellei entered.

"I've named the ship Tattermoath," he told her.

She scrunched up her nose, then looked to Nimb who was hopping up and down and grinning, showing no teeth for he had none.

"All right," she said, her lips curving upwards.

Later that day while Falsen and Unela babysat Nimb, the two lovers returned to the rock door with the hole in it...

Ranglu looked into the hole. He could see the sandy rocks that truly were on the other side of the door. He stuck his arm through. It disappeared.

"Are we sure this is the right one?" he asked, pulling his arm out.

"Yes, you dick. Have you ever seen any others? Have you ever stuck your hand into another dimension or whatever it is?" his partner replied.

"No...we must be able to do something...find out something...we can't live the rest of our lives knowing there's something like this but not knowing anything about it. Do you understand me, woman?"

"Yes, man."

Ranglu looked back at the hole. He stuck his hand through. This time, it did come out the other side. "It's not working, woman!"

She looked. "Oh..."

He took his arm out and then put it back through. It appeared out the other side.

"Let me try," she said. She put her arm through the other side and it appeared on the other.

"You've broken it," the young woman told him.

"You broke it," he returned. "With your fat wrists."

The corners of Fellei's lips lifted. "You're lucky I'm over here," she said quietly. "Otherwise...I'd murder you."

Ranglu's eyebrows lifted. Then his eyes went to the ground as a pale-blue and dark-purple snake slithered through a crack in between a couple of rocks. It lurched forward, bearing its fangs. It didn't reach Ranglu, but it sent him tumbling backwards. He fell, managing to twist. He put his hands out in front of him and cut one of his palms as it struck the side of a sharp point. Fellei's normal looking, straight and sharp, cross handled, silver bladed sword cut through the long, quite thin snake.

"Ow," Ranglu complained, getting back to his feet.

"Are you okay?" she asked, moving over to him.

"Yeah."

"Very good. You're aware your hand is bleeding, yes?"

"Yes."

"Do you have anything to cover it up?"

"No."

"Okay."

"Good."

"Umm…snake skin?" Fellei asked.

"Not really in the mood for snake skin."

"You don't have to eat it."

"I don't?"

"No."

"What do I do with it?"

"Just put it up your butt."

"My butt?"

"Yeah. Your hand will be completely healed in no time if you put it up your butt."

"Does the snake need skinning first or should I just put it up there head first?" Ranglu questioned.

"Just head first. All the teeth must pierce the flesh."

"Urgh. Terrible sense of humour," he said chuckling, wearing a mocking disgusted expression. Fellei exhaled, amused. "Should we head back?" she asked.

"Yeah. I'll just have to hold my hand up in the air till we get home."

"Okay."

"Just check the hole again."

Fellei walked over and put her arm through. It appeared on the other side of the rock. "Not working," she told him. "We'll come back again another time."

"Okay," he agreed. "Let us go." They started to traverse back to the dark-green Hoat. "Weird snake," Ranglu commented as they walked, their eyes on the rocks.

"Not from here," the young woman replied.

"The hole?" Ranglu turned to her with wide eyes.

"Maybe indeed," she replied.

"And so, the intrigue rose in my head, like the heat in my mother," he said raising his voice louder and louder, one bloody hand in the air. Fellei laughed.

When they arrived home, Ranglu went to run his hand under the tap. Nimb jumped onto the kitchen top and watched as he did so.

"Anything interesting other than the snake?" asked Falsen.

"The hole stopped working," replied his son, hand still under the tap.

"What do you mean?"

"Our arms would disappear when we first got there but then minutes later, it seemed to just be a normal hole. We could see our arms on the other side. We tried a few times." He started washing his hand with soap. After this, he dried his hand with tissues.

"Oh. Very strange. Very intriguing."

"Indeed, it is Father."

"Yes…"

Ranglu spotted Nimb waving a hand at him.

"Hello?"

"Hello," replied the creature. The young man's eyebrows raised.

"I taught him that," said Unela. Nimb hopped up and down excitedly.

"He's definitely a quick learner," she added.

"I think he's a genius," Falsen interjected. "Genuinely. It's fascinating."

Ranglu eyed the little one curiously. He slowly stretched out a finger towards him. The Boob suddenly turned serious as it approached. Then as it got too close, he slapped it with both paws and went leaping onto Fellei's shoulder. Falsen smiled. The others chuckled.

Before evening arrived, Ranglu, Fellei and Nimb went to Fellei and her father's home. Paiht – her father – had been living there with Fellei for a little while now. It was located in a secluded spot with only a few other houses nearby, lower down in the rocky, sandy region. There was nothing unique about the outside of the house. The walls were stone, there were a few square windows and an average sized rectangular door. The handle was round, black and rusty.

Fellei knocked a specific knock. Nimb watched from her shoulder. Paiht opened the door and smiled a little. He was a dark-brown haired man with tanned white skin. He wore nothing unique. He gestured silently for them to enter and he shut the door behind them. They entered into a small, mostly empty room. A wooden chair was sitting in one corner. Some sheaths were sitting in another. A shield hung on one of the walls. A picture of their family hung on another. There were a few books piled up in another corner.

They walked through this room, opened a rectangular door, walked through, closed it behind them and then Paiht spoke. They were in the kitchen. It was a circular room, the sink and tap were bronze coloured, the tops were clean, black marble.

"Who is this?" he asked softly gesturing at the little creature.

"We're pretty sure his name is Nimb," his daughter replied. "And we think he is a Boob."

"Oh, yes. I think I've read a little about them."

Fellei nodded. "Ranglu's father found a rock that was shaped like a door. It had a hole in it. But when you put your hand through the hole, it doesn't appear on the other side of the rock. It disappears. We think it might be some kind of passage into another dimension or a portal or something. That is where this fellow comes from. He latched onto my hand on the other side, and I quickly pulled my hand out and he came out with it."

"That is very interesting," said Paiht with a smile, still speaking quietly and softly. "I would love to see this door."

Fellei nodded. "I can take you there tomorrow. But it did suddenly stop working. The hole. We returned to it later and when we got there, our hands would disappear like before but then minutes later, they didn't, and we could see our arms on the other side. So I don't know if it'll work tomorrow or not..."

"Okay," said Paiht. "That's okay. We can still have a look. It's possible for things like that to appear from nowhere and then disappear...into nowhere. Though I don't really know anything about them so...yeah, I don't know, but it's very interesting. And Nimb is very cute."

"Indeed he is," his daughter agreed. "I think he's a little sleepy now," Fellei said, eyeing him on her shoulder, "but earlier he was coming out with lots of cryptic things."

"What do you mean?"

"He can speak our language. Very slowly but he can speak it. We think he might be a very clever being. A fast learner."

Fellei then told her father some of the things the creature had said.

Paiht looked at them all with furrowed eyebrows. "Well…I'm not really sure what to say," he told them with a small chuckle. "Maybe he will be an important figure in your lives. Maybe things are about to change. But neither of you should think about it. Of course, you can a little but don't think about it too much. Just relax and go with the flow. Otherwise, you won't be able to enjoy your lives. Anyway, sorry." His feet shuffled, and he looked to the ground for a moment. Both the young ones smiled. "No need to apologise, Paiht," said Ranglu. "That was actually very helpful for me. I could feel myself beginning to worry a little about it all."

Paiht smiled. "Okay, I'm glad."

"Do you want to come and watch the red moon tonight with us?" Fellei questioned.

"Umm…no, that's okay. Thank you, daughter. I think I'm going to just stay here. Or go on a small walk maybe."

"Are you sure, Father?" she asked.

"I'm sure," he replied with a smile.

"Okay. Well, I'll see you tomorrow and you can spend some more time with Nimb and we can go to the rock door."

"Okydoky."

Fellei hugged her dad goodbye.

Paiht stood alone in the kitchen, thinking silently…

It was night. The moon was red in the black sky. The group had walked on the track beside the cliff wall which stretched quite a long way. They had travelled to Swoolah; the tavern for the best view of the moon would be there. Many beings did the same thing on this night. The place was full, and the opening outside the flat roofed tavern was full. Full of deep-violet hooded figures. They all looked to the moon as it reached the perfect spot. It was huge. It seemed close. It was magnificent. They began to mumble words under their breath. The others there carried on chatting and admiring the moon, as these beings prayed or did whatever it was they were doing.

Ranglu, Fellei, Nimb and Ranglu's mother and father came out of the tavern's entrance with drinks in hand. Nimb didn't hold a drink of course, he just stayed quiet, hidden on Fellei's shoulder, looking around, waiting…

"Pretty cool," said Ranglu, walking around the crowd of hooded figures.

"Yes it is," Fellei answered, her eyes going from the bowed heads to the moon and back.

"This is what you saw," Falsen said, stepping closer to Fellei so she heard him.

"Yeah…" she replied. She felt a little…nervous, frightened.

"Everything will be okay," Unela told her, laying a hand on her arm. Fellei nodded and smiled. That was when a group of loud, deep voiced beings approached the crowd of hoods. Their deep voices could be heard over everything else. Fellei's eyes widened and she began looking for the girl she had seen in her vision. She was on the wrong side of the crowd. She couldn't find her. A moment later, one of the cloaked beings retaliated. Black burst forth from his palm, knocking one of the men off his feet. The young, dark skinned, red haired, blue eyed, twelve-year-old girl named, Wing, struck her head on the rocky ground and fell unconscious. Fellei scooped up the girl's body just in time. Something knocked Fellei's arm, but she didn't see what. She ran to safety with the girl in her arms. She sat down in a very small cove like area in the cliff wall and laid the girls head on her lap. It was bleeding. She had obviously hit her head on a bad rock. Ranglu and his family were there with the young woman, helping, over filling the cove area. Ranglu took the bandage off his hand and gave it to Fellei who folded it up and dabbed and then held it on the young girl's head. They started to hear Lightpistol's going off at the Tavern. Then one ray flew by behind Falsen and Unela – a very small blur of pale yellow. "We need to get away from here," said Unela. Fellei, got up, still holding the girl. As fast as possible, they made their way along the track, single file, Fellei at the front. They hugged the wall, not wanting to get hit by a ray – the Lightpistol's ammo – when the wall curved a little and the path too, Falsen, who was at the back of the single file line, breathed a little easier. Then all of a sudden, there was a bang. It sounded as if a bomb had gone off. All of their eyes went wide. They carried on moving as fast as possible, not looking back. They soon decided to make their way down the hill when they saw an okay opportunity. A bit of the hill which looked less treacherous than the rest. Ranglu helped Fellei make her way down. Nimb was still holding on to her neck and hair. When they reached the bottom, they all relaxed a little more but still they moved fast and felt frightened and confused. They travelled on, heading for home…

But before they reached their home, the girl woke. Wing quickly rolled out of the stranger's arms and hit the ground. She leapt to her feet and took out her Lightpistol. Dizziness and terrible pain sent her off balance as she shot. A yellow blur scraped Ranglu's arm instead of hitting Fellei. The segment of his clothes which it hit burnt off and the ray had burnt his arm. He let out a painful shout. Wing tumbled to the floor again, the dizziness sending her down. "It's okay!" shouted Fellei drawing her sword as the girl took another shot. The blade blocked the very thin ray. The ray vanished in an instant. The girl shot again. Fellei's senses were buzzing with energy. She blocked with the blade of her sword and the ray vanished again. Fellei was slowly approaching the girl. "Stop!" she cried, blocking another shot. Suddenly, the girl froze, as did Fellei. Ranglu looked between them. Neither was moving an inch. Nimb was still on Fellei's shoulder. Falsen was already running to grab the girl's weapon. He successfully took it from her. Then both girls began to move once more. But Wing only moved a little. Her eyes were on Fellei's and Fellei's were on hers. They both stared at each other. Neither was frozen anymore. But they stayed still, staring.

Fellei had seen true darkness, true pain, true sorrow, true hopelessness, loss, struggle, strength, hunger, passion, anger, weakness, revenge, regret, torture, death and hope…

Wing had seen true hope, true love, true supportiveness, true joy, true happiness, true pain, true loss, true sorrow, passion, fire, rage, kindness, softness, generosity, forgiveness and no hatred.

Fellei fell down to her knees beside Wing. She began to sob. She embraced the young girl and kissed her cheek. Wing felt real peace for the first time in her entire life. She felt a kind, patient, loving, not judgmental, understanding spirit intertwine with her own. She felt it washing away the dirt, washing away the pain, washing away the regret, the shame, the guilt, the anger, the darkness. There was a fire, a light beginning to simmer, to shine.

"It's okay now. I'm proud of you and I will always love you," Fellei told her.

Wing began to weep and weep and weep. She shook in Fellei's arms. The voice of high hope and wind had finally come, and it was filling her sails, as the Word had said it would.

Chapter 4
A Nod and a Wink

Paiht woke to loud knocking. It was his daughter. He knew by the pattern. He made his way down the wooden stairs – which were wide both left to right and front to back. There were open gaps between each step – at a faster pace than usual. He was a little worried for it was still night and he wasn't expecting her home until the next day.

He opened the door and saw her, standing beside a girl he had never seen before. Fellei had insisted Nimb stay with Ranglu and his family for the rest of the night. Nimb had reluctantly agreed. They entered and Paiht shut the door.

"I'm sorry, Dad," said Fellei before entering the kitchen. "I didn't know what to do. And umm, Wing" – she gestured at the girl – "needs her head looked at by someone."

"That's okay. Umm well, we'll go in the sitting room. I'll go and get my stuff."

"Okay."

Fellei and Wing left the kitchen, opening and closing a rectangular door and stepping onto stone and then onto a pleasant, patterned rug. Fellei switched on the main light which was surrounded by a nice circular shade. Then she turned on a tall, curve necked lamp too and fetched a cushioned, wooden stool for the girl to sit on.

"How are you feeling?"

"Okay."

Fellei smiled at her. The girl looked to the ground.

Paiht soon appeared with a bag in one hand.

"What happened?" he asked.

"A lot," his daughter answered. "There were moon worshipers at the tavern and then um, these macho, asshole, small minded men arrived and started shouting and pushing them around. The moon people retaliated and one of the men was sent flying and he knocked into Wing who then fell and hit her head on a rock. We got her away from the mess but then rays started flying and so we moved further away as fast as we could. Then we heard a bomb, or we think it was a bomb. But umm, yeah. I don't know. There's more I need to tell you as well but it's probably best we just relax and patch up Wing's head."

"Okay," her father replied. He had already begun tending to her head.

"I will try my best to make this all as pain free as possible," said Paiht to the girl. He could feel a mix of very strong emotions emanating from her.

"Okay," the girl replied softly and quietly. Her eyes became wet with tears once more.

When Ranglu arrived home, he made his way to the workshop, Nimb on his shoulder. His mother and father had insisted he didn't, but he managed to mostly convince them he would be fine. Nimb wanted to go with him. He whipped the cover off Tattermoath, pressed the camouflaged segment, pulled the slanted top up further and hopped into the front seat. After checking that there were indeed binoculars underneath the seat, he put a Looce Shard – a shard of Looce Metal with a number of specific ridges running up its body, the shards end being a point and the shards top, a flat circle – into a circular hole. It fitted perfectly, and things began to light up. Nimb watched with wide eyes. Ranglu pressed a black button which had a small white picture of a house with an open roof on it. The roof did not open but the back wall of the workshop did. Tattermoath slowly began to back up, its wheels rolling. Once he was out, Ranglu pressed the black button beside the other button. This one had no picture on it. The two halves of the black wall started closing. Tattermoath then lifted off the ground, almost perfectly smoothly. The wheels beneath disappeared into the body beneath, segments opening up and then closing over them. Ranglu lifted the ship up further into the air. The ship was quiet as it lifted. Then when he was quite high in the sky, he willed the vehicle onwards, heading for Swoolah, the tavern. Tattermoath's back end lit up a little brighter as he flew forward. Nimb hopped up and down, grinning, his toothless, dark mouth open. Ranglu soared at a quite leisurely speed through the sky. Before he got close to the Tavern, he pressed a blue button which had a small white drawing of a figure, wearing a cloak on it. Tattermoath cloaked, mostly, slowly, so he could almost not be seen by the naked eye.

When Ranglu could see the tavern below, he grabbed the pair of binoculars which were located beneath his seat. He rubbed the lenses with a sleeve, flicked on night vision and then put them to his eyes. The night vision technology turned night into day. It did not literally turn the moon into the sun, but it showed everything in its true colour, as if nothing was hidden by darkness. The place was a mess. The building had collapsed. There were bodies, rubble, rocks, unidentifiable objects, fire. Surely, a few provocative assholes could not have been the cause of all this. Ranglu zoomed out to look at the surrounding areas and that's when he spotted something on the top of the cliff wall, above the ruined Tavern. There was a skinny looking fellow dressed in bright red and pale green. He wore a mask with vicious red eyes. A single red horn curved upwards from the right side of his head. The whole mask was red. The upper body area of the suit he wore was all red. The legs and feet were pale green. The skinny fellow looked up at Ranglu. Red covered his eyes. His black lipped mouth was the only thing that was visible; the mask covered everything else. The fellow grinned, showing a mouth full of sharp fangs. He waved at Ranglu. His feet swung back and forth, hanging off the wall of the cliff. Ranglu froze. He didn't know what to do. He took the binoculars away from his eyes for a moment. He felt frightened. He looked through them again. He caught the bright-red and pale-green coloured figure skipping off into the darkness. Ranglu shivered, he shook his head. Nimb was watching Ranglu. He placed a paw on his face. Ranglu eyed him and smiled a little. The young man turned the ship and quickly made his way back home.

Wing was not expecting to fall asleep, but she did, on the sofa. Fellei fell asleep in a smaller but still large, cushioned brown chair. Paiht stood, leaning against the brick wall opposite the sofa where a fire place sat surrounded by pale-orange, yellow and red bricks – the fire place held no fire – he was looking at the two girls, thinking about everything Fellei had told him on this night. There was only one lamp on now. It was glowing warm orange, making the room feel, cosy and sleepy. Paiht grabbed a cushion and placed it on the rug. He laid down on his back, his head on the cushion and after a moment, he closed his eyes.

Before Ranglu began quietly descending back down to the ground, he spotted something in the distance. He put the binoculars in front of his eyes and looked. The young man saw a big, dark-blue and white ship. This ship was shaped like an arrow, but the entire back was curved, then the wide sides made their way inwards until they made a pointed front. The entire body was dark-blue except for one wide white stripe which ran down the entire middle, coming down the nose and then running back along the body beneath. Ranglu dropped lower as it approached; it was going neither fast nor slow as far as he could tell. When they passed over his head, he raised back up and quickly sped up after them. He was following the mysterious group named, Blue Eye. Ranglu had heard many rumours about the group. He quickly caught them up but then had to come to a swift halt when they themselves halted. Though the young man found he couldn't stop. Something was pulling him closer and closer to the ship. He had lost control. He could do nothing. Nimb's eyes were suspicious. When Tattermoath got close to the big, dark-blue ship, he found himself being forced upside down. His underside was pulled up to the underbelly of Blue Eye – Blue Eye also being the name of the space ship – and the big blue ship swallowed him up. The seat harness had kept Ranglu in his seat. The young man had grabbed Nimb so he didn't bang his head on the top. Tattermoath was being twisted back around. It was pitch black. When Ranglu was sitting the right way up, once more a segment opened up above Tattermoath though the young man didn't notice. It was still pitch black. Tattermoath was lifted up through the open segment. Then, all movement ceased. Ranglu couldn't see anything until a big door parted in front of him and pale light shone into the room. Ranglu looked ahead of him. There stood five beings. Behind them, the corridor looked bluey grey. One of them, a green skinned, bald fellow with a slim face, orange eyes and diamond, black pupils, walked to the side of Tattermoath. Suddenly, the clear top of the white ship opened, making Ranglu jump a little. The green man just stood there, looking at Ranglu and the creature.

"Are you here to kill us?" Freece questioned.

Ranglu met his eyes and raised his eyebrows. Nimb was watching the green one suspiciously.

"No," said Ranglu.

A woman with black hair, warm orange skin, green serpent eyes and a red forked tongue said, "If what you say is true, you and your Boob may exit the ship."

"Yes," the green one agreed, folding his lean and muscular arms. He wore a white, sleeveless shirt and grey trousers.

"And if you are lying, death will greet your first step," said another. She had purple hair and big violet eyes. Her skin was pale. She wore a black leather jacket with a black shirt beneath. Her baggy trousers were deep green.

Ranglu sat there for a moment and then slowly started to get out of the ship. When his feet touched the floor, nothing happened.

"Please tell me you are the Blue Eye people. The good hero people?" he asked.

"Who's asking?" asked a fiery haired man with entirely purple eyes and grey lips. His skin was tanned white. He wore a black blazer with a black t-shirt beneath. He wore red shorts.

"My name is Ranglu and this is Nimb," he replied.

"Nice," said the fiery red haired one.

"Yes," the green one agreed.

"I…um…have heard rumours about you. I saw you and um…was curious," the owner of the white ship told them.

"Likely story," said the black haired, serpent eyed woman.

"Likely story," the green one agreed. "Nobody likes us."

"He never said anything about anyone liking us Freece," the purple haired and violet-eyed one told him. Her name was Annife.

"What did you say to me?" he questioned.

"Don't worry, you sexy hunk."

"Thank you," said Freece in a solemn fashion, bobbing his head. He had quite a deep voice.

"Where did you find the Boob?" the black haired, forked tongued lady questioned. Her name was Harhk.

"Umm…"

"A hole in…a rock…shaped like a…door," said Nimb. His speaking was already getting better.

"Well, shit on my face that's a cute creature," said Freece.

"Drop the weapon," said Annife.

"Yes," said Freece with wide eyes.

Ranglu slowly unsheathed his light pistol. None of them moved at all. He placed it on the ground.

"I think he's good," said another woman who had been lying down on the ground this entire time, staring at the ceiling. A pale-blue pirate's hat sat on her belly. She had pale-blue eyes and blue, frosty skin. Her hair was very pale-blue, almost white. It dazzled a very little amount in light. She wore white, flared trousers and a pale-blue baggy shirt.

"What were you doing?" she – Enfuin – questioned, still lying on the ground, her eyes looking up.

"I was at a tavern and things started to go crazy, and me and my family had to run but I was obviously curious as to what had happened so I just was going back home from looking…at what had happened to the tavern."

"It adds up," Freece, the orange eyed, diamond pupil one decided.

"Likely story," said Harhk sarcastically, her forked tongue flicking out.

"What did you see at the tavern?" asked Enfuin.

"A creepy man wearing a red mask and a red suit with pale-green legs—" Ranglu decided was the best thing to say first.

Enfuin suddenly sat up. "Is he still there?" she asked.

"Oh umm, no. Well, I don't know. I saw him skipping away," he replied. Freece stamped his foot. Annife, the purple haired one, stared at Ranglu with her big eyes. Harhk spat on one of the walls. Raggyshal – Raggy for short – the fiery haired one, he blew raspberries. Enfuin threw her pale-blue hat at Ranglu. Ranglu caught it.

"Come with me, stranger," she said. "If you cross us, you will die," she warned.

The young man cautiously took a couple of steps forward. "I thought you didn't kill? Justice and…"

Enfuin got to her feet. "Yes," she replied.

Ranglu didn't know what that meant.

Enfuin approached him at a normal, easy pace. This made Ranglu nervous. She lifted a hand. "I am Enfuin," she said. "I am the captain of this ship."

Protests suddenly erupted forth.

"I am not the captain of this ship!" she shouted above the noise. The other voices died down.

"I am the leader of this group," she told Ranglu and Nimb.

Protests erupted once more.

"I am merely dust!" she shouted after a handful of seconds. The voices died down again.

"I am my own father's son!" Freece suddenly cried, his voice going up some octaves. He got overly excited.

Harhk ran at him with a furious look on her face. She tackled him to the ground.

"Come," said Enfuin ignoring them. Ranglu followed nervously. His eyes going to the fight for a moment and then ahead of him. He walked past Raggy and Annife who smiled at him in a possibly friendly manner and then started

36

following him. Ranglu's eyes slid all around the place. The lights were making the clanking corridor a blueish grey colour. Soon they turned right, took some more steps and entered a circular area with a black floor and curving grey and black walls; some of the walls were made of dots of lights, varying in colours, covered by grates. Corridors led off left, right, onwards. A big black pillar stood in the middle of the room. Ranglu quickly found out the pillar was open on one side. "Don't worry," said Enfuin before she entered the tube, after pulling a red leaver on one of the walls. She entered and was lifted off her feet. Ranglu couldn't see what was sending her up. She quickly disappeared.

"It's safe," Annife told him. Raggy nodded and winked.

Not able to do anything else Ranglu stepped in. Beneath his feet was some kind of black material. It didn't look like anything special. There was likely something beneath it. An invisible force sent him up. He could feel it. He began to hover on the force once he reached the next floor which wasn't far up at all. There were no more higher floors. The ship wasn't so huge. He stepped onto the floor. Annife led the way to the cockpit which was rather large. The seats were black and grey but they were elegant and precise, comfortable and sleek. Ranglu wanted one. The clear front window was huge. The deep-blue dashboard was huge, covered in many buttons and switches. The rest of the cockpit was also dark-blue except for the dark-grey floor.

"So," began the pale-blue young woman. "I saw you in one of my frosty visions. That is why you have made it this far."

"Oh," Raggy said from behind. "Right, very nice." Ranglu and Nimb looked to him and then back to the young woman.

"Here, let me show you." She walked over to him and blew in his face. Pale, dazzling breath hit his skin and suddenly Ranglu could see himself, standing inside a circle of blue fire. His vison was pale and cold. It was night. Some kind of a sand storm was coming his way. The storm had red, vicious eyes like the fellow who was sitting on the cliff wall above the tavern. Ranglu held a sword. It had a cross handle but the ends of the arms of the cross-travelled upwards, either side of the blade a small distance. The dark-silver coloured blade was straight, then suddenly it dropped down and then went straight again. It suddenly rose vertically up and then went straight again. Ranglu didn't know why anyone would shape a sword in such a way. Suddenly, the weapon turned into a magnificent bow. Ranglu took an arrow from the quiver that sat on his back and he hitched it onto the string of the bow. He pulled back on the string, aiming up and onwards. He let go. The arrow flew through the air. Suddenly, the vision stopped. The young man came back to reality.

"The weapon you were using was one Annife has already made," the blue one told him.

"One I've already made?" the violet eyed one asked excitedly.

"I think that's what she said," Raggy replied calmly.

"Nice," said Annife.

"And the storm may very well be that devilish fellow you spotted. Meaning maybe you are supposed to help us. Yes?" Enfuin continued.

"Yes," said Nimb.

"Umm," said Ranglu. The young man turned to find Annife right behind him. He jumped and moved away from her. She put out a hand. "I am Annife. The clever one. The one who is clever with some things. The one who knows things about…some things," she said slowly. "I am a whizz," she ended.

"And me," said Raggy from a distance. "I am the captain of this ship," he told Ranglu sombrely. He bowed so low he tipped forward and hit his face on the ground. It looked like it genuinely might have hurt.

"Raggy's talents are unexplainable," said Annife, sounding impressed.

"That's not true at all," Enfuin argued.

Raggy got to his feet. He clicked his fingers and then ran his hand through his mad hair. "What's your opinion on belly buttonless women, Ranglu?" he asked quietly. "Those fine flat skinned belly women?" he pointed a finger at the young man. "You can be honest with myself, young one."

"They are nice," Ranglu found himself saying.

"Pull your shirt up, Annife," the grey-lipped one said calmly. Annife did so. She had no belly button. Raggy stared at Ranglu, looking amazed.

"Put it away," said Enfuin. "Let's get to work." She hopped into one of the most central, furthest forward seats. None was obviously the leader's seat. And in a moment, Ranglu found himself flying with the group of heroes that called themselves Blue Eye. Though he still wasn't sure if it was actually them. He really didn't know what to do.

The Blue Eye stopped above and a small distance away from the tavern. They all looked out of the massive clear front. Freece and Harhk joined them. Ranglu spotted Raggy closing his eyes. The fires below started speedily dying down until there was no fire remaining. Ranglu looked back to the calm faced fellow. Did he just do that? Enfuin suddenly disappeared in a dazzle of light and…smoke?

Mist? Spirit? Out of the dazzling mist, or whatever it was, appeared a beautiful white dove, the inside of the dove's body acting as another dimension of sorts. When Enfuin returns to her usual form, she will be fully clothed and looking perfectly like her normal self. Harhk turned around and held out her arm and hand in a strange twisted manner. Suddenly, she twisted both her hand and arm and a black portal of some kind opened up a handful of steps away. The dove flew through the portal. They all turned as the dove came out of another black portal located outside of the ship. The dove flew down towards the tavern. Ranglu could see the green one concentrating. His body was tense and his eyes were closed. In an instance, his entire body twisted and he disappeared in a puff of green smoke? He reappeared down below in another puff of smoke, next to some rubble. He stood completely still for a couple handful of seconds. Then he slowly began to lift off the ground. He was shaking a little. It appeared as if pale-green light began to leave his body and dance away from him, covering the land around. Ranglu saw that the light was somehow highlighting every single being it could find, including creatures, both alive and dead. Harhk held a hand out towards the dark portal in the ship. The portal outside began to move down, getting closer to the ground. Harhk and Raggy then walked through. It was just Ranglu, Nimb and Annife on the ship now. Annife took a seat in one of the seats located in the corner to the right. A decent sized screen was in the dashboard over there. She pressed a button and a controller came out of the dashboard, sitting on a platform. The screen turned on. A large drone dropped out of the bottom of the ship and flew forward and down towards the fallen tavern, its grabbing mechanisms ready. The young man could see its point of view on the screen. The woman was controlling it. Ranglu decided he would stay on the ship. He watched as the team worked with incredible speed and efficiency.

Every single body was soon recovered. But not a single man, woman or child had a heart that was still beating. They were all dead.

Enfuin was flying through the darkness, up above the cliffside, searching the nearby areas. Her vision was pale and cold, it pierced through the darkness with ease.

The dove stopped when it found a massive fiery picture on the ground. There was a triangle of fire surrounding two watchful eyes and above them, on the right, was a curving horn like shape. The dove swooped down to the ground and suddenly Enfuin returned to her normal form. She ran towards the fire, letting out a battle cry. She ran right through the flames bringing up her arms as she did so. The flames leapt up with her arms and in an instance, they froze over. She leapt and a roof of freezing air appeared above her and as she came smashing down, the freezing roof came down too. The flames were vanquished in an instance. Enfuin stood there for a moment. She felt rageful, sad, regretful, confused…in a puff of light and what she simply called dazzle mist, she turned into a dove and made her way back to the ship, surveying her surroundings as she flew.

When she arrived back at the fallen tavern, she spotted the black portal and flew through. She was back in the Blue Eye. All the others were waiting for her. She had been searching around for a short while, but she found nothing except for the flaming picture. She returned to her normal form.

"It was definitely Vyan," she told them.

Chapter 5
Hectic

"We are Blue Eye by the way," Enfuin told Ranglu. They were back in the room where Tattermoath was.

"Okay," he said nodding. "It was hard to be sure."

"Yes," she replied. Then she tipped the front of her hat further down and bowed. "Goodbye, Ranglu and Nimb. Take care of the weapon."

"I will," said Ranglu, getting into Tattermoath. At the moment, the weapon, the one he had seen in the vision, was a dark-silver dagger, sheathed in black. It only had three forms. The odd shaped sword, the dagger and the bow.

Ranglu secured himself into the chair and then shut the top. Nimb held on to him as Enfuin pulled a lever and the white ship began to slowly drop down. Ranglu soon found himself on the underside of the Blue Eye, upside down once more. A voice suddenly came out of the dashboard. It was Annife's. "Are you ready to correct yourself?" she asked.

"Ummm…yes," Ranglu replied.

"Okay."

Suddenly, the white ship was falling. Ranglu tugged at the steering wheel and span around so he was the right way up, diving down. He kept the momentum, swooping down a little and then flattening out and flying onwards, turning in the direction of home. He really needed some sleep.

Once Ranglu had parked Tattermoath in the workshop, he opened up the top and clambered out.

"I'm sorry," Ranglu began, looking at both his mother and father. "That group called the Blue Eye flew past me and I followed them out of intrigue, naturally. I didn't know they could see me because I was cloaked but their ship sort of sucked me in and then I met them and they were looking for this man who I told them I had seen at the tavern on the cliff above. And things turned out well though. One of them had had a vision of me and they ended up giving me this before I left." Ranglu unsheathed the dagger. He held it out and closed his eyes. Suddenly, it turned into a dark-silver, strong looking, curved bodied bow. The young man accidentally dropped it on the ground. He picked it up. "I don't know how it works. I think it reads my thoughts…umm…a genius woman made it…is this all a good enough excuse?"

"You promise with all your heart that it is all true?" his father questioned.

"Yes," he answered.

"Then yes, it's good enough."

"Mother?" Ranglu asked.

"Yes," she replied quietly. "It's quite a good excuse. And how are you doing, Nimb?"

"I am tired," the little creature replied. "I would…like to…sleep."

The mother let out a sigh. "Take him and yourself to bed," Unela said to her son. Ranglu let out a sigh of relief.

"Thank you for being such great parents," he said, walking towards them.

"Yes," said his mother. "We will speak more tomorrow."

"Yes," Falsen agreed.

Ranglu smiled and then they watched as their son walked to the other side of their room, turned around to smile at them again and then exited.

Ranglu made a quick cosy little bed made of blankets and cushions for Nimb in his room on the floor. The young man didn't want to squish the little creature so he thought sleeping in the same bed wouldn't be very safe. Then he stripped into his underwear, got into bed, said goodnight to Nimb who he then discovered was already asleep, then closed his eyes. His second to last thoughts before falling asleep were how he needed to brush his teeth well the next day. His last thoughts were about the Blue Eye. He made sure not to think about the fellow in red and pale green. He tried his best not to anyway.

Ranglu woke. He turned over onto his back so Nimb had to hop a little to stay on. The little creature had been sitting on him, staring at the young fellow's face for a short while.

"Oh…hello," said Ranglu.

"Hello," Nimb replied. "How are you…feeling?"

"Okay," he replied with a chuckle.

"Okay," said Nimb.

"How are you feeling?" Ranglu questioned, still lying on his back.

"Good."

"Good."

Nimb grinned at him and began to jump up and down. Luckily, he was a very light creature.

Ranglu slowly sat up, putting a pillow behind his back. Nimb was now on his legs.

"I had dream," Nimb said.

"What happened in the dream?" Ranglu questioned.

"My sight was...pale. You were standing in...circle of...fire. You shot an...arrow at sandy...storm...with red eyes."

"That was the vision I saw when Enfuin blew that misty stuff in my face," Ranglu told him.

"Maybe...some...touched me." Nimb wondered.

"Maybe," Ranglu replied.

"Very...intriguing," the little creature said, staring into the young man's eyes.

"Yes," said the dark-blonde haired one, chuckling a little.

Ranglu looked Nimb over. The black and white being looked a little scruffy and dirty.

"Would you like a wash?" asked the man.

"No," said Nimb. "Look."

Ranglu's eyes went wide as all the dirt and scruffiness vanished completely. The creature in front of him was now all fluffy and clean.

"What else can you do?" he asked.

"Who knows," the small being replied.

Ranglu exhaled in amusement. "Right, let's get some food and do some more explaining to the old pensioners."

"Okay," Nimb replied.

Ranglu got dressed and then visited the bathroom to brush his teeth and wash his face. After that, he made his way to the kitchen where he found no one.

"Nobody," said Nimb.

"Indeed."

Ranglu looked in the dining room. Nobody. His mother and father's bedroom. Nobody. There was noise coming from the workshop. In there, he found a good few more people than just his mother and father.

"Ah the young Ranglu," said Raggy, the red haired one, with a bow. Harhk, the one with snake eyes and a forked tongue, stuck up a middle finger. Freece,

43

the green, lean, muscular one just looked at him. Enfuin tipped her pale-blue hat and bowed. Annife looked at him with her big violet eyes and waved.

"We wanted to make sure you recognised us so we wore the same clothes," the purple haired one said, wearing a black leather jacket, black top and deep-green trousers.

"Well…thank you," Ranglu replied.

"You're welcome," said Freece with his deep voice.

"No more explaining is really needed anymore," Unela told her son.

"Right," said Ranglu, looking as bewildered as his mother.

"The reason we came back," Enfuin began, "is because I saw that you had possibly come into contact with a girl with a lot of power?"

Ranglu was silent for a moment. "Umm…not that I know of."

"She looked around maybe eleven, twelve, thirteen years old. I saw you walking with her. And on the other side of the girl was another girl, around your age I think. The young girl had a beautiful face. I think she was dark skinned and red haired. The younger one. I felt…something like power resonating off her. I felt, she was destined to help us take down the devil fellow you saw. Like you are. I felt things from all of you in that vision. It was a little too much. I couldn't tell…things. But something strong was coming off the girl."

"I'm really sorry. I haven't met anybody like the girl you're describing," Ranglu lied. His mother and father eyed him. Harhk eyed them.

"Okay," said Enfuin. "Well, that means you will one day to come. When that day comes, contact us by pressing that new dark-blue button on the dashboard of your ship, with the picture of the eye."

"Okay," Ranglu replied nodding.

"You can trust us," said Raggy. "I promise you."

Ranglu nodded. "I do."

"Okay," said the red haired one.

"You can," Enfuin added. "We are heroes. Not villains."

The young man nodded.

"Farewell," said the pale-blue one, bowing and then turning and leaving surprisingly swiftly, through the open back which they had somehow opened themselves to get in. The others said farewell in their own special ways, and exited, heading for their ship which was parked not far away, in the open land area. Ranglu shut the back once they had left. He rubbed his face with his hands.

He looked at his mother, father and Nimb, who was standing on Falsen's shoulder.

"Why did you feel it wasn't right to tell them?" Falsen questioned.

"I don't know," his son replied. "It just didn't. I think the girl belongs with Fellei and Paiht for now. They can help her better than anyone else."

"I stand behind your decision, son," said Falsen. "Now, let's speak about how intriguing every single one of those beings are."

Ranglu chuckled. "The Blue Eye group?"

"Yes."

"Wait…why were you in the workshop with them anyway?"

"They…broke in."

"You seem calm…"

"Yes, well, I feel a little odd after meeting them all."

"Me too," Unela agreed.

"Yeah…" said Ranglu. "I guess they can track me now. Or maybe it's the ship they tracked. Anyway…I think that's fine. I do trust them. I watched them recover every single body at the tavern. And all the rumours say they're heroes. So…what do you think, Nimb?" Ranglu asked, curious.

"You can trust them," he answered.

As the Blue Eye group were making their way back to the ship, Harhk walked to Enfuin's side and said, "I think he was lying."

"Maybe," said Enfuin. "But that's okay. Things will fall into place. I feel it."

Fellei, Wing and Paiht began on their journey to the door shaped rock. Wing quietly said she was happy to go and see this intriguing hole they spoke of. She had slept peacefully for the first time since she could remember. Now she felt close to good. She couldn't remember ever feeling like this. Unfortunately, there were still things nagging very quietly at the back of her head. But she had a strong mind. A powerful mind. She was managing to block it all out.

While they were in a more populated area, Wing kept her head down. But when they reached the open land she looked up and enjoyed the wind blowing on her skin, cooling her a little.

They soon came to a halt and got off the grey Hoat. They quietly clambered up and across the rocks and made it to the door shaped rock with the hole in it.

"Stick your hand in, Father," Fellei said.

"Okay," he replied. He stepped closer and did so. His hand came out the other side.

"Damn it," said Fellei.

"It might be close by," Wing commented. This was probably the fourth time she had said anything so far today.

"They can move," she added softly.

"Have you seen one before?" Fellei asked.

"Once. They are rare…if it's okay, I might be able to feel it."

"What do you mean?" the young woman asked.

"I think I can feel, or umm, sense things like this."

"Okay," the brown haired one replied. "Go for it."

Wing walked towards the door and put her hand in the hole. She didn't put it the whole way through. She kept it still, inside the hole and closed her eyes.

To Fellei and Paiht's intrigue, Wing said, "I can see it."

She took her hand out and opened her eyes. "It moved." She started walking, a finger pointing at the ground, like she was following a trail. Paiht and his daughter followed. They didn't have to go far before they found it, swinging around to the opposite side of a neither small nor large rock. This hole looked into the inside of the rock. It looked as if your hand would hit stone if you were to put it into the hole.

"That's amazing," said Fellei, looking at the dark-red haired girl. She made eye contact for a short moment and smiled a little in reply.

Fellei gestured for her dad to try this one. He knelt down and reached in. His hand never touched stone.

In Angelfole a hand appeared out of a hole in a cliff wall. The magnificent waterfall falling down the cliff wall quickly splashed it and the hand withdrew.

Paiht looked at his hand and then at the two behind him, wearing a happy, surprised expression.

"Amazing…I've never come across this before." He put his arm in further and held it there for a moment longer. It quickly got drenched. He pulled it back out and lifted it up to the girls and said, "I think the other hole could be under a waterfall maybe. Unless the rain is…crazy over wherever there is."

"Would you like a go Wing?" he asked. She shook her head. The father nodded. "Daughter?"

"Sure." She moved closer and knelt down once Paiht had moved away.

Once through she moved her hand around, seeing if she could feel anything other than water. Other than the rock either side of her arm, she couldn't. Her arm withdrew and she stood up smiling.

"How did you find it? Can you explain it?" she asked Wing, curious.

"Umm, first I could feel it and then I could see its sort of track in my mind. I don't know why."

Fellei nodded.

"I think you are definitely like Fellei and me," Paiht began, softly. "That means you will be a part of an interesting ancient family tree," he said softly. "It's very cool," he finished, trying his best to speak in a reassuring, easy to process way.

"Is it magic?" the young girl asked.

"Umm…n-y-not exactly. Kind of." He smiled. "It's umm more…it's deeper than magic I guess you could say."

Wing nodded, not making eye contact for more than a second.

"Some might describe it as spiritual," he continued.

"You're connected with the mind and the soul and the body and nature," added Fellei.

Wing nodded again.

"Our minds connected," Wing said, speaking to Fellei.

"Yeah, they did," she replied. It was quiet for a handful of seconds.

"How do we find out more about this hole?" Paiht asked, looking to his daughter.

"I do not know," she answered. "Can we?"

"I have no idea," he said.

"What shall we do now then?"

Paiht looked around. He spotted, possibly a small fellow perched on a large rock, a good distance away.

"We might have a peeper," he said. Wing looked at him and then in the direction he was looking. Her vision travelled towards the rock. In her mind's eye, she could see the small fellow clearly. He or she was a hairy and white being and had a pair of binoculars over their eyes. In this moment, Wing felt something inside.

Wing suddenly bolted. "Run!" she said.

"What?" Fellei called after her. Both she and the father started traversing the rocks as fast as possible, trying their best to keep up with her.

"It'll just be a Sund!" Paiht kept saying. But Wing kept moving, until she reached the sandy, rocky ground beside the Hoat and collapsed, weeping.

"Please save me. Please save me. Please save me," she kept repeating. Fellei knelt beside her and embraced her. "It's okay; it'll just be a Sund. There just nosy, harmless explorers." Fellei kept trying to reassure her. "They live all over this area, tucked away in caves and other places like that. There's nothing to fear."

Wing got to her feet, wanting to get onto the Hoat and drive away. That was when she had a vision of a terrible man wearing a red mask with a horn curving up from the right side of his head. "No no no," she began. "No no no. Please drive, please drive," she begged, looking back at Fellei and Paiht.

A black portal suddenly opened up around thirty feet away. A skinny man dressed in red and pale green stepped out of it and started running straight for them. Wing let out a terribly cry and then suddenly, she froze. The man with vicious eyes froze too.

Wing started shaking, grunting, shouting, screaming. Her head burned hot and suddenly she was knocked off her feet.

"Dad!" Fellei called, her fear growing and growing.

"Look after her," he said, walking past his daughter and toward the being. Paiht sent his feelings, his senses, his mind, what he called his Inner Body, forth. He sent his Inner Body hurtling towards the being who had a deep, dark, twisted, purely evil spirit. Purely evil Inner Body. Paiht's Inner Body struck his and the devilish man froze. Paiht's light pierced his darkness, began to invade his body. But then, something unexpected happened. Paiht started to feel fiery heat. Visions of his dead wife started to appear on the edges of his mind's eyes vision. The son he had lost at such an early age materialised there too.

Paiht blocked it out. He took a step forward, breaking through a barrier that had shot up in an instance. The masked one started to shake. Unwillingly, his suits pale-green feet started scraping backwards, marking the ground. Then he came to a complete halt. He could barely move anything.

"You're weak," said Paiht, moving forward. "You're a weak little man with no power. No purpose. No life," he began quietly, anger in his voice. "Your days in this world have been for nothing. They will always be for nothing!" His voice was gradually getting louder and louder. "Your life is meaningless! Your loss is inevitable! The light is blinding you! Justice is here!" Paiht was managing slowly to make his way towards the demon. The father was drawing his sword. The silver blade and silver cross handle shimmered in the sunlight. "Hope is here in the form of a sword and it will cut off your head!"

Suddenly, the devilish one went flying sideways as two thick rays blasted the ground beside him, sending him, the sand and a number of rocks flying. Paiht had got close and so the force knocked him onto his back.

Harhk had sensed the opening of her ancestor's portal – this ancestor being her only relative still alive as far as she knew. The title of their relationship she didn't know. Her species and all species closely related were all nearly extinct. There were a number of reasons why – she had sensed the portal's opening, its distance from her. She could never come up with a precise location but she could always get them close. Fortunately, this time, they had been nearby.

Paiht had lost his connection to the demon.

A cloud of green mystical energy appeared beside the motionless body of the one in red. And then a moment later, Freece, with the body, vanished from Paiht's vision, in another puff of mist? Luckily making it back into the ship, though he had nearly failed to do this. It had taken more than a lot out of him. Freece put the limp body inside a unique cell made just for the masked one.

Paiht watched as the dark-blue and white ship disappeared into the sky.

He had been so close to ending the terror that was trapped in the form of a humanoid being.

While Paiht tended to Wing's wounds, Fellei handed her a small black circular object with a dark-red flat centre.

"This is a beacon," she told her. "If you press the red centre three times, then my beacon" – she held hers up – "will start flashing red. I can then plug it into a ship, a Hoat or a device and there are programs that will be able to track your beacon using my beacon. You can also press it six times just to let me know that you're okay." Wing had been nodding while she talked.

"Will you remember all of that?"

"Yes," said Wing.

"So three if you need me and six just to let me know you're okay. Though obviously hopefully you'll never need to click it three times."

"Okay," the young girl replied.

"And there is one last thing," Fellei said with a smile. "If you hold the red button down, then you can speak to me." Fellei held the middle of the object down and spoke into it. Out of the bottom of Wing's device came her voice. Wing then held the button down on hers and spoke into it. Her voice came out of Fellei's beacon device.

"Though give me a warning by clicking three or six times before speaking to me using it. And if I want to contact you, then the beacon will buzz and shake a little too. The buzz isn't overly loud but it's loud enough."

"Okay," Wing replied.

"Okay, good," said Fellei. "If you forget or have any questions, then just ask me whenever."

Wing nodded.

"There are probably better things," Fellei said, looking at her beacon device, "but we don't have a whole lot of up to date technology."

"I like it," said Wing.

"Okay, good." Fellei sat down, sighing heavily. Paiht smiled a little. It was quiet for a bit.

On the Blue Eye, the atmosphere was hectic. Enfuin was battling with her own thoughts. She knew there were things that didn't add up, didn't make sense but she didn't care. This would all be over soon.

The team were heading for the Ancient Towers located low in the Waysem Mountains. There they would find an acquaintance named Shaip. He was a priest of an ancient kind. He was the only one they knew who might be able to vanquish their prisoner once and for all. The team had found that ending the being's life was not something that was easy or simple. The demon would always survive, escape, hungrily search for a willing, strong, powerful host. Once the host's body was his, he was trapped inside until that body was no longer usable, no longer strong enough to be his vessel.

The masked one lay still on the cell floor. The demon was still unconscious…

When Vyan finally woke – his time of sleep extended by the cell which was a constant drain on his energy – he opened his eyes to the sight of the bluey-grey cell walls and then his head turned in the direction of the clear front, made of Varz glass. Through it, he could see Enfuin and Harhk. Vyan, the demon slowly got to his feet. He walked closer to the clear front, looking between the two female beings. Calmly, with a smirk on his face, he leant his masked forehead against the Varz glass. He closed his eyes, but all the ladies could see was his mask's whole red, vicious red eyes. Harhk suddenly lurched forward, striking the glass. Vyan's forehead lifted off the glass; he looked at the warm orange skinned, dark being. She smiled at him in a patronising manner. Suddenly, he began striking the glass over and over and over. His inner body couldn't break free from the cell. His outer body couldn't either. He found it impossible to ignite, to burn, to reach the heat required to produce fire. Soon he found himself feeling so fatigued he dropped to the ground. Harhk put up her middle finger and then she and Enfuin left the room. Thick parts of the circular door appeared from out the tall and wide, chunky door frame. The parts spiralled closed, meeting together.

Annife was there standing in the corridor to meet them.

"How is the lovely fellow?" she asked.

"You call him lovely again, I rip your face off," Harhk replied.

They started walking down the corridor.

"I'm so sorry," the purple haired one replied.

"You don't think he's nice?" asked the pale-blue one, sounding serious, looking at Harhk.

"What?" she shouted.

"I've always liked him personally."

"What?" the dark one shouted even louder, looking furious, coming to a halt.

"I'm joking, woman!" she shouted back.

"How dare you!"

"How dare you!"

"How dare I? You silly bitch."

Enfuin burst into a dove and started pecking at Harhk's head. The orange-skinned one repeatedly attempted to swat the bird away.

"Vyan has escaped!" Annife cried. Both the beings stopped and looked her way.

"I'm just joking," she said. Harhk ran at her and tackled her to the ground. Annife had managed to quickly take out a small silver object from her own pocket. "Embrace," she shouted, putting it against Harhk's back and then quickly letting go. The silver, small rectangle suddenly grew around the two women, embracing them in its metal walls. The two beings found themselves in pitch darkness, stuck together, barely able to move a muscle.

Enfuin, still in dove form, looked at the still metal, rectangular box, turned back into her usual self and walked away.

Soon she was in the cockpit with Raggy and Freece.

"Young Enfuin," Raggy began, looking her way. He was sitting in a pilot's seat. "How are you?"

"Yes," she replied. Freece looked from Raggy to the young Huing – Huing being the name of Enfuin's species.

He said, "Have you ended Vyan's life?" He was standing.

"No, Freece," she answered.

"Why?"

"What do you mean why?"

"Tell me why."

"Have you not been listening to anything?"

"So are we just going to keep him in the cell forever?"

"No, you tit."

"Tell me why."

"We don't have the power."

"Physical power? I have the power!"

"No. Power to power the cell."

"Power to power the cell," Raggy repeated calmly.

"So why aren't we ending his life?" Freece asked.

"We are trying but we can't do it."

"I can."

"No, you can't."

"Why?"

"Look, you green dick, we are taking him to that priest we met not too long ago."

"What priest?"

"The priest," Raggy replied.

Freece paused, thinking. "Why?"

"Because he's a devil."

"The priest?"

Raggy shook his head wearing a solemn expression.

"Where are we going now?" the green one asked.

Enfuin walked up to him and started clicking her fingers either side of his head, beside his ears, while making meowing sounds with her voice. Freece went very still and started lowering down into a crouching position. Slowly, he backed away from Enfuin, looking around with wide eyes. Suddenly, he bolted and disappeared.

The Blue Eye soared on through the sky…

Chapter 6
Silence

"Do you want to talk about anything?" Paiht asked Wing. They were still in the sitting room.

She shook her head.

"Okay. That's fine," he said.

It was quiet.

"Do you want to see something cool?" Fellei asked.

The young girl's eyebrows raised a little. "Okay."

"Okay," said Fellei, not sure what she was planning to show her. Her father looked at her with raised eyebrows. Then he walked over to a wooden desk located at the back of the room. He opened its top and took out a plain silver coloured, simple and elegant looking pen. He walked to his daughter and passed it to her.

"What do I do?" she whispered.

Wing smiled.

"Click it," he answered.

"Okay…"

"You have to push it hard."

With strength, she clicked the bottom of the pen which at the moment was pointing towards the ceiling. It practically burst into a majestic looking shield shaped as a head of an eagle. It even had eyes and a furry head engraved into the metal. Wing's eyes were wide, as were Fellei's. She had dropped the object and jumped backwards in surprise.

"Holy crap! You could have warned me."

The older man smiled in a friendly manner. "Yes," he said.

"When did you do this?" his daughter asked.

"Recently."

"It's cool."

"Thank you."

"Congratulations."

"Thank you."

Fellei held the shield up and looked at Wing, then to her father. "How do I turn it back into a pen?"

"That's a little trickier. Hold it up in front of your face so you're looking at the inside of it. Then while you're breathing on it, say the words, Cleenhin Hee, and at the same time, push in on the sides."

Fellei did this. A pen dropped to the ground. "It's hard not to drop it," she said.

"You're just not very good at it," her father replied.

She pulled a disapproving expression, then looked at Wing. "Do you want to try?"

"That's okay," she answered, a small smile on her face.

Raggy looked out from his seat. Through the clear front of the Blue Eye, he could see mighty, strange mountains stretching high, and low on their odd bodies was a small city made of stone. An invisible protective barrier stopped heavy objects from falling onto the city. Raggy slowed the Blue Eye right down and passed through the barrier.

"Pretty," he commented.

"Very," Enfuin agreed.

"Umm, where should I land?"

"Maybe over there, in that big empty square," Annife pointed.

"Or in that empty space," Freece gestured.

"Or in that one," Harhk interjected. They were approaching closer and closer.

"Everywhere is empty…" Enfuin commented.

The ship landed in a stone square and the group exited. While Enfuin and Raggy had a look around, the others stared up at a massive, majestic black stone clock tower, which stood on one side of the square. House size grey stone buildings surrounded the rest of the square except for where there were paths.

It was eerily quiet. There was no one in sight.

"Where are the people?" Raggy asked.

"Because I know," Enfuin replied, sarcastically.

"This is a cool thing!" Freece called. The pale-blue one and the red haired one ignored him. They walked up to windows located near the front doors of two separate buildings. The curtains were open. Neither could see anyone inside. The bell suddenly started ringing in the clock tower. Harhk let out a little surprised chirp. Freece screamed and then once he had calmed down, he cleared his throat and mumbled something manly.

"Me and Raggy will go try and find the priest. The stairs up to the towers aren't far from here," Enfuin told the others. "Stay with the ship," she said in a slow, purposeful way.

"Don't patronise me," Harhk growled.

"Yeah," said the green one.

"Goodbye," said Enfuin, walking to the left of the black clock tower.

Raggy bowed to them as he passed. The red and blue one disappeared down a wide path. Strong, beautiful, grey stone buildings sat either side of them. They grew more and more majestic as they travelled forth, weaving their way to the bottom of the neither wide nor narrow white stone staircase which led up to a massive black and brown circular door. The two began to climb. They had noticed the stairs and the city seemed to be pretty much spotless. They didn't know that a being named Oddu was the one that kept it this way…this being could feel something right now…he was concentrating…

"I don't know if we should enter that tower," said Raggy, as they climbed the steps.

"I know but…we'll be fine. We just need to find him and take him to Vyan. Then it'll all be over. No more devil chasing. Wouldn't that be nice?"

"Mm, yes," he replied. "We look around for the priest as quickly and quietly as possibly."

"Yes."

He nodded then rubbed his face with one of his hands, still climbing. "It is probably my nerves making it worse," he quietly thought aloud.

"I think we can look after ourselves no matter what we come against," Enfuin told him.

"Yes." He nodded.

"Do you think it is a spell keeping this place so clean?" Raggy questioned.

"I would guess so. Or maybe they have an army of cleaners. That would be cool."

"Yes, it would," he agreed. His eyes went to the brown trunked, yellow leafed trees growing to his left. "They are nice," he commented.

"They are pleasant," Enfuin agreed – climbing the steps on his right. She then turned her head to her right and looked at the city which she could see a lot of now she was higher. The two had started climbing the steps with haste.

"The whole city is pleasant," she decided.

"Indeed," the red one agreed.

Up and up they went, swiftly stopping their chatter.

When they finally reached the massive, circular, black and brown door, white stone beneath their feet, they looked it up and down. Then Enfuin decided to simply twist the black, hanging, circular handle and push. She had to push hard, and the door smoothly, slowly and silently glided open, revealing a truly massive pile of bodies filling most of the large, very high ceilinged, circular room. The floor was marble, decorated in mosaics though the shocked two couldn't appreciate their beauty for they couldn't see them. Raggy and Enfuin took fighting stances as a being came sliding down the pile and hopping off to land smoothly on his two deep green covered feet. The being wore a green suit, mostly deep green. It looked to be exactly the same kind as Vyan's. He had one horn curving up from the right side of his head – from Enfuin and Raggy's point of view – and another deep-green horn going up from the middle of the top of his head and curving backwards and then downwards a little. Raggy and Enfuin didn't know if the body beneath the suit truly had these horns or not.

The name of the being was Oddu.

"Hello," said the demon with a slithering voice. The body which was his vessel had a forked tongue like Harhk's. It was black. "Have you brought me a partner?" he questioned genuinely.

"Did you do this?" Enfuin questioned.

"Yes," he answered.

Raggy's skin went blazing hot, his hair too, his clothes protected by a spell. His eyes turned a fiery orange colour and fire burst from his hands and body, the flames passing through his clothing as if it were not there. It had taken much time and burnt clothing in the past for this to happen successfully. The demon raised his hand and with it appeared a veil of deep green. The fire was too strong. The one in green was sent backwards, coming off his feet, hitting the bottom of the pile of bodies.

"Who do you think you are!" the serpent voice shouted. He sped forward at an unnatural speed and pinned Raggy against the wall. A deep-green wall suddenly shot up around them, surrounding them. "What are you?" asked the demon.

"Your doom," said Raggy, having swiftly been growing hotter and hotter. His eyes shone and fire burst forth from them, his mouth and the rest of him. The demon hit the green wall, unable to hold on to Raggy. He didn't try to keep the cage around them. He let it break and he rolled across the floor, managing to scurry with speed to safety. His deep-green suit was almost still in perfect condition. Raggy's blurry, fiery, tinged vision took a few moments to return to its clear self. Enfuin hadn't been able to keep her eyes on the green one, he had disappeared behind the bodies. Both she and Raggy, cautiously, readily, started walking…searching…it was possible Oddu had left the room. There were three possible exits, in the form of tall, stone, curved topped, empty doorways, not including the entrance which Raggy and the pale-blue one had come in. The two didn't see when the demon scurried swiftly and silently across the ceiling like a spider, above them. He crept down the wall and out the entrance, they had come in. Then he silently dropped down and started running down the steps – Unfortunately for this one, he couldn't teleport or create portals – Raggy and Enfuin continued to look, ready to spring into action…too many seconds later, not having found him, they left through the entrance and sprinted together, deciding staying together was the best choice. They were heading for the Blue Eye.

No one stood outside the ship but the green one could feel there were beings inside. He could feel that a possible new friend, a new partner was in there too. He zipped inside, running up the ramp and quickly and silently searched the ship, swiftly finding Vyan, standing in the middle of a Cell.

Annife had seen him on camera footage when he opened up the chunky circular door, before the Cell. She started running, running, running…but when she got to the Cell, it was open and empty. She couldn't put the ship on lockdown in time.

Enfuin and Raggy made it back to the Blue Eye too late…

The demons had escaped together. Maybe Oddu didn't have to be alone anymore…maybe he did…he took the still a little fatigued, Vyan to his ship. Maybe it was time to leave this city behind. *I will miss it,* he thought to himself.

When night arrived, it started raining quite heavily. It rained at night relatively often. Falsen and his son were in a cave. They had been energetic with wonder and intrigue. Doing anything less exciting than being in a cave was very boring and useless to them at the moment. Nimb of course had also wanted to go with them. He was perched on Ranglu's shoulder.

The young man began to whistle. Falsen joined him. There were small echoes for at the moment, they were in a space not quite big enough for them to stand at full height. Nimb attempted to join in but he found he couldn't. Ranglu could feel his breath as he blew.

"That tickles," he said.

"Sorry," the little creature replied, rubbing his paw on the side of the young man's face, in hoping it would itch the ticklish area.

"Thanks," Ranglu said, smiling. His foot caught on a rock. "Ah." He walked on, knees still bent.

"First time you've done that in a while," his father commented.

"Indeed it is. I am quite the expert traverser."

"This is quite a long tunnel," Falsen commented.

"Well observed," his son replied.

"Oh. There we go. Good timing. I see a turning." He was walking in front of his son, shining his torch onwards.

"A left turning?" Ranglu asked, his torch pointed at the ground in front of him.

"Indeed, son."

"Nice one, Ranglu," he complimented himself.

"Is this…the right time for a high five?" Nimb questioned.

"Yes!" Ranglu exclaimed happily. He put the torch in his left hand and held his right hand up, palm facing Nimb. Nimb high fived it with a small paw, concentrating. Then he grinned happily.

"Twenty steps, I reckon." Falsen decided.

"Till the turning?"

"Yes."

"Let's see if you are correct." They began counting.

With some steps varying in size, the man in front arrived at the turning in twenty steps.

"I'm smart," he said, looking at his son. Ranglu shone his torch in his father's face. "You're a disgrace. Now walk on, sir."

He did so, entering a massive cave room. They started shining there torches around. Ranglu opened his mouth to say something when his light landed upon a deep green, lonely Sund.

"Excuse me," said the Sund. "Do you mind? Imbecile."

"I apologise," said Ranglu, moving the light off his hairy face.

"Father and son?" asked the Sund, able to see them.

"Yes," Falsen replied.

"Explorers?" the Sund asked.

"Yes."

"Are you enjoying yourselves?"

"Yes."

"I am Jor," the green, hairy one told them.

"I am Falsen."

"I am Ranglu."

"Very strong," he complimented, talking about their names, looking at the father.

"Thank you," Falsen replied.

"You won't find anything down here," Jor told them. "The cave also floods easily. I would go now if I was you," he said with a hint of something. Both Ranglu and Falsen were unsure of what that something was.

"Okay," said Falsen, not wanting to cause or experience any problems. "Let's head back home," he said, looking at his son, then walking out and turning. Ranglu followed. They began their way back through the long, rocky corridor.

Once they were a good way away from the cave room, Ranglu asked, "Do you think it does flood easily?"

"I don't know. But I think we should head home now anyway. We've been down here a good while now."

"All right," Ranglu agreed with no objections.

Soon water was running under their feet but only a little. The two of them made it back to the cave entrance without any trouble. They started clambering over rocks, making their way back to the Hoat. That's when they met another Sund, perched on top of a particularly tall rock, happily sitting in the rain which at the moment was light.

"Good night, explorers," he greeted, making them jump.

"Hello," said Ranglu. His father was no longer in the mood to talk.

"Have you found anything?" the small being questioned.

"No, sadly," the young man replied.

"A shame. On you go."

"Uh-uh. Yeah. Okay." Ranglu unsurely turned away and he and his father walked on.

"Sund's aren't usually dickish, are they?" the son questioned, sitting beside his father on the quietly hovering Hoat, the rain picking up again, hitting his face.

"Not sure," Falsen replied.

Nimb disappeared beneath Ranglu's clothing. He had had enough.

"Whoa," said the young man chuckling. "You can't just do that without asking."

Nimb silently stayed in warm safety. Ranglu let him.

When they got home both men and Nimb got ready for bed. They were thankful for the comfort and warmth. It swiftly became clear that Ranglu was more tired than he had thought.

Wing, Fellei and Paiht were in the sitting room. It was night. A single lamp cast a warm orange light. None of them could sleep. Wing had something on her mind.

"I wish the violence would stop," she said quietly, her head on a pillow. She was lying on the sofa and unsure of whether the others were awake. "I hate it."

"I do too," Fellei replied softly.

"Everyone should hate it," Paiht said from the floor. This had been on his mind tonight too. "It's something that belongs in stories, as a fun or gripping thing. A thing of entertainment. But no one should bring it into the real world. Nobody should have to carry weapons because they fear other people. And even the demon in red. His head must be swiftly taken from his neck, but he must not be made to suffer. His life must be ended because he is a devil, pure evil, I know it and I know you do. But he must not be made to suffer. You should not yearn for revenge, Wing."

He said all of this because he had felt this yearning resonating strongly off of the girl. She was silent.

"How can someone like me change people's minds?" the girl asked. The other two could hear she was crying, trying not to. "No one has ever listened to me. I'm not someone that people will ever listen to."

"Neither am I," Fellei said. "But that's...so beautiful. You will always be humble. You will always be kind. You will always be hope to those who aren't loved, who aren't listened to, who feel they don't have a voice, who feel powerless. As long as you stay in the light, you will be an angel, bright enough

to scare away any darkness, wise enough to turn that darkness into light…I…I…"
Fellei went quiet.

"Both of you has more chance of changing the world than anyone," Paiht told them. "As long as you always keep the passion burning and you, you hold on to what you believe and you…you never give up, you never let anyone stop you, you always get back up after you fall. Your passion, your purpose, your dreams will come true. You will see the world change. You will see people change. You will open minds. You will bring heaven closer to everything…I need to do something…I need to try harder…we all need to always try our best to be peaceful. Things need to change."

Chapter 7
Angelfole

Ranglu woke to the sounds of nature and animal calls. He opened his eyes and saw Nimb sitting on him once again. Beyond Nimb were trees with long, healthy, twisting and tangling branches, the leaves a bluey green. The lighting was enchanting, blue with a slight greenish tint. Ranglu's eyes went wide. Nimb had to quickly hop onto the ground as the young man got to his feet. Ranglu quickly bent down to pick the little creature up. Once on his shoulder, Nimb said, "We're in Angelfole."

"Don't move," he added.

"What?" Ranglu asked. That's when he spotted a blood red, wingless griffin, creeping to the left of him, beyond a couple of trunks and greenery.

"They are blind and death," said Nimb. "They have…heightened senses. Do not move. And no more speaking."

Ranglu stood as still as he could, thoughts dancing around his head. A moment later, he heard maybe a couple of screams from far ahead of him. Then suddenly, there was a nearby crash and crack and snap. Through the branches above the wingless, blind and deaf griffin came a massive dragon, pterodactyl like creature, coloured red, black and grey. The griffin attempted to jump away. Talons ripped at the back end of its side and it fell on its other side. Before it could get back up, the dragon like creature stomped and grabbed, then burst back up through the trees, griffin in its grasp, making a racket and a mess. Ranglu was standing completely still, shocked and frightened to his core.

"Move now," said Nimb. "Find a cave. That is probably the safest. I will protect you."

Ranglu didn't move for a moment. He heard more screams and shouts from the same direction. "Move quickly," said Nimb. "Look for caves."

Ranglu took a step to his right. He began to walk, then he started picking up pace.

"It will be okay," Nimb said quietly. "It will be okay," he repeated. "It will be okay," he said again.

The young man hopped over fallen branches, pushed greenery out of his way. There was noise everywhere. He was panicking. An animal was going to pounce on him at any second…a dragon was going to swoop down from above…a hoard of angry birds were going to peck him to death…animal noises sounded all around. Running water was nearby…someone running hit Ranglu's side. Ranglu tumbled to the floor, frantically made sure Nimb was still on him, got to his feet and sprinted on, not looking in any direction but ahead.

"It was another person," Nimb told him. Ranglu kept running.

"There!" said the Boob. The young man halted and looked to where he was gesturing. He couldn't see a cave. His feet fidgeted. He was sweating. He batted at his bare skin. He only wore a T-shirt and sweatpants. He was ticklish all over. Then he spotted the small, dark entrance to a cave. He darted for it, cutting the bottom of one of his bare feet as he rushed in. He let out a moan and tumbled to the ground. He crawled to a wall and sat with his back against it. He looked at the bottom of his foot. There were smaller damages too. His thoughts went to infection. His mother and father had made sure he got all the highly recommended vaccinations, but this place was unknown. He didn't know what kind of things lived here. Ranglu tried to concentrate. He needed to wrap his foot in something.

"Grab leaves," said Nimb.

The tanned boy hobbled out of the cave entrance, swiftly grabbed several big leaves, and then returned into the darkness, sitting down again. As he attempted to wrap his foot in leaves, his eyes darting up and around and back down again, Nimb told him to "Stop".

Ranglu watched the little one drop down to the side of his foot. "Put pressure on one leaf," the creature told the young man. Ranglu did as he was told, his eyes still flicking around. When one big green, quite thick leaf was beneath his foot, Nimb asked him to "fold the ends on top and hold".

Ranglu did what he thought Nimb was asking him to do. He was correct. Then the Boob got up on his foot and placed a paw on the overlapping ends, telling Ranglu to "let go".

Ranglu noticed a faint enchanting blue light escape from beneath the Boob's paw, and float away. When Nimb took his paw away, the leaf's ends were sealed together. They then proceeded to wrap both feet in a number of the same leaves which Ranglu quickly grabbed more of.

"The leaves themselves…are tough," said Nimb. "Hopefully, your feet will be okay for a while."

"Nimb," Ranglu began. "How did we get here? Do you know?"

"I believe the hole has swallowed us."

"What do you mean? The hole in the door rock?"

"Yes. Not only us. It can choose anyone who has touched or passed through the hole."

"W—h—"

"It is a being with a mind," Nimb told him. "It lives to connect. It hunts and feels."

"I don't understand, Nimb," the man said. "Did you know all of this? Know this was going to happen?"

"Not completely. But it is okay. You are supposed to be here."

"I…" Ranglu didn't know what to say. He didn't know what to do.

"So, does the hole connect only with beings with minds and feelings and that kind of thing? It wants to connect with us?"

"Yes," said Nimb. "Be in you, around you—"

"Might it take us back home?" the young man interrupted.

"It might," the Boob replied.

"At any time?"

"Yes."

"And then it could bring us back here again?"

"Yes. Unless it…decides to leave you."

"How likely is that?"

"I do not know. Everything I learnt is from…voices in my visions."

"Okay…um…what am I supposed to do?"

"I do not know. But it will be okay."

"It will be okay? You're certain?"

"Yes. We will be okay."

"Okay…you've seen that?"

"Yes."

"We make it back home?"

"I do not know."

Ranglu definitely felt something touch his neck. He lurched forward and got to his feet, swatting at his neck. He still felt panicky. His head felt tired and full, unable to function anywhere close to well. The boy looked out of the cave entrance, seeing greenery bathing in the enchanting blue light.

"What do we do?" he asked.

"Be you," answered Nimb. "Be yourself. Feed…your curiosity. I think you should go exploring. In caves. Caves are safest but still dangerous. Keep your eyes peeled."

"Is this what your visions said I should do?"

"Um…I'm not sure, Ranglu. I am sorry. I think so."

"But I have no torch or anything? Do you not think I also need shoes?"

"Oh…okay…I will try."

Ranglu wasn't sure what he meant. Suddenly, the creature shone like the sun. Ranglu looked away. The light swiftly dimmed. When the young man looked back at the Boob, a bright-yellow light was surrounding him, lighting up the darkness.

"That would have been helpful last night," Ranglu commented, a little surprised, but starting to suspect this little creature was more than just an adorable, cryptic, fluffy little being.

"Sorry," said Nimb. "I don't like doing it. It makes me tired."

"Your feet will be okay," he added. "The leaves are strong enough. Be as careful as it is possible."

"Well…okay…" replied Ranglu, letting out a heavy breath. "Though I'm pretty terrified, I'm also insanely intrigued and excited. I feel completely insane. But that's okay. Let's go freekin' look in this lovely cave, in which," he continued, raising his eyebrows, "we will find treasure, scrolls, maps and freekin' magical…chickens."

Nimb jumped up and down, wearing that toothless grin. Ranglu could see his little white tongue.

"You are truly adorable," the young man commented, letting the creature up onto the top of his head. "Truly, I could squeeze you very hard."

"Please don't," Nimb said quietly.

"No, I won't," Ranglu reassured.

The young man began to walk, Nimb lighting the way. He made sure to lift his feet off the ground and then lower them back down as lightly as possible, while still trying to walk as normally as he could, trying to keep a reasonably good pace.

"Any ideas or guesses as to what we might find?" Ranglu asked Nimb.

"A…map."

"Of?"

"Mmmm…a sandy place. The inside of the friendly storm demon."

"The friendly storm demon?" Ranglu started descending a slope that wasn't too steep.

"The sandy storm you saw in vision," said the creature.

"From the vision Enfuin showed me?"

"Yes."

"You think that storm is friendly? And it has an inside?"

"I think so yes."

"So you don't think it represents the horrible, red, masked man I saw on the cliff? The one the Blue Eye are trying to catch."

"Oh…no. I do not think so. I do not think you will see him again."

"What? Really?"

"Yes. In the vision, I think the fire around you is a sign that you will be protected, safe. The arrow you fired maybe means there will be a battle of some kind. And the friendly storm is the friendly storm."

"Which has an inside?"

"Of a sort," said Nimb.

"Of sorts," Ranglu corrected. "Actually, of a sort is fine. Sorry."

"Of sorts," said Nimb.

Ranglu quietly thought.

"Wing won't see devil again either," said Nimb with a smile.

"The girl with dark skin and red hair?" asked the young man.

"Yes."

"She has seen him?"

"Yes. She has seen him twice. Once when she was escaping her master, she encountered him but got away. The devil didn't realise her strength. The second time she was with Fellei and her father—"

"What?" Ranglu questioned, stopping before a right turn, no longer on a slope.

"Wing felt broken in that moment. She had…cracked strength and the red one overpowered her. But then, Fellei's father overpowered the devil. He nearly

66

vanquished him. But the Blue Eye shot at the devil and the green one stole him away."

"So Fellei, Paiht and the girl are safe?" asked the man.

"Very safe."

"Okay…and do you know what the green one did with the devilish man? The green one being Freece I assume?"

"Yes. Freece put him in a special cell."

"Anything more?"

"Yes. They took him to a city in mountains. They wanted a priest to vanquish him but all they found was another devil. This devil was tricky. He managed to free the red devil from the cell, then he took him to his own ship. I think he wanted a friend maybe. A partner. The red devil convinced the green devil to leave the planet. The red one had had enough of this planet. The green one at first seemed unsure but then seemed happy with leaving. And they left. I do not think they will return."

"Nimb…" Ranglu said, still not having started walking again. "How do you know all of this?"

"I've seen it."

"In visions?"

"Yes. In my mind."

Ranglu started walking. He made the right turn, walked a couple handful of steps and then the rocky corridor suddenly widened for no apparent reason. Ranglu hadn't looked up since Nimb got on his head. But Nimb looked up now. His light revealed many, many white bats, hanging above. Ranglu and Nimb passing through didn't seem to bother the bats. The young man swiftly reached the other side of this wider area and entered a rocky corridor of a similar width as the ones before. Ranglu was very curious…about the cave, and everything else.

"Are the Blue Eye group okay?" he asked.

"Physically yes," said Nimb.

"Emotionally?"

"No."

He turned left and down another slope. Fortunately, these slopes weren't steep. A good way down the slope he had a choice to make. "Left tunnel or right tunnel."

"Left," Nimb told him.

"Okay," said Ranglu. "You should always make these decisions," he added.

"Okay," the little creature replied.

Then, further down he could turn left or carry on forward. Nimb chose left. They were still going down a slope.

"When you said, Fellei, her father and Wing were safe, that meant they're not in here, right?" asked Ranglu.

"I do not believe they are," Nimb replied.

"You don't believe they are? Does that mean they might be?"

"Unlikely. If they are, they will be okay."

"Completely good okay?"

"What does that mean?"

"I mean, will they be better than okay? Will they be good, healthy and well?"

"Yes."

"Oka—" Ranglu had reached a definite dead end. There was nowhere to go but back the way he came. The ground was less sloped now.

"Oh..." he said.

"No," Nimb said.

"No?"

"I feel something is here. A secret. Can you not feel it? This is the right way. You trust me?"

"Yes, I do, oh wise one."

"Oh wise one," Nimb repeated with a grin. "Feel wall roughly," he added.

"Roughly?"

"Roughly."

"Okay." Ranglu put his palms on the wall and moved them around as roughly as he dared. Shining, Nimb watched with suspicious eyes from on top of his head.

"Right hand," said Nimb.

"What?"

"Let right hand wander right more."

"Okay." Ranglu stepped to the right, his hand moved that way and up. Before he needed to stretch high, the side of his hand knocked off a small piece of rock which fell to the ground. Small bits of rock had fallen off before but when this one did, Nimb said, "Stop. Feel for something there."

Ranglu did, finding a small hole which his pinky could fit inside. He felt around and found a thick bit of string. He scraped the loop out of the hole, then put his pinky through the loop and pulled lightly. Nothing happened. He pulled a little harder. Nothing happened. He pulled harder. Nothing happened.

"Much stronger," said Nimb.

"Pull much stronger?" Ranglu questioned.

"Yes."

The young man grabbed the string with both hands and pulled. A deep click or crack that Ranglu could barely hear sounded, and the wall began to move. To the young man's surprise, it moved upwards. He quickly darted through. When the rocky door had almost disappeared into the ceiling, it started coming back down, a little faster. Ranglu moved onwards, finding himself in another rocky corridor.

"I think we're in the right cave," Nimb said smiling.

"I'm glad," Ranglu replied. "Because as exhilarating as it is, honestly, I don't feel like doing it again. Plus, this is something that just popped into my head, we are going to have to get back out."

"We'll be okay," Nimb reassured.

"I believe you, young one. Wait, are you young?"

"Yes."

"Okay. So will your voice change as you grow older?"

"Maybe."

"Maybe?"

"Maybe."

Ranglu stopped. "Right or straight on?"

"Right," the creature replied.

He went right. Soon he found himself in an open space. There was nowhere to go but straight on. He walked and found a gap. A gap in the floor that led into darkness. More ground lay ahead. Jumping over the gap would be easy. It was quite small. He might've been able to just step over.

"Shall I hop over?" he found himself asking.

"No," Nimb decided. "Climb down."

"Climb down the gap?"

"Yes."

"Oh shit...really? Are you certain?"

"Yes. Be brave, Ranglu."

"Okay, *sensei*. I'll be brave."

"I will see if I can see how far down the ground is."

"Okay," Ranglu replied, crouching down to let the creature make his way to the ground. The little one walked to the edge, got down on his belly and looked over. Ranglu felt very nervous watching him, like a father watching his child. The creature shone a little brighter. Then he got to his feet and started walking back to Ranglu.

"So you are aware," the Boob began. "I do not need the water you give me. I just like the taste."

"Oh," said the young man, laughing a little.

"Sorry," Nimb added. "It was just a thought that passed in my mind."

"That's all right." Ranglu realised for the first time that he could do with a drink.

"The ground is not very far down," Nimb told him.

Ranglu let the creature back onto his head, then said, "Wait. Wouldn't it be best if you got in a pocket or…hung your armpits on my shirt collar?"

"Yes. Pocket." He clambered down into one of the sweatpants pockets, his shining head poking out. He brightened a little.

The young man walked forth and cautiously sat down on the edge of the gap, looking down. Finding good looking hand and foot holds, he twisted and lowered down, his hands and feet successfully finding the holds. Below the rest of the wall was completely, strangely smooth. Something or someone must have smoothed it out. Ranglu looked behind him to the other wall. He stretched one leg out towards it for a moment and his foot touched the wall, then came back into its hold. He could see good holds on the other wall.

"Okay, three, two, one." His left side twisted towards the other wall and once his left foot hit the hold, he pushed off the wall with his right hand and foot and swung around, his left hand grabbing a hold and then his right hand and foot also successfully grabbing holds.

"Yeah," he exclaimed quietly. The rest of the way down was quite easy. He found the next holds easily and then the next.

His feet hit the ground in no time. The leaves wrapped around them were still holding up extremely well. In fact, to Ranglu's surprise, the leaves on the outside of each foot, the ones wrapped around all the others were still just about enduring on.

On one side of the young man was a wall, on the other, a rather narrow corridor leading into darkness. The two walls he had just climbed down were located in front and behind him. He twisted and started down the narrow corridor, helping Nimb back onto his head.

Soon Ranglu could see the end of this narrow corridor. He was able to hear running water.

They reached the end and stepped out of the corridor onto a very large slope. A quite big stream ran down the middle of it. They could either go up or down. Nimb chose down.

And so, Ranglu started down once he had taken a drink from the stream which Nimb had told him was "clean and good". They walked to the side of the stream. Nimb lay on his belly on top of the young man's head.

They had been walking down this slope for a little while when the Boob noticed a tunnel entrance over the other side of the stream, on the other wall. He told Ranglu they should go into that tunnel. So the young man looked for a rock or a couple rocks to hop on, to get over the stream, so to keep the leaves as dry as possible. Once he had found some not too ragged looking rocks, poking out of the water, he hopped across and made his way into the tunnel, stepping up onto a ledge and walking onwards.

"Right, left or forward, Nimb?"

"Right."

"Okydoky."

Ranglu walked for a while down this curving tunnel. He was a little tired when he reached the poolroom. The poolroom seemingly being a dead end. Curved, smooth stonewalls surrounded a not quite circular pool of water.

"What do we do now?" Ranglu questioned.

"Look into the water."

Ranglu leaned over the water. Nimb's light turned off in an instance, leaving them in pitch black.

"Nimb?" Ranglu called.

"Yes?" he replied calmly.

"Did you mean to do that?"

"I did."

"Okay. Please warn me next time."

"Okay."

Ranglu spotted red deep in the water. Two red things maybe. He moved around the side of the pool cautiously, looking in. Two red eyes looked back at him. Before he could panic, Nimb said, "Friendly storm."

"Friendly storm? The eyes?"

"Yes. His eyes."

"What does that mean? What do I do? Are we safe?"

"Yes, safe. You need to dive."

"Shit on my mother. You're joking?"

"Shit on your mother?" the little creature asked. "Why? I can't."

"No. Sorry, Nimb. Umm…you think I need to swim down? To the eyes?"

"Yes. Can you not feel it? It is clear."

"Mmm…can you swim?"

"Yes, but slowly."

"You can just get in my shirt. I'll tuck it in. Then you should be able to just sit in there while I swim down."

"Very good."

"Wait…you're certain about this?"

"This certain."

"Okay. Right. There are no creatures in the water?" The young man asked.

"I do not know. You will be okay."

"Well, you haven't led me wrong so far Nimbolobo. As far as I know."

Ranglu sat down, dangling his legs in the water. Hopefully, the leaves will be okay. He then made sure his shirt was properly tucked in. Nimb's soft, hairy body tickled the young man as he clambered in.

"Wait, how long will I need to hold my breath for?"

"You will be okay."

Ranglu looked into the water. As far as he could tell, the eyes didn't look too far away. "Ah poo. Haha. Alalalalala. And drop." Ranglu plonked into the water. Then swiftly took in a big breath and dove in. He kicked and pushed as fast as possible, heading for the eyes. He didn't like opening his eyes in water but he was doing it. Nimb was floating against the bottom of the young man's stomach, not needing to hold his breath under water.

With one last kick, his stretched out hand touched the ground in between the eyes. Ranglu had no idea what to do. But as his hand touched the ground, the eyes suddenly brightened. Red filled Ranglu's vision. It was so bright he had to close his eyes.

When his eyes opened again, he was lying on hot sand, soaking wet and cold. Wisps of Red light were floating away, off his body. Nimb quickly clambered out of his shirt and jumped off the sand onto his back. Ranglu moved the creature to his shoulder as he got to his feet and looked around. In all directions except one was vast, empty land. In that one direction was a great, mighty pyramid with the big, yellow stone head of a Seruthineira. Also known as the Great Sandbeast. Its eyes were calm. Its face and head was covered in short fur. Its nose was a powerful nose. It had two, long, thick, sharp teeth coming down either side of its mouth. Its ears were big and pointed, facing Ranglu. The young man was close enough to be able to see maybe a circular door of some kind at the bottom of the pyramid.

"I'm assuming that's where we go next?" he questioned.

Chapter 8
Skull and Crossbones

Ranglu reached the door which was circular and seemingly made of black stone. Red lines that to Ranglu looked like blood ran down the door's body. In the middle of it was a skull and crossbones.

"Looks nice," the young man commented.

"Scary," Nimb replied. "Scare away others."

"You're certain we need to go in here? We won't die?"

"We will be okay."

"Okay, from now on I won't ask if you're certain again. Or if we'll die again."

"Okay..."

Ranglu cautiously reached a hand towards the door.

"Be careful," the Boob added.

The young man retracted his hand. "So I do definitely still need to be careful?"

"Yes."

"Okay. Am I all right to touch the door?"

"I do not know. But I believe we need to go through it."

Ranglu reached for it again, wondering how heavy it would be. When his hand drew incredibly close, the skull and crossbones shone incredibly bright red and Ranglu jumped away and had to close to his eyes for a moment. When he opened them again, the skull and crossbones were gently glowing blood red.

"Good," the young man commented.

"Try again," said Nimb.

The boy blew some raspberries in complaint. Then once more, cautiously, he reached for the door. His hand made contact, nothing happened. There was no handle or anything so he just started to push. It wouldn't budge at all. He put his other hand to the door and pushed harder and harder and harder. Suddenly, he fell forward, through the door as if it weren't there. He tumbled into darkness and swiftly got to his feet which were still wrapped safely in the leaves, though the ones on the very outside of each foot had fallen off. Nimb hadn't realised how durable they would be. It was pitch black. "Nimb?" Ranglu asked.

"I'm okay," the creature replied. He had fallen off.

"Can you brighten?"

"I do not think that is necessary."

"Wh—" Ranglu then realised the darkness around him was fading. Just the darkness around him though. He became able to see the ground and Nimb. He picked the creature up and put him on his shoulder. They both looked around. The darkness had only faded very nearby, like a wide, dim spotlight was shining on them. And so, nothing had yet been revealed to them except the yellow stone floor. The young man stepped and looked back towards the door. It was still there, closed, apparently solid.

"Which way should I walk?" he asked.

"I do not know," the creature replied.

Ranglu, slowly and cautiously kept stepping forward, the spotlight following him, the darkness only around him fading to reveal more floor until he saw a…reasonably small wooden table in front of him. On it was a golden, old-fashioned lantern. He had no way of lighting it.

"Pick it up," said Nimb.

Ranglu hesitated, then did so, cautiously. Nothing happened. He and Nimb looked it over. They found nothing until they looked at the bottom of the lantern. Words were engraved on the bottom. *I will light the path to the revealer of paths.*

"It will light the path to the map," said Nimb.

"How?"

"I am not sure. Hold on."

"Hold on to the lantern?"

"Yes. I think, keep your eyes peeled for more lanterns."

"Okay. Which way should I go now?"

"I do not know. Any way. You feel. You decide."

Ranglu went right, around the table and onwards, lantern in hand. He saw nothing but the floor for a minute or so, but then in the corner of his vision, he noticed the edge of another table. He stepped right so the light revealed what was on it. A silver plate. Ranglu slowly picked it up and looked it over. On its bottom were the words, *Follow me and you will find the feast you yearn for.*

"For the greedy," Nimb said. "Follow only the lanterns. Now I know quite surely there will be more. But hold that lantern still. Until the end maybe."

Ranglu stepped left again and carried on onwards. "*The end* sounds ominous, Nimb."

"End of this…event."

"I understand."

Ranglu stopped for a moment when the floor started slanting down. Then carried on forth. A few minutes later, the floor flattened out again and the man reached the back of a chair. He moved around, revealing more and more of a rather large, strong and thick wooden table. A chair sat at each end and a chair sat at the middle of each side, facing one another, all tucked in beneath the tables brown, wooden top. Somehow, the wood and the items sitting in front of the chairs were all pristine. At one end, the right end, sat a silver plate. At one side sat an emerald-coloured dagger. On the other side sat a large, golden key. And at the other end sat another golden lantern.

"Go that way," said Nimb.

"The way the end of the table is pointing?" Ranglu asked, gesturing at the end with the lantern on it.

"Yes," the creature replied, smiling. "Follow the lanterns."

Ranglu nodded and started that way. He was feeling less scared now and more excited. More comfortably excited and of course intrigued and bewildered.

He walked forward until he reached a wall. He followed this wall, one hand stroking it as he walked. It curved smoothly until he seemingly reached a dead end. His hand touched the end wall and he moved around, trying to light it all up. A deep crack suddenly sounded. It was loud. It made both Nimb and Ranglu jump and exclaim. The young man had to quickly jump away when he noticed the floor was moving, opening up a passage. Once the segment in the floor was fully open, torches suddenly blazed on yellow stonewalls, lighting up the darkness below for a long way, revealing a slim, silver slide which led down and onwards.

"I wasn't expecting a slide," Ranglu commented. "This feels like the right way to go?" he checked with the creature.

"It does."

The man took a seat at the top of the slide and placed Nimb on his lap. The Boob was grinning. Then he pushed and started down the slide, still holding that first lantern he picked up. As he fell lower, going quite fast, ahead he saw a room.

The slide sent him into that room, where a golden, unlit lantern hung off the low ceiling, and on the wall ahead which was lit up by a torch, was an engraving of the two eyes of the 'Friendly storm'?

"Friendly storm," Nimb confirmed.

In front of Ranglu's very eyes, engravings that looked like branches began to grow from the eyes. Leaves grew on those branches. The branches glowed a healthy brown and the leaves a healthy green. The eyes suddenly went red. Then all the engravings disappeared in an instance and letters began to appear. Nimb and Ranglu watched, unmoving.

Ranglu Niefonpa. Your life shall not end now. Your legacy shall continue. You must prepare before you begin the journey, though you are already a warrior, you must prepare. Be patient. Be wise. Be bold. Be good.

The wall cracked and crumbled and fell. Out of the darkness beyond flew a rolled up, tanned paper map. It flew right into Ranglu's hand without him attempting to catch it. The darkness beyond then blazed with a white light, blinding Ranglu.

When Ranglu could see again, he was standing in his bedroom back at home, map in hand. It was morning.

When Ranglu was no longer inside the pyramid, the mysterious pyramid vanished. There was only vast, yellow land all around.

Ranglu Niefonpa's legacy shall continue.

Chapter 9
That Hole

Ranglu got down onto his knees beside his bed. Nimb jumped off his shoulder, onto the bed and watched as the young man unravelled the map and stared at it with wide eyes. His feet were still covered in sandy leaves. Ranglu could see nothing. The thick, tanned paper was blank. He flipped it over. Blank.

"Unexpected," said Nimb. "Patience," he added.

Ranglu blew raspberries in a manner which meant he was pondering about something. He flipped the paper and then flipped it again. He poked it with a finger, put it under a light. He heated it with a flame, though of course he did this safely, very much not wanting to burn the paper. Nothing worked.

"Well, Nimbulous," he began, "let us…show Father…wait, what time is it? How long have we been gone?"

The two went upstairs to find both Unela and Falsen in the kitchen.

"Hello," said Ranglu questioningly.

"Hello?" Mother replied.

"Anything weird happen recently?" he questioned.

"Quite a lot," said Falsen. "You have leaf around your feet."

"Have I been missing?"

"Have you?" Father questioned.

"Have I?"

"How are you, Nimb?" Unela asked, bypassing the oddities.

"I am well," the creature replied.

"Very good. And also very good speaking."

Ranglu snorted. "Yeah," he said in a knowing, sarcastic manner. But Nimb was grinning, hopping up and down.

"What?" Unela asked, looking at her son with furrowed eyebrows. "How could you have gotten so dirty already? I didn't realise you had even been outside yet."

"Well…it's just…I was stuck in, maybe another dimension, maybe just a strange part of the planet where time moves differently, maybe something else, I don't know. Nimb's been with me. The fact he can talk really well now is old news, Mother…hence the yeah comment, and the leaf feet, and dirtiness, sandiness. And this rolled up, so far blank map."

Falsen stared at his son. Unela looked generally unsure.

"Confirm me, Nimb," said Ranglu.

"I confirm what has been said," Nimb told them.

"You're serious?" Father asked. "Please tell me you're serious. That would be fricking awesome."

Ranglu laughed, hearing his father say "fricking awesome."

"Yes, I am completely serious. I swear it on…Fellei's life. How else could I have these sandy big leaves around my feet and smell the way I do? Have you smelt me? Truly, it's nasty. How could I possibly look like I do already, this early?"

"I was wondering if that was you," said Falsen, speaking about the smell.

"Why in all of this world were you…where were you? You should have been at home in bed," said Unela.

"That hole apparently can sort of, swallow you up if you've touched it, connected with it. It's alive and it's all a bit creepy and probably best you don't know anything about it, Mother," he replied with an innocent look and an innocent smile.

Falsen's eyes widened. "Might it take me?" he asked.

"It might. I have no idea."

"Where does it take you?"

"What is it called, Nimb?"

"Angelfole," Nimb answered. "Dangerous."

"Dangerous?" Unela asked. "What kind of dangerous? You're not going there again, son. I've had enough of all this, this nasty stuff going on."

Ranglu laughed. "I can't help it, Mum. I didn't decide to go there."

"What do you mean?"

"I just said."

"Well then…stop the thing. Disconnect from it."

"I don't know how to."

"Do you know how to, Nimb?" she asked.

"I do not. But I believe it would be a rare thing for it to take Ranglu again. It is uncommon for such a thing to take anyone. But this time, it took I think a group of people. Ranglu will be okay."

Unela took a moment, trying to understand and process what was just said.

"Okay…" she began.

"Ranglu will be okay," Nimb said again.

"What was it like there?" Falsen questioned. "What happened? Just slowly tell us everything and then we can…process…is that okay, wife?"

"Yeah," she replied.

"Okay," said Ranglu. "I need food and water first."

And so, Ranglu got food and water and he got some water for Nimb so the little creature could enjoy the taste. After, he told his parents everything that had happened and all the extra things they needed to know.

"Best story I've heard in a long time," said Falsen. "Really grips you when you know it's your son's life on the line."

Ranglu laughed at this. Unela managed a tiny smile.

"What do you think prepare means?" Falsen asked, seriously. "Do you need to get fitter? Practice your swordsmanship? Or prepare mentally?"

"I'm not sure," his son answered. "I'll do all you've just said to be safe."

"Don't overthink," Falsen told him.

"I won't."

"It's a good job Nimb's here," said Unela. "You've made me feel much better than I would have, hearing all this."

Nimb grinned excitedly. "You are welcome."

There was a knock at the door. Unela answered it, revealing Fellei, Wing and Paiht.

"Fellei!" said Ranglu happily. He swiftly got out of his chair and sprung towards her. He embraced her.

"What do you want?" she asked, her body squished against his. "Urgh," she added, able to smell him. Ranglu let go and stepped back. Fellei sniffed herself and then him. "That's terrible," she decided.

"Sorry. It's not my fault…"

"What the hell have you been doing?"

"Damn it…do I have to? I'm very tired and I would like to get changed."

"Do you have to what? Why are you so tired?"

"Shut your pretty mouth…everyone enter. You all need to know things that only wise man Ranglu knows…and Nimb, obviously. Nimb knows all."

Though Wing could feel they were good people, she stayed nervously silent until the red devilish fellow was mentioned, when she heard everything that Nimb had earlier told Ranglu, about the demons leaving the planet. She still stayed silent. But the nervousness went. Her head buzzed, thoughts danced. The news completely distracted her for a short while. Sadly, her thoughts weren't all good, optimistic and hopeful. She still had many doubts and questions. Though she didn't ask those questions. But she felt better, and that was nice.

After, Ranglu had a wash and got changed. A little after he had finished getting changed, there was a knock at his door.

"Yep," he called.

"You decent?"

"Yep."

Fellei opened the door and with her was Wing. "I wanted to show her your room," said the young woman. Ranglu bobbed his head.

"You may touch or mess around with anything you wish to," he said, looking at Wing. Fellei shut the door behind them.

"Are you sure?" the young girl asked.

"Completely certain," Ranglu replied.

"Really, it is fine," Fellei confirmed.

Wing smiled a little and began slowly looking. If she touched anything, it would be very gently and with great caution.

"So I am of course coming with you on this great adventure of yours, yes," Fellei stated.

"Just Nimb," Ranglu replied.

"What?"

"Just Nimb," he said, sounding deadly serious.

"No."

"Yes."

"No."

"No."

"No?"

"No."

"Good. Asshole." The two didn't see but Wing smiled at this.

"Of course you're coming, woman, you dangus. As long as the friendly storm allows it anyway."

"The friendly storm will love me," said Fellei.

"I'm sure it will, dear."

"I'm actually quite angry at you," she told him.

"Why?"

"I don't like the fact you went on this pretty incredibly adventure without me. Plus now I don't even know if I'm Nimb's favourite anymore."

"That must be hard for you," Ranglu consoled.

"It's not."

"No? It sounds like it is."

"You sound like it is."

"Yes, that's a good point."

"Your mother's a whore."

"Whoa."

"Sorry. I blanked out for a second there. Did I do something?"

"You're lucky she didn't hear you. She would kick your butt."

"Debatable. What time is it for you?" she asked.

"What do you mean?"

"If time moved differently there? How long were you there for?"

"No idea," said Ranglu. "But I am knackered. I'm probably going to sleep for the rest of the day, once you've left me in peace."

Fellei slapped him around the face.

"Ow!" he complained laughing. "Why?"

"Just…life," the young woman replied.

Wing was chuckling quietly, her eyes going from object to the two of them, object to the two of them. She found them quite entertaining. Their energy, their love, their feelings, they emanated off them. She could feel them.

"Forgive him, Wing," said Fellei. "He's less developed than us. A bit dumb."

Ranglu nodded serenely. Wing was smiling, creases by her eyes.

"Where's my son?" Ranglu questioned.

"Who?"

"Nimb."

"He's not your son. And he's hanging out with our fathers and your mother I think," she replied.

"What a cool little dude."

"Indeed."

Fellei walked over and grabbed the map off the bed. She unravelled it. It was blank.

"So you've definitely tried everything?" she asked.

"That I can think of."

Fellei put the thick, tanned paper close to her mouth and breathed on it whispering the word, "Ryval."

"Anything?" Ranglu questioned.

"Nothing," she answered. "Wing," she said, stepping closer to her. "Do you see anything?"

Wing shook her head. Fellei flipped the paper over. Wing shook her head. Fellei then breathed on that side, doing the same thing again. Nothing showed up. She scrunched her nose. "Frustrating."

"Patience, young one," said Ranglu. "I have learnt much on my travels with Nimb. Patience is indeed a virtue. One you should learn."

"Shut your mouth," Fellei told him. "I've been patiently waiting for you to pass away for a long time now."

"Mmm," Ranglu replied, smiling, amused. "You shall have to practice swordmastery with me please," he added.

"All right. When?"

"Some soon time."

"Not today?" she asked.

"No. I need sleep."

"Okay. Well, you enjoy yourself."

"I will."

"Good."

While he slept, Ranglu had a vivid dream. Some kind of puzzle floated in front of him. The young man was surrounded by floating grains of sand in every other direction. Then the puzzle suddenly changed form. In front of him stood a growling lion with sharp teeth. Then the lion disappeared. Next, he saw a mountain with many steps going up its great body. Then everything calmed. A cobbled path weaved in front of him. Lovely short grass grew either side of the path and there were trees gently swaying in the wind. A shield lay in the middle of the path. Then he saw faces. He saw Fellei, Wing, his mother and father, Paiht, Nimb, the Blue Eye team, a unique looking stranger with long brown hair and a beard. And then, he woke. He turned over onto his back to see a pale wisp of light dancing above him. The light was clear for the room was dark. He sat up slowly and his eyes followed the light as it floated down and passed through a solid drawer in his bedside table. Ranglu opened the draw and saw the map was glowing with a faint, pale-white light. The light swiftly faded. Cautiously, the boy reached into the drawer and took out the map, unravelling it after turning the light on. It was still blank. Ranglu sat there for a short while, thinking. He came to the conclusion that he needed to prepare his mind and body. But there were other parts of the dreams that he couldn't come to a conclusion about. He didn't even know if the lion and the puzzle meant what he thought they meant. Really, he hadn't come to any conclusions, but he was definitely planning on preparing his mind and body as best he could. The rest he could ask Nimb about, and the others, but Nimb mainly for Nimb saw things differently and probably more correctly than anyone else. And the glowing map…the floating wisp of light… *Had they given me the dream?*

Ranglu had found that Nimb wasn't in his room, sleeping where he normally did. So the young man left his room and went up the stairs to see if it was day or night. It was night still. He hoped morning would come soon…Nimb was probably with Fellei. *What can I do?*

The young man returned to his room and grabbed a small silver machine that had a round body and a small snout. He also grabbed the sheathed dagger which Annife had made and returned upstairs. The tanned fellow put the machine down at the bottom of one of the walls in the dining room and unsheathed the dagger. He managed to keep hold of it when it practically burst into the strange sword with the cross handle that grew up either side of the blade for a short distance. Ranglu turned on the machine which was almost completely silent and prepared himself. A small, relatively soft white pellet silently shot out of the snout of the machine. Ranglu attempted to block it with the sword. He failed. Another pellet shot out. He missed it again. Then another. He clipped this one. Then another and another…

Ranglu practiced this for a long time, at one point having sped up the machine. He was trying to get used to the sword and sharpening his reflexes. Then the irritating time came when he had to collect the pellets and put them back into the machine. Afterwards, he went through all the pellets again, and put them back into the machine.

Then he made the sword change into the bow. He grabbed a quiver not quite filled with arrows and went outside. He set up a target. The sky above was lightening. He began to shoot, then move and shoot. Then collecting the arrows and doing it again.

Falsen drew the curtains and spotted his son outside. The father opened the door and watched him for a moment. Then asked, "Hungry, son?"

Later that morning, there was a knock at the door. Ranglu answered it. His mother and father were working. The young man opened the door and saw what was beyond. He stared silently for a moment. The Blue Eye team stood there, Freece, the green one, with a big lizard hanging on his shoulder. It was dead.

"Hello," said Enfuin. "We brought you a lizard as an apology for disturbing you again. We just need to ask you something and then we'll be on our way."

Freece dropped the green and brown lizard at Ranglu's feet. "I found it over there," said Freece gesturing towards the nearby empty, open land area. "So it's home-grown. So cooking it won't be a problem."

"What?" Enfuin questioned, looking confused.

Freece didn't know she was speaking to him so he didn't answer, he just carried on looking at Ranglu.

"Freece!" she called.

"What?"

"What you just said didn't make any sense."

"It did to me."

"And that's good enough?"

"What?"

"Urgh, nothing. Sorry, Ranglu. Umm, what we wanted to know was if you had seen Vyan? The red devil you saw."

"Oh, no I haven't. Umm, do you have, um, any clue as to where he is?" Ranglu replied.

"No, we do not."

"Okay, umm, well I do, sort of, but it's a long story. Do you want to come in and sit down?"

Freece bustled in happily, not saying anything. Harhk followed him.

"Okay," said Enfuin. "Anything would be helpful." She walked in. Annife followed quietly, giving the young man a small smile. Raggy looked at Ranglu and then down at the lizard. "Would you like some help taking it in?" the red haired man asked.

"Um, yeah."

Raggy nodded, bent down and picked up one end, Ranglu picked up the other. They brought it in to the house. "Freece put a spell on it that repels bugs," Raggy told him, as they entered.

"Oh okay, cool, thank you," the young man replied. They put it down in a corner of the dining room. Ranglu felt a wave of pity for the thing and told himself he would make sure it all got eaten and made the most of.

"A lovely home," Raggy complimented.

"Thank you."

"Tell us what you know of the red bastard," said Harhk, leaning against one of the walls.

"Okay." Ranglu looked at them all. He wasn't sure where to begin. "Umm…" They were all staring at him. He swiftly found himself talking.

Harhk began cursing over and over. She was about to strike the wall when Raggy lifted up a hand and out of one of the stones suddenly protruded more stone, this bit of protruding stone struck Harhk very, very hard in the head and she fell unconscious.

"Sorry," said Raggy, looking at Ranglu. "She would have wrecked your home."

Something suddenly clicked in Ranglu's head. "You can command, more than command, you can umm, be stone, fire, water, wind, umm…wood and leaves and earthly stuff. You're a…um…"

"I am a Sheaperrihaiker," the fiery haired one told him.

"A Sheaperrihaiker," the young man repeated. "You're…legend type stuff."

"Yes," he said humbly.

"Ranglu, how certain do you think it is that Vyan and the other have left the planet?" Enfuin questioned.

"I'm pretty sure. I have enough reason to trust Nimb with that kind of stuff."

"Okay…" She thought for a moment.

"How will we find him now?" Annife questioned. "Harhk won't sense him if he's too far away, will she?"

"No," said Enfuin. "He could be anywhere. We'll never find him."

"We may have to forget," said Raggy. "Live our lives and not think about it. But if Harhk does sense him again, then of course we will try our best to find him and stop him for good."

"We're the reason he's still alive. That man, your partner's father" – the pale-blue one looked at Ranglu – "he really has the power to end Vyan? He was really going to?"

"I'm pretty sure, yeah," the dark-blonde young fellow replied.

It was quiet.

"There's nothing that can be done," said Raggy. "Begin letting go of it all now. The sooner the better."

"I actually think your futures do um, lie elsewhere," Ranglu began. "Something happened to me, very recently and I've had a dream and…do you mind if I just tell you the whole story. I feel like I need to."

"That is fine, Ranglu," said Enfuin. "Please do."

When Ranglu had finished, he fetched the map and brought it to Raggy. Annife watched with suspicious, violet eyes, over his shoulder as he sang an ancient, ancient song which he had said was called "A Voice of High Hope, Enlightenment and Revelation". As he sang, his skin started to glow angelic yellow, his eyes too. And then, the map began to reveal some of its secrets. Ranglu watched in awe struck silence.

When Raggy came back to reality, it didn't seem like he really was back in reality. He seemed dreamy and wobbly and elsewhere. He laid the map out on the table, holding the sides. "This is not all of its secrets," he began. "It won't show them all. I know it."

"I must come with you on this journey," he continued, looking up at Ranglu. "I must."

"Okay," said the fellow, unsure of what to say. "I think you will be coming with me in some way no matter what."

Raggy nodded. "You all must let go of the past and look ahead," he told his team. "Trust me. You need to."

"How?" said Enfuin. "How are we supposed to do that?"

"I will help every single one of you. I believe you'll be able to. Don't second guess. Do not overthink. Trust your guts and hearts. Don't listen to your heads for now. Trust me."

They had found on the back of the map were the words, Three months' time…they guessed this meant they would either encounter the friendly storm in three months' time or start the journey to the friendly storm or…but if they were to be starting the journey to the friendly storm, they would need to know where it was but as far as they could tell, the map so far gave them no clues. This was because the map seemed to be a map of the insides of a building of some kind…maybe…probably…

"Do you remember what surrounded you in the vision?" Raggy asked Ranglu. "Do you remember?" he asked again, looking at Enfuin.

"It was land similar to everywhere near here," said Enfuin.

"Yeah," Ranglu agreed. "I don't remember seeing anything specific."

"Okay," the red haired one replied. "Maybe it will come to you…or maybe you will see it on the horizon and you'll need to travel to it. You didn't see any houses in the vision?"

"No."

"But then visions aren't literal," Enfuin added. "Well…it looked like a sand storm and you were standing in a sandy place. But there was also no one with you, and…I don't know. It's just unlikely you will find answers in the vision Raggy, I think."

"Okay. Good point."

"But obviously we have no answers in other places, so the vision is fine," she said. "Sorry," she added. "I'm going to shut up."

"Never shut up," said the purple haired one, stepping close and patting the pale-blue one's back.

"So," Freece began. "This storm…do I need to viciously attack it when It comes for us all, like some DAMN PIG!"

Harhk slapped the green one. "Listen, you oaf! Where have you been? The shitting thing is called a FRIENDLY STORM."

The green one stared at her, angry, ready to strike back. Raggy raised a hand and the stonewall threatened to get them. They looked at it and then Freece eyed Raggy. The red haired one raised his eyebrows. Freece crossed his arms. Then quietly added, "I'm not scared of you," looking at the fiery fellow.

"I believe you, Freece," he answered.

"Good."

Annife had been looking at Ranglu for a short while now. "How is my weapons in one?" she asked. Ranglu assumed she was talking about the strange sword, bow and dagger, transforming weapon.

"Wonderful," he answered.

Annife smiled happily. "Thank you."

"You're welcome."

"Freece," said the pale-blue lady. "Can you do any of your Inhast?" she asked, gesturing at the map.

"Why? What?" he questioned grumpily.

"To try and reveal more of the map?"

"It might be that we're supposed to leave it alone, let it reveal in its own right time," Raggy interjected.

"I know," the lady answered. "But it might also be that we are the ones that reveal the map. The ones that help Ranglu by revealing the map for him. Yes? Of course that's not the only part we're going to play in his little adventure. I forbid it," she said with a smile, looking at the young fellow.

"Give it to me," the green one demanded.

"Be very gentle, please," said Raggy.

"This means a lot to Ranglu and us," Enfuin added.

"Mm," he replied, taking the map. He was standing. He held it out in front of him and stared at it. Ranglu watched, a little nervous. He had no idea what might happen.

Suddenly, it looked as if green lasers were shooting out of Freece's eyes, hitting the paper. Ranglu gasped and stepped back. The others kept watching as if this was absolutely fine. Then the lasers disappeared. Freece's eyes were glowing green, as was the map which had no holes in it. The green one looked to be in a Zen like state. Green light danced from his eyes and from the map, intertwining in the air. Then it all vanished. Freece came back to reality, looked at the map for a moment, then handed it to Enfuin, wearing a lazy expression.

"There's more," she said. "It worked," she added, looking at Freece and then Ranglu.

"Amazing," said Raggy.

Ranglu stepped closer and looked, as did everyone else, except for the green one. Now they couldn't tell whether everything was there or not.

Still, after a little while of looking, there was no indication of where the storm might be located. It was definitely showing the inside of a very complicated, vast, intricate, precise structure, building of some kind. There were small pictures of different things located in different areas of the building.

"Fascinating," the red haired fellow admired.

The back of the map read:
Three months
Two months
One month
Then the weeks counted down...
Then the days...

Chapter 10
Listen to Me

There was an angry man named Kolwel. It was morning. He pushed open one side of a two door arched doorway. He walked through the nearly empty tavern, towards a rough looking, muscular green fellow with a grey horn curving up from his forehead. His upper body was bare and inked. Kolwel was shirtless. He too was muscular. His skin was tanned, yellowish-brown, his eyes were entirely blue. His hair was long and brown and he had a long, shabby beard. He had pointy, elf like ears and a single, black horn curving up from the right side of his head.

"Don't move, Yab!" he called.

Yab, the green, rough looking one looked up from his drink. He saw Kolwel, sprang up and ran for the back door. "Damn it!" shouted the pointy-eared one, running after him. Yab burst through the back door and started running across the sandy, rocky ground. Kolwel was catching him already. Yab ran down a track and entered a small, sandy, skinny treed forest. He sprinted and weaved as fast as he could. But Kolwel could dart and weave like an animal, his bare feet unharmed. He swiftly caught up and leapt at the man's back. They tumbled to the floor. Kolwel pinned him to the ground. He gripped his neck with a hand.

"Just listen to me," he growled. "I'm not going to hurt—"

Yab let out a shout and wildly struck the man in the head. Kolwel's hand left his neck and his forearm hit the ground, trying to keep himself up. Yab attempted to scramble away but he failed. The blue-eyed one struck him against the ground.

"Listen, asshole. I just wanted to tell you I know you were paid good money to do the job. I understand it was just stealing one thing from my home. That was it. I forgive you. All I wanted to say was that I forgive you. I'm not here to kill you or hurt you. Just never go near my home again. If you tell anyone else where it is, I will hurt you." Kolwel stayed on top of the man, pinning him down. He had let go of his neck. Now he was just looking at him, making sure what he had said had sunk in. Then he got to his feet.

"Why?" asked the horned, green fellow, also getting to his feet.

"Why what?"

"Why me? Why spare me?"

"Because you're a good person."

"The others—"

"Maybe they were," Kolwel interrupted. "But it was my life or theirs. Leave now."

Yab looked at him for a moment. Then turned and started walking. Kolwel turned too and began walking. After a couple handful of seconds, Yab turned to look back. He couldn't see Kolwel. He would never see him again.

Kolwel ran and ran and ran, not because he was in a rush or being chased. He just didn't want to waste time walking. Still at such a constant pace, it took him a good while to get home. His home located in a bizarre, dangerous wood named, BeastSpawn Wood. The trees trunks were deep red and brown and the leaves were too. As was the grass which grew out of the rocky ground here. Kolwel slowed down once he entered the wood. His thoughts were on how he had lost control when the men had come to his home, his long hidden home, and attempted to steal a specific item.

The beasts of the wood, some known to be dangerous – these being some of the reasons other beings never came in these woods – others not so much, let him pass without a glance. He walked on, deeper and deeper into the wood until he reached his wooden home which was tucked in between a mess of red and brown nature, almost all covered up. The animal man brushed past the leaves and plants, to his wooden, arched front door. He walked into the house, onto wooden floorboards. He walked into the mostly bare sitting room, picked up one already packed, big black bag from off the sofa and put it on his shoulder. Then he walked out of his home, never to return, heading towards the other end of the forest.

Kolwel had been swiftly travelling for a while when he spotted a very large spaceship in the distance.

He eyed it as he passed. It was dark-blue and had a white stripe. It was triangular shaped but with a curved back end. He walked on, houses ahead. His plan was to quickly pass through this area, head down. But that didn't happen. He stopped, sensing something unusual behind him. He turned and saw a woman wearing a simple pale-blue dress which was a little dirty with sand. He felt peaceful looking at her. He sensed an animal presence. A gentle, beautiful, peaceful, truly feminine presence.

"Yes?" she asked, stepping forward from the ships door after closing it.

"I apologise," he said. "You are very beautiful."

Enfuin's eyes gave him a suspicious look.

"You are very handsome," she returned.

The blank map that sat in Kolwel's bag started to reveal its secrets for the first time. Its secrets were different to those of Ranglu's map. He had obtained the object in a pyramid that had revealed itself to the Hunter. The map was a mystery Kolwel still longed to unravel. The experience he had had in the pyramid had been truly incredible.

"What is your name?" the Hunter found himself asking.

"Enfuin," she answered.

He bowed. "I am Kolwel."

"Where do you come from?" she asked, walking a little closer.

"Nowhere," he answered.

"Ah, as do I," she said.

"You are a traveller?" he asked.

"Yes."

He nodded.

"Your bag seems to be glowing green," Enfuin noticed. Kolwel looked at it. Green light suddenly spilled out of it and swallowed the two up, then the green vanished.

Ranglu threw a stone up in the air. Fellei aimed her metal bow; holding on to a deep-green grip with one hand and pulling the string back with another. She let go and the arrow flew, striking the stone in the air. Nimb was sitting in a shaded spot, beside a rock, watching.

Fellei threw a stone into the air. Ranglu hitched an arrow onto his bow's string, pulled back while aiming and let go. The arrow struck the stone.

"Nice!" Fellei complimented.

"Yeah!" said Ranglu, jumping up like a child.

"You always ruin it!" she complained. "You're not cool enough!"

"You're not cool enough! You're heated like the sun! Hahahaha!"

Fellei quickly picked up a stone. Ranglu didn't manage to hit this one. He fumbled.

"Haha!" she exclaimed. "You're terrible. You're going to die!"

"Wow!"

"That's right, son!"

"I'm not your son!" he exclaimed incredulously.

"You are. I had sex with your father!"

"NO!"

"DEAL WITH IT!"

"I THINK I'M GOING MAD WITH THE HEAT!"

"BECAUSE OF THE HEAT!"

"YES!"

"YEAH! ME TOO!"

"HAHAHAHA!"

Nimb was in hysterics, rolling on his back.

Chapter 11
The Boy on the Throne

Enfuin and Kolwel stood in a beautiful, green forest, decorated with plants ranging in lovely colours. There was pleasant bird song and water calmly running nearby. Ahead of them, the trees made a pathway, one which led to a large, smooth surfaced, upward slanted rock. They couldn't see what lay beyond the rock. In every other direction was wild, seemingly untouched, gorgeous nature, no other paths in sight.

Enfuin watched as the animal man dropped his bag to the ground, opened it and rummaged around. When he brought out the map – which had nearly dimmed back to its normal, not glowing self – and unravelled it, she said, "You have the same map." But then almost immediately realised. "It's not the same. Where has it taken us?"

"It has been blank up until now," he told her.

"Are you a good man?" she asked.

He looked up at her. "Yes. I have not stolen you away. I swear to you. I discovered this map. I discovered it in a way. But it is more complicated than that. It was a while ago now. I have wanted to know more about it ever since but it has never revealed anything more to me before now…is it because of you?"

"Me?" she asked. "I…have no idea."

"But I have been looking at one of a similar kind over the past, around three months. Maybe, I don't know, they have something to do with each other."

"Can you tell me anything more?"

"Not until I know I can trust you."

"Okay. That is fine. Here," he said, handing her the map. He already felt he could trust her. "In the bottom left, it shows these lines of trees, I think," he said gesturing to the tunnel of trees ahead which led the way to the rock. Sunshine pierced their canopies every now and again down the tunnel, casting patches of sun on the green ground.

"Okay," said the lady. "And then beyond, there's a valley."

"You agree we should head that way?"

"Yeah. But why? Do you know what the goal is?"

"I don't."

"Okay. I think…yeah, let's just start walking."

"Okay."

They began, entering the enchanting walkway. Enfuin felt like she would be greeted by a king or queen at the end of it and be given a medal. Kolwel's thoughts were on nothing of the sort. A blue and white bird landed on his head. Enfuin eyed it and smiled. Kolwel didn't seem to notice, or maybe he just didn't mind. The bird fluttered away. They carried on walking, sunlight occasionally splashing on their heads. When they reached the rock, they walked onto it and looked out. They saw a heavenly vision. A majestic valley with a river running down the middle of a grassy plain, a tall, strong cliffside stretching upwards to the side of it. On the other side, also a little way away from the river was an ocean blue and warm yellow forest. Beyond the open green were more trees. A wood made of green and orange colours. And on the horizon, far, far away – Enfuin was surprised by how far she could see – were mountains.

"That's nice," said Enfuin.

Kolwel chuckled a little. "Yes."

"How do we get down there," she wondered, looking around and down. Below the rock, she found a clear path. It weaved all the way down the steep hill to the ground.

"Is there any chance you can fly?" she asked.

"Sadly not. You can though?" he suspected.

"Yes. But I will stay with you on foot."

He nodded, then looked to clamber down from the rock, but stopped. "Wait," he said, "try."

"Try what?"

"Try and turn yourself into the dove."

"How do you know it is a dove?"

"I can sense it."

She looked at him suspiciously.

"Trust me. I could sense it when we first spoke. The name of my kind is Xvallos." He waited to see if she had heard of such beings.

"Makes sense," she said, looking him over.

He bobbed his head then asked her again to try and transform. She couldn't do it.

"This place is blocking your ability to transform," he said.

"You sure it isn't you?"

"I would never. I promise you."

"This is very clearly a magical place. You know it is."

"So it doesn't want me to be able to fly," she observed.

"I assume so."

"Good," she said sarcastically.

"Let's move now. While it is still light," he decided.

"Yep," she replied, both of them moving to clamber down from the rock. They stepped onto the thin path, Enfuin behind Kolwel, and made their way down the steep hill, occasionally looking up and out, admiring the beauty ahead. The sky above was blue completely, not a single cloud in sight.

When they reached ground below which was made of healthy green short grass, they carried on walking, now beside the winding river.

The pale-blue one looked to her right and admired the grey cliff that was a little ways away. She heard a splash. Her head turned. She looked back down the river and saw a small fish jumping out of the water and diving back in.

"Look at the cliff," Kolwel said. He had come to a stop.

The lady also did. She looked where she thought he was looking.

"There." He pointed. "There's a hanging silver handle." His eyes could see much further and better than Enfuin's. She couldn't find it. The Hunter started stepping towards the cliff. Enfuin followed, still trying to spot the handle.

When they reached the hanging handle, they could still see no sign of a door or anything. Just a handle hanging low on a cliff face. Enfuin went to grab it before Kolwel did; he was still looking over all the nearby stone. Somehow, it was pleasantly cool to the touch.

"Be careful," said the Hunter.

The woman cautiously twisted but didn't pull. As she twisted, the handle felt as if it clicked but there was no noise. It was a soundless click. Enfuin paused…the cliff vanished silently. In front of them now sat a magnificent throne made of vines. Behind the throne stood tall, thick, immense trunks stretching up and up, higher than the clouds. Their canopies couldn't be seen. When Enfuin and Kolwel were gazing up, they spotted something. Someone. A child. A boy with an innocent face. He gracefully floated down, landing in the throne, sitting. He looked at them and said, "If you hold on to rage, it will stop you. If you hold on to the past, it will stop you. Your hearts are good but your minds have faults. Innocence is what you should teach. Innocence should be longed for. Have a voice of hope and act with burning passion but be slow to anger. Thrones lay far ahead of you. My words will stay with you forever as long as you let them. Trials and hard times are not what is wanted. All lessons learnt in pain can be learnt in love. All lessons can be taught by a wise, gentle voice and a loving embrace. You are forgiven. Now take control."

Both Enfuin and Kolwel fell to their knees, tears in their eyes. Their bodies hit the ground and their eyes closed.

Enfuin and Kolwel now shared a vision as they slept. They saw a young man stabbing another. The one who had just been stabbed fell down to the ground, dying. But then, another man appeared. This man lay his hand over the man's wound and closed his eyes. "You are healed," he said softly. And the man who had been stabbed got to his feet, embraced the fellow and kissed his cheek. "Thank you," he said.

The vision changed. They watched as a woman slapped her daughter across the face. The girl began to cry. The woman struck her again and stormed off, cursing. Another woman appeared and walked up to the girl. The girl looked into her eyes. The woman lay a hand on the cheek that had been struck and said, "Be at peace, little one. You're safe now." The girl embraced her and sobbed in the woman's arms.

The vision changed. There were two boys. One bullying the other. Pushing and shoving, calling names, punching and hitting. Then the boys turned into men. They were older now. The victim answered the front door to his home. The former bully, now a man with bags beneath his eyes was standing at the door. He began asking the man for forgiveness, tears in his eyes. The other one said, "I forgive you." The bags disappeared from beneath the man's eyes and his face brightened.

Enfuin woke surrounded by floating grains of sand. Enfuin got to her feet and stood very still. The place was reacting to her arrival.

"Kolwel!" she called. There was no answer. It was silent. Eerily so. All the floating sand disappeared in an instance. Enfuin was in a high, curved, stone ceilinged room. A yellow stone pave was beneath her feet. She stayed completely still on this pave, for she spotted a few stone figures and then something or someone else. Her eyes were wide; her thoughts were dancing manically. Up on a platform between two pillars was a stone throne. Sitting on that throne was a long, thick snake with the head of a woman. The woman's head was up, staring at Enfuin, moving side to side. The pale-blue one found the sight disturbing. She held eye contact with the snake woman. The head began to hiss at Enfuin.

"You think you can banish me from my home?" she questioned. "You think you have the power to do that? Because you have encountered something holy…" She was quiet for a moment. "You are nothing. You have no strength." The head spat, grey liquid flying from her mouth. Enfuin had to move. She managed to just dodge the liquid. The snake woman had already leapt off her throne and she came for Enfuin with alarming speed. She lurched and snapped her pointed teeth but all her teeth touched was the stuff Enfuin called, dazzle mist. A dove fluttered above the head, dodging and diving. As the head lurched again, the bird darted for an eye. It made contact. The snake woman began to scream. The head swung back and forth manically. Enfuin changed back into her normal form and sent two beams of ice from her hands. The ice made contact with the head and wrapped around it. But the snake woman swung her body so the ice broke and cracked on impact with the stone. This the serpent woman barely felt. The piercing peck in the eye had caused her more pain than she had felt in a long time. Enfuin turned back into a dove. In the same moment, the snake shrunk to a much, much smaller size, as did the head. The bird dove down towards her, only just twisting and dodging another spit. The evil being lurched out of the way in the blink of an eye. She was faster now. Frighteningly fast.

"You can't stop us," she screeched. "My uncle is a devil and he lives here too! You cannot defeat me! This is our home! If you take me away from it, I will haunt you forever! Stay away and I will let you go in peace!"

"Free my friends and I will leave you alone!" Enfuin returned. She could sense they were here.

"No!" she replied.

Suddenly, Raggy broke free from the stone that encased him. His form was fire. His blue flame eyes darted around the place. He was panicked. He wasn't sure of anything. Where he was, what was happening. The serpent lady earlier had hidden, watched and surprised them. She now, seeing Raggy, went darting out of the room, through an empty doorway located beside the platform on which the throne was sitting. Enfuin didn't chase her. She swooped down and changed form so she could speak to Raggy. Though before she could, he sent an orange fireball flying her way. Having no time to think she put her hands up and an ice wall began to form but when the fireball struck, it sent her tumbling backwards. She hit the floor. Quickly, she transformed once more and darted into the air.

"Enfuin!" exclaimed the fiery figure. "I'm sorry! I'm sorry! I, I, I, something attacked me! I." He calmed the flames that shaped him and put his hands behind his back. Slowly, he started to look like himself again. Enfuin quickly transformed and stepped a little closer, ready to defend herself, her head turning from the doorway to Raggy, doorway to Raggy.

"Don't let down your guard," she warned. "You are in control of yourself?" she questioned.

"Yes. I promise you," he answered. "I felt more frightened than I ever have, encased in that stone or whatever it might be. I would have shot anything that moved in that second I broke free. I didn't know what to expect."

"Okay, okay," she replied. "Just forget about it. How do we break the others free? Quickly. I don't know what to expect."

"Yes um…freeze the stone and break the ice."

"Obviously. Okay."

"Make sure you're careful. Concentrate."

"Yes. Watch the door."

"I'm sorry. I might hurt them if I try and break them free."

"That's fine. Just watch the door." Enfuin had begun freezing one of the other stone figures, the cold and the ice infiltrating even the inside of the thick, unusually strong stone. She was concentrating hard, trying her best not to let the ice harm the body inside.

"Who was with you?" she asked.

"The rest of the team," he answered.

"Okay. Good. This won't harm Freece and Harhk. It's just Annife."

"Though any of them could be Annife so be careful."

"I realise that."

Raggy and Enfuin looked as one of the other stone figures started to crack more and more.

"Make sure they don't do anything stupid," said the pale-blue one.

Freece came bursting out. He saw Raggy first, ready to fight, then his eyes went to Enfuin.

"What happened?" he shouted angrily.

"Be quiet," said Enfuin, making the ice break and crumble, the frozen part of the stone figure doing the same. Harhk's body could be seen. "Freece, can you tear the rest off?" the pale-blue one asked. "It's Harhk," she added. He walked over and started pulling at the stone. When the dark haired one was finally free, Enfuin had begun working on Annife. Then Freece came over and did the same again. Soon they were all free. Annife and Harhk had come out, cautiously, ready to fight but because of Enfuin's warnings, as they were being broken free they didn't attack.

"What is happening?" asked the orange skinned being. She looked tired. She seemed…strange.

"Are you okay?" asked the one in the blue dress.

"Yes."

"I don't know what is happening. I…how did you all get here?" Enfuin questioned.

"The map," Raggy answered. "It started glowing red, the glow getting stronger and stronger and then the light swallowed us up."

"And where did it drop you off?"

"In a room. Not this one. We were surrounded by floating sand for a moment and then it disappeared. We started looking around but I don't remember clearly what happened once we found this room."

"Where are the others?"

"I don't know."

"Do you know if the light brought them here too?"

"I'm almost sure it brought Ranglu and his father and Fellei and Nimb. They were close to me when it happened. Though I didn't actually see if it took them or not."

"Were the rest of you close to Raggy too?"

They answered by either shaking their heads or saying, "No."

"I was with Paiht," Annife told her. "I think the light swallowed him up too."

"How certain are you?"

"A little."

"Okay."

"You seem different," the purple haired one added.

"What?" said Enfuin.

"You seem different."

"You do," Raggy agreed.

"You do," Freece agreed.

"You do," Harhk agreed.

"Sorry," was the first word that came out of her mouth. "My head is…weird and full and buzzing like a freeking big ass bee. I feel strange. I'm not really sure…I don't know. Let us just go and search for the others. Do whatever we're meant to do in this place. Everyone keep your eyes extra peeled. According to the niece of a devil, there is a real devil in this place, and a creepy shrinking snake with a woman's head."

"Is she looking for a mate to breed with?" the green one asked.

"Probably," the blue one answered.

He nodded.

"Just watch out for anything that moves." She started walking towards the empty doorway. "And anything that doesn't move," she added.

"Yes, ma'am," said Harhk. "I despise how leader like you are trying to act."

"Yes," everyone agreed.

"You are a bitch," said Freece, looking at Enfuin.

"Yes," everyone agreed.

The blue one laughed quietly. "Fine. All of you lead the way. I'll stay behind."

They all moved in front of her, walking cautiously beyond the door and down a stonewalled corridor. There had been two choices, to turn down one corridor or go forward down another. They went forward. Midway down was a door on one of the walls. At the end of the corridor was a left and right turning. They walked to the door.

"Shall I kick it?" asked Freece.

"No, I will," said Harhk.

Annife twisted the handle and opened it up. They all looked in except for Enfuin and Raggy who were keeping an eye out behind them. What they could see was a lab of some kind. It looked like a lab of some kind anyway. They entered, the fiery and icy one following behind. They shut the door behind them.

"Creepy," said the genius of sorts, her eyes even wider than usual.

"I like it," the forked tongue one added, walking over to a thick looking glass jar that held a big black insect of some kind. It was still alive. Trapped. The forked tongue lady reached for the lid, twisted, yanked and put the glass jar on its side.

"Wait!" said Annife, trying her best to stay quiet. "You don't know what it is!" Everyone was looking now, eyes wide.

"Oh, stop whining," Harhk hissed back. "It's a Truzzkohlyu. It should not be trapped in a jar."

"What does it do?" asked the green one.

"It's very dangerous. It burrows into skulls and feasts on brains," she answered seriously. Annife suddenly sprinted for the door. Freece followed her, as did Raggy and Enfuin after giving the room a quick, panicked looked over. Harhk was left alone with the long legged, long bodied creature. She stroked its back gently.

"Enjoy yourself. Don't let anyone trap you again," she told it. Annife poked her head back through the door. "Get out here now," she said. Then her head quickly disappeared. Harhk muttered curse words, as she walked to the door and left the room.

"That has been one of my favourite places we've ever been to," she complained.

"We don't have the time. As delightful as it was," said Raggy. "There was no one in there."

"There might be something important," she argued. "I will look for something important. You all stay here." Before anyone could say anything, she returned into the lab. The place was covered in glass jars and bottles, holding specimens, liquids, plants…her eyes followed pipes and tubing…she looked in cupboards and drawers. She passed basins and taps, one or two expelled some strange kinds of gasses maybe. She quickly turned them off and stepped away…

Once she was satisfied, she exited, meeting the rest of the group outside. "Nothing," she said, walking past and starting down the corridor. They followed, Freece stepping to her side, chest puffed out, chin up.

"You really took nothing?" Enfuin questioned quietly.

"I did not. I was sensible. Most of what I liked probably would end up killing someone. I decided not to take them."

Enfuin nodded suspiciously. "Okay…"

"It is the truth."

"Fine, I believe you."

"Very good."

At the end of the corridor, they turned right and saw another door in one of the walls.

Harhk cautiously opened it up. Beyond were stone stairs leading down into darkness. But before Raggy made some light there was a shout. It didn't come from below. They moved quickly further down the corridor, making a left turn and running onwards. There were no doors on the sidewalls, just one much larger arched one at the end. It was black unlike the others which were brown. They sped up to it and Harhk twisted the hanging silver handle and pushed, then pulled. It opened, revealing Paiht standing off against a large black devil named, Dionyvash. Both beings were groaning and sweating, standing almost completely still. Dionyvash had two horn's curving up either side of his black, muscular looking head. Neither of the men looked toward the Blue Eye team as they entered unsure of what to do. Then, in the opposite corner of the massive, grand, majestic room opened another door. Wing, Fellei, Nimb, Ranglu, Falsen and Unela entered. The large black one felt the presence of Fellei and Wing. A tinge of fright tickled at him and in that moment, he broke off the connection between him and Paiht and he filled the room with smoke in an instance, blinding everyone. Raggy acted quickly, making the smoke disappear. The black devil was running towards Wing. Before he could reach her, Fellei reached out with both her sword and her inner body, Wing joined her. Ranglu let an arrow fly. Falsen and Unela shot their Lightpistols. Dionyvash stopped in his tracks and threw up a wall of black fire. They all leapt backwards. The black one wasn't prepared when Raggy brought the fire crashing down on him, sending him to the ground. This was when the snake woman came through yet another door, bigger then Enfuin had seen her. The black one made the fire disappear. Using his hands and arms, he leapt up, leaving the ground and charged towards Raggy across the vast stone floor like a lion. Raggy willed stonewalls to protrude from out the ground to block him but he charged right through them. Harhk managed to open up a portal which Dionyvash charged straight through. She sent him crashing through another door. There were seven doors in total. One in each corner, another two on either side wall and one opposite and far away from the large black throne which sat on a blood red stone platform. Hanging from the ceiling was a dangling cage. Inside this cage were two silent beings – silent for their tongues had been taken from them – squished together, watching, hoping, praying that these strangers would end the devil's life and free them from this hell. The recently made half-blind serpent woman had been stopped by Freece, who managed to quickly teleport up to her head and strike it multiple times before being swung into a thick stone pillar. A segment of the pillar broke off as his back made contact. Enfuin was a dove again, making Reeshune – the snake woman – nervous, successfully distracting her. Ranglu managed to pierce the snake body with a metal tipped arrow. Fellei managed to drive her sword through the flesh. This was when Reeshune realised she wasn't getting any help. Her uncle had left her. He had ran. Surely he hadn't fled? But he had. These opponents were a force unlike any he had faced before. The snake tail whipped and sent Fellei skidding across the floor along with Falsen who had managed to hit the snake body with a Ray, Unela too was hit, Wing too but before she was she too managed to shoot the serpent body with a ray. Nimb couldn't hold on to Unela so he flew off her shoulder and hit the ground. Reeshune shrunk down and slithered away, dodging and weaving, at an alarming speed. The arrow fell out of her body and fell to the ground. She was badly wounded but still had enough in her to spit at Freece, successfully hitting him, and Raggy too. The minute it touched the material of their clothing, the spit grew thick around them almost in an instance, turning to stone. As the serpent zipped out of the corner door, which the Blue Eye team had entered through, a bare foot stamped down on her. It was Kolwel's foot. He too had earlier been encased in stone by Reeshune but his strength had broken him free. He had just reached the door a moment earlier. His instincts had told him to wait. The woman let out a screech and she grew and grew at a great speed, sending Kolwel into a wall. Then she shrunk back down. This had nearly taken all she had left in her. Her energy was nearly drained. She would have died if it were not for the StoneBurrower hole – a StoneBurrower being a species of Sandmouse. A hard, tough but tasty snack that she enjoyed. She made it into the hole located at the bottom of the wall, forcing herself to shrink down further. She soon collapsed. She needed to heal. Fortunately, she healed faster than most, though not as fast as she would have liked. At least she was safe now, as far as she knew. She was right. Her opponents had lost her.

Chapter 12
Bite

While Enfuin dealt first with breaking Freece free from his stone prison, the others began working out a way to free the silent caged prisoners up above. At first, no one knew whether to speak or not. The atmosphere was a terrible one. Everyone felt strange.

"Can your arrows break the chain?" asked the stranger with the beard, quietly. The other man Ranglu had seen in his dream.

"Umm, yes, probably," Ranglu replied, his eyes darting to his unconscious father who was being propped up by his wife.

"If you shoot I can jump up and catch the cage, so they don't get hurt."

"Okay. How high can you jump?"

"About as high as this ceiling," he answered, looking up.

"Okay." Ranglu hitched an arrow onto the string. He aimed for the chain, hoping it would break in one shot. It did. Kolwel leapt up and caught the cage. He landed sturdy on his feet and put the cage down on the ground. He broke the cage open with his bare hands. When the two, bony, scared, big-eyed beings were free, they mouthed the words, "Thank you," over and over and over but they kept their distance, watching everyone and everything with wide eyes. Completely at a loss of what to do. Kolwel fetched his bag which had been transported here with him. He quickly took out some food and water and the few items of clothing he had, the water kept in a strange, flexible kind of glass called, Flune Glass. The beings were very almost completely nude. Slowly, he reached out to give the water and food to them, after sliding the clothes to them. They didn't approach. They just looked at him with their big eyes, tears falling down their faces. He left the food and water on the floor in front of them. Others added all the clothing they could spare to the pile. No one had any more food or water though. The ones who had been surrounded by stone once more were now free again. Everyone's eyes were darting around the place, expecting surprises. All were quiet. No one knew what to do next. Falsen was still unconscious. His head was bleeding a little. But he was being looked after. He would be okay. The two caged prisoners swiftly began eating and drinking. One of them was thinking, shaking his head, talking silently to himself...suddenly, he ran across the floor, using both his hands and feet. He was weak and wobbly. He stopped beside Kolwel. He gestured at his mouth, trying to tell him something. "More," he was trying to say. "More of us. More of us. Slaves. More Slaves. Down below. Down below..."

Kolwel nodded. "More slaves down below?" he asked quietly.

The being kept nodding mouthing. "Yes, yes, yes."

"There are slaves down below," he told Enfuin. The bony being had returned to the food.

"We saw a staircase leading down," the pale-blue one said.

"Okay. Let's go there now."

"Okay. Everyone should stay together. I will get everyone together."

Enfuin did this successfully. The two beings stopped eating as soon as they heard those who had saved them were planning to save the rest. The two were desperate to save the others. Kolwel asked them if they were strong enough to walk. They nodded, saying, "Yes." The only problem was Falsen was still unconscious.

"I will carry him," the Hunter said. As he went to pick him up, feeling a sense of urgency, he sensed danger. A moment later, Falsen in his arms, five large, entirely black, bizarrely muscular looking wolves came crashing through one of the doors. Behind them came Dionyvash, running with them. The two bony beings went running for one of the other doors. Even the Hunter had not seen wolves like these before. They looked unnatural, monstrous. They were not monstrously large, though bigger than a common wolf, they were monstrously formed, their muscular figures deformed and disturbing. Smoke filled the room as Kolwel jumped into the air with both Falsen and Unela in his arms. Raggy once again dealt with the smoke, Enfuin sent beams of ice towards the wolves. A wall of black fire went surging towards Paiht, Fellei, Wing, Ranglu and Nimb. They were all sent to the ground as Raggy stopped the wall in its tracks, before it could consume the family. It carried on burning, completely still. From the ground, unable to see the black demon Paiht reached out his inner body and managed to seize Dionyvash's. The wall of fire vanished. Three wolves came charging for the group. Paiht couldn't see them. He was on his feet, standing completely still. Before the wolves reached Ranglu, Fellei, Wing and Nimb, Freece managed to dive into the back of the side of one, just catching it and grabbing it, swinging it around and throwing it against the ground. One of Ranglu's arrows struck one in the head but the arrow didn't pierce it, the arrow just fell to the ground. Wing managed to shoot two Rays. They burnt off the fur of the wolf and damaged the flesh but the wolf kept running, making no sign of being hurt. A portal opened up in front of the creatures and another sent them crashing into a wall. But another was heading for Harhk. She had to leap into the air. She only just dodged its snapping teeth. Kolwel was protecting both Falsen and Unela. He had been scratched four times already. If he were Ranglu or Fellei or Falsen, then the wounds inflicted by the dogs would have rendered him useless. He would be rolling around, screaming on the ground. The wolf lurched with an open mouth. Kolwel moved forward, twisting, grabbing the beast by the head and swinging around. The beast's back end hit Unela in the head as it swung around. Kolwel slammed the beast down. Stamped his foot down on its body and ripped and twisted at its head with all his strength. The beast's incredibly strong neck snapped, its head twisted and went loose. It was dead. As Fellei's inner body took hold of Dionyvash's, the room shook and the ground cracked. Parts of the stone floor turned to sand. Harhk's feet sunk in sand. A wolf leapt at her, knocking her down. She dug her thumbs into its eyes before it could bite her and it let out a cry. Next, she did something that hurt her. She made a sound that sounded as if she was about to throw up. A black liquid called Saneeck came up into her mouth and she spat. This affected the dog in an unexpected way. The liquid spread with speed and obliterated all of the wolf's fur. His flesh started to feel like it was burning and the creature started running around like a maniac until it dropped dead. What Harhk didn't know was that the dogs had been subjected to many experiments. The usually and incredibly hazardous, painful, possibly deadly poison that Harhk could produce reacted with the enhanced dog's body in a much more extreme fashion to how it would usually react with a normal wolf, a bear, a person or anything. All of the others were keeping the wolves busy enough for Wing to be able to join Paiht and Fellei in vanquishing the black devil. As her inner body invaded Dionyvash, the entire floor turned to sand, as did parts of the walls and roof. All this sand fell down, then a small amount of it began to float. Kolwel and Freece ripped a wolf in half. Enfuin froze the sand under one of the beasts so he got stuck. He was soon dead. Raggy managed take control of some remaining stone and wrap one of the now slowed down wolves in it. Using much energy, he managed to crush the beast. Annife had thrown her small metal rectangle and shouted, "Stomp!" It turned into a large, thick, metal platform. This metal platform slammed down on top of the beast and sent it beneath the sand. It suffocated down there and died. Many times, everyone had shouted, "Leave Paiht and the devil alone! Leave Fellei and the devil alone! Leave them alone! Keep them safe! Protect them! Don't let them get hurt…"

Now everyone watched as Paiht slowly drew his sword, staring down the devil. He took one step forward. He took another step forward. Then another and another. He was drenched in sweat; he was more tired than he had ever been. He could have collapsed there and then. He took another step forward and another. Then another and another. He raised his sword up. He reached the devil. He didn't go for the neck for he knew his sword couldn't cut through the black one's neck. Instead, he thrust his sword through Dionyvash's eye. Dionyvash couldn't hold on any longer. Paiht, Fellei and Wing broke down his inner body completely. He fell down to the ground and he was dead. In the moment of his death, the building turned to sand and the sand rose up, purposefully dodging the heroes as best it could. The sand brought up the slaves from below, so they did not suffocate. It began to swirl and dance around all the beings. Two red eyes appeared in its vast body. Then all the grains of sand swooped up further and then started plummeting down, disappearing and forming a being. The light from the red eyes travelled with the sand, filling the being's whole red eyes.

There was no more building. No more storm. Just a blue, sunny sky above and a male being whom the storm had seemingly created. The man was completely nude. His eyes were open and entirely red. Everyone stared at him silently, as he mumbled over and over, "Many beings must act in unity for the universe to be saved."

Part 2
Volume 1

Prologue
Leiyal

An extract taken from a children's book named, *Stories Cosmosian*, which was written on the planet Leiyal by a man named, Jeyl Mooti:

In the deep, deep, vast darkness of space, many stars and planets floated and danced for nothing held them down. For a while, they knew only their own stories but slowly as the universe began to grow, tales, legends, myths, truths and lies came in abundance. And one of these tales told of the birth of the planet Leiyal.

She was once only a star, but she held a beauty like no other. She did not have hair of gold like those around her and her eyes were not glinting with silver. No, her eyes were the deepest yet sharpest of greens, and her long, waving hair was a deep, dark-red. Her graceful movements caught the eyes of those around her, her gentle voice echoed in their ears, her youthful charm began to capture their hearts. As she danced, they began to near, as she sang, they came closer still and as they drew close enough to look upon her glowing form, they felt almost hypnotised. Seneth was the first to reach out his hand in an attempt to touch her, but as his fingertips felt the softness of her skin, a rage awakened inside of her. She looked around and, in every direction, she saw that she was surrounded, trapped, without the freedom to move as she wished. The angelic white glow that embraced her figure turned to a dark, fierce red and this light grew outwards, flickering with dark bolts of lightning, shadowing over all that surrounded her until suddenly all the stars were pulled in close to her body. Then came the mighty explosion. Fortunately, the sound was trapped in its own pocket, otherwise the small sensitive beings who lived on planets even a reasonable distance away may have been deafened. Leiyal's red light filled with crackling arcs of red, white, silver and gold lightning until in one sudden moment, everything vanished leaving behind a new and nervous eeriness and a planet whose body was an enchanting mix of gold, white, silver and a deep, dark-red. At its heart was a gentle soul whose anger was fierce. Her name was Leiyal.

Chapter 1
Halt

Halt, the common man, was how he wished for people to think of him. But what he was known as most commonly was Halt the traveller. Fortunately, this was also fine. He was a tall, muscular man, though more lean than bulky. His hair was a very dark-brown, almost black. This was the case for his eyebrows, eyes and thick stubble too. His average day consisted of riding on and on and on into the beyond. His horse, Thela – a name neither rich nor poor – was a great companion. Faithful, cunning, scared of very little. She had great stamina which was fortunate as she was the traveller's partner, destined to cross many lands of many kinds. They had travelled far on this cold day and after leaving what few people knew as the Vast Forest – the largest forest upon Leiyal – behind them, Thela had broken into a canter. The final sprint is where we will now join them.

Up ahead was a village, a village that appeared to possibly be mostly made of huts. All Halt could see was vast green and grey land, cold and wet. Only in places did a little amount of snow lie on the ground. Mountains grew tall in the misty distance, creatures prowled unseen, few birds flew above looking over the land below with watchful eyes.

Halt pulled on the reins and slowed Thela down, as they drew closer to the village. The soft brown-haired horse happily slowed and trotted forth.

The travelling partners entered the village. They passed stonewalled hut after stonewalled hut. The locals watched them curiously but politely as they passed, the sight of a stranger not being completely bizarre. And when Halt finally spotted the stonewalled inn – the first place not designed as a hut – he dismounted, took the two large bags off of the horse and made his way to the front door, not needing to tie up Thela before entering. She would wait for him, able to defend herself.

The innkeeper, an old, round, grey and longhaired dwarf, stood upon a step ladder behind the bar peering at the stranger as the stranger walked closer, eyeing the place all around. Grent, the dwarf couldn't decide whether he looked like bad news or not. He was tall and broad and wearing a big, heavy, dark-grey coat which made him look even broader. His hair was short and messy, as was his facial hair. His grey trousers were dirty, as were his big black boots and the long black scabbard hanging at his side, mostly able to be seen. *He is certainly a traveller,* thought Grent.

Before Halt reached the bar, he had already seen the room and the entirety of its contents. *Nothing to fear. No need to worry. A safe place at the moment.* The only thing that caught his gaze and his intrigue was a woman sitting alone in a corner, wearing an enchanting deep, dark-green cloak. Her hair was long and dark-silver. It was beautiful. He had rarely seen hair like it in the twenty-seven years he had lived. But a strange thing happened when their eyes had met. She had shifted as if about to bolt but when the new face turned away, she quickly settled again. "Greetings, traveller," said the Dwarf with a low voice.

"Good day to you," replied Halt with a lower voice, nodding and smiling. The innkeeper laughed.

"That's a mighty voice you have."

"Thank you," replied the stranger.

"What can I do for you?"

"Do you have a spare room for one night, maybe two nights?"

"We do. We're not exactly in the busiest of locations. We get a few travellers like yourself who stay for a night or two then move on, and I expect a runaway or two, though I think those end up staying here permanently. In fact, I reckon most of the village is populated by runaways."

"It is likely," Halt agreed. "It would be a good place for them." Grent nodded. "Let me get you your key." He did this and then gestured to the stairwell saying, "The keys and doors have numbers on them. It's just engraved in the key there." He gestured. "You won't need any help finding it."

"Thank you," said the traveller. "And is there space in the stables?"

"There is. Just take the beast around the back and you'll see." Halt nodded. "I'll be back for a drink."

He walked towards the exit – bags in hand – beneath thick, dark, wooden beams, and eyed the cloaked lady once more. She was looking out of the window, the pale light shining upon her fair skin. Once outside, he began to lead Thela towards the stables and when walking past the window on his left, he glanced in and at the same time, a raven landed on his padded left shoulder. The silver haired woman's eyes suddenly widened as they met the stranger's eyes and then saw the raven. A white mist suddenly filled Halt's vision; it was the most bizarre thing. He rubbed his eyes and then looked back through the window. She had vanished, nowhere to be seen. The traveller jogged around the side of the building, Thela by his side. The woman had not come out of the back exit. Still she was nowhere to be seen. Halt rubbed his eyes again. *Was his mind messing with him once more?*

He thought deeply, as he guided Thela into a stable nook and took off her kit with a promise to get her some food. Then, once done, he swiftly made his way back inside. No such unique silver hair anywhere in sight.

Halt first walked up the stairwell and then down a creaking corridor until he found his room. He unlocked and opened an old looking, rectangular, dark, wooden door and entered. It was small and pleasant. Nothing more, nothing less. After placing his things on the floor beside his bed, including his coat – downstairs being warm enough to be able to do so – and sword, the simple but strong cross handle flashing in a moment as light stretched through a rectangular window to touch it, he exited and returned downstairs, a thick, black jumper upon his broad back.

As he sat down on a wooden stool at the bar, Grent looked at him and asked, "Everything well?"

"Yes, thank you again."

"You're very welcome. Now what can I get you?"

"Just an ale for now, please." The Dwarf stepped off his stepladder and then a moment later, he popped up above the bar once more, a tankard of ale in hand. He placed it down and Halt picked it up and took a drink. "Perfect."

"Jolly good."

"Where have you come from? If you don't mind me asking?"

"I was in the town, Naeh, last."

"Do you know where you are now?"

"I do not."

"Neel. Though most people these days just call it Hut Village." The traveller nodded and was quiet for a moment, then he opened his mouth but hesitated before speaking. "Feel no need to answer this, really, but do you know anything about the woman who was sitting in that corner?" he gestured. "Silver hair, dark-green cloak."

"Honestly, I do not. I would very much like to though. I do love a mysterious woman. My wife is still a puzzle to me."

Halt chuckled. "Is she around?" he asked.

"She's out but you'll have the pleasure of meeting her later."

"Any children?"

"Fully grown. Fully short adults now and all in faraway places." Sadness flickered in the dwarf's blue eyes. Halt thought of how he could never live in such a place as this one, so secluded. "But as long as I have my lady, I'm a happy, lucky man," added Grent with a smile.

"I will pray that your happiness always stays."

"Thank you, sir. You are a good man. That I can already tell."

Halt nodded in thanks and raised his tankard.

"The fair lady is quite the looker, isn't she?" said Grent after a second of quiet. The traveller looked at him questioningly.

"Silver hair," said he.

"Ah, yes. She is indeed," answered Halt.

"She arrived early this morning. She asked me if there was room in the stables and then much time later, she appeared again, ordered a drink and went to sit in the corner. I don't even know her name."

"A mystery indeed."

"Maybe she'll return this evening."

"Maybe." For some reason, Halt doubted this very much.

"Anyway," said Grent. "It'll be time for supper soon. Is there anything you're particularly craving?"

"I would be happy with anything. Cook me up your favourite dish."

"I will do exactly that," the dwarf said with a grin.

Minutes later, Grent's wife – Dillie – returned home and met Halt before Grent went off to prepare supper. Then a little later with a small bag of treats, the traveller returned to his partner, Thela.

Halt, being the man he was, saw that a horse was missing. There was definitely another in the stables before. *Maybe it is the woman's horse that has vanished.* He felt strange. Uneasy. Unsure.

After he had fed Thela the treats and said farewell, he journeyed away from the inn – the Wandering Lamb – and began to look around the large village. His reason for doing this was half because he wanted to find the woman though he knew he wouldn't and half out of curiosity for he enjoyed seeing these new, odd places.

One of the first things that caught his attention was an old wizard dressed in deep, dark-blue robes, sitting outside the arched front door of an average sized, stonewalled hut. Kids sat at his feet watching him with wide eyes as he flicked his hands and spoke old, strange words, creating sparks of light and out of those sparks came more. Then the sparks intertwined, softened and flowed, beginning to take a form. In seconds, the beautiful head of a strong stag was floating above the children. Then suddenly, sparks flew out of its nose and they jumped, and all began to laugh. Halt stood and watched for a little while longer. He met the wizard's eyes once and they shared a smile. Then he moved on and quickly found himself prowling the markets which still stood. He walked, watching faces, listening to conversations, intrigued by folk and the way their strange minds worked, often so differently to his. It didn't take long for him to fall into a dreamy state. And when he awoke, he realised that he must get back to the inn for his food may be ready and waiting.

He arrived in time, swiftly took a seat and in a few moments began to eat.

The meal was truly delicious, made of perfectly cooked Hei Bird meat – an odd-looking creature – and roast potatoes and the strange but delicious vegetable named Ferl. And of course, there were seasonings and gravy. Halt believed gravy to be one of the greatest inventions. Once he had devoured this meal, Grent quickly appeared by his side. The dwarf had been waiting. "How was that?"

"Truly delicious. The best thing I've eaten in a very long time. Possibly the best thing I've ever eaten. I do not know your secret but it all really did taste…heavenly."

"Thank you, sir. That really means a lot."

"Man!" shouted Dillie from the bar. "Leave the fellow alone! Stop trying to feed your ego and get back here!" Grent grinned, bowed and went to his wife.

His horse having been seen too, the traveller journeyed onto the cobbles once more. It was getting dark now and colder. There was a peaceful atmosphere in the village. Halt wandered slowly around, weaving past hut after hut, just enjoying the fresh air and the peace…the wizard he had seen earlier suddenly appeared in front of him. "Hello, stranger. I saw you through my window. Would you like some company?" the long, grey haired man asked. Halt chuckled a little.

"Company would be nice," he said.

"So where do you come from? Faraway lands?" asked the man with a twisted walking stick.

"The town Naeh is where I was last."

The wizard nodded. "And where are your origins? In fact, tell me your name first."

"Halt," said he with an amused smile. "And yours?" The old man stopped walking and stared at the traveller's face.

"You don't look like a Halt." He decided after a moment, beginning to walk again. "I am Therai," he added. "Now where did you originate?"

The traveller hesitated. "I was born in Helma." This is what he said to all who asked.

"Ah Helma itself," the wizard said thinking back. "A great city."

"Indeed."

The old man tapped his twisted walking stick twice upon the cobbles at his feet and said, "That's enough walking for me." Halt thought surely not for they hadn't gone far at all, but maybe the old fellow was more crippled than he looked. "It was intriguing to meet you," said Therai shaking the man's hand.

"And you," Halt replied with a smile. "Maybe I'll see you again."

"Maybe."

And the wizard returned to his front door, entered his home and took a seat upon an old, rocking chair that was located near the fireplace which was holding a hot and healthy orange fire. He didn't enjoy the company of liars.

The traveller walked on unaware of the fact he still had company. A good distance away, watching, following, was a young dark-skinned, dark-haired boy named, Tellamo. He had seen when the raven had landed upon the stranger's shoulder and the woman in the inn had ran away. *The man looks a little scary. He is probably a bad man. I hope the woman is safe.* The boy crept from hut to hut, watching curiously, a little drunk on adrenaline. Not many exciting things happened around here. He followed Halt all the way to the border of the village where the dark stranger stopped and looked out, admiring the vast green and grey plain. *It is beautiful and quiet, cold and lonely, secretive and dark, mysterious and intriguing.* Halt stood there for far too long. The boy got bored, adrenaline now having melted away. He returned home. And so, he missed it when later another raven landed upon the man's shoulder. For a few moments, the *common man* didn't notice. When he finally did, he cursed, snapping out of his dreamy state. "Bastard bird." He hit the bird and it flew away cursing back at him. "Damn it," he murmured, coming back to his senses. He looked around. It was far darker than he had realised. The village was silent. He fidgeted around. A feeling of unease swiftly entered and danced around his body. He felt the dark begin to cling. "Go away, go away, go away," he murmured, as he speedily made his way back to the inn.

Chapter 2
Athaiel Began to Write
Athaiel

My Introduction

My name is Athaiel Lethu. Though I have been putting it off for many years, I am now writing this down on paper because I do not know how much time I have left ahead of me, and I refuse to leave this world behind in its current ignorant state. I have heard hundreds of rumours saying hundreds of different things about myself and the life I led. The inns run wild with false stories about me, those who surrounded me and the times we lived in, but though I am very old, I still hold a hope. And it is that this tough, rough, testing, mysterious, important, purpose filled, magnificent, truly beautiful universe will know the truth of me, my friends and family, and the history of Leiyal which I took part in.

Before I start, you would be wise to remember that I am part Senva, part Naytha. Except obviously for my birth and many parts of those early years, I remember every day of my life, every single day. This does not mean I remember every single detail of every single moment though. Not every word that comes out of my friends' mouths will be exactly what they said, but do not think that any part of what I write is exaggerated or untruthful or anything like that. Also know that the place I come from is fond of its stories, extremely fond, and storytelling is known as an art, an art that should be learnt and practiced. Meaning I shall be writing my story as I would write any. So, do not let any poetic wording that might sound pretty to the ear lull you into forgetting that everything I am about to tell you is true.

Now let us begin on a truly magical evening when my friends and I were all around the age of eighteen for this is when our stories really began. We had recently left the safety of education behind and now the world was our oyster.

We were free, and we were happy, only just stepping onto the long, long twisting paths on which, at this point in time, we could see nothing but cobbles.

Chapter 3
A Magical Evening

I slowly wandered towards the Piper Inn that was without a doubt already filled with many of the locals, and I hoped maybe a traveller or two also. In a strange way, I felt warmer just looking at it. Smoke rose from out the tall, strange, twisting chimney and into the sky where the wind changed its dancing form over and over until it seemed to disappear, and a comforting orange glow highlighted both square, frosted windows either side of the Elleth lamp lit, arched wooden doors which alone seemed to carry a warmth to them. Whether it was because of their familiarity or just the look of the wood itself, I do not know, it was likely a mix of both.

As I drew closer and closer, wearing my beloved long, deep, dark-green coat, snow fell lightly from the dark, violet tinted sky above, adding to the sheet of white that already lay at my feet, almost reaching the top of my tough black boots but not quite. The sweet sound of music flowed like water through any gap it could find in the form of a golden light that few in the world would have been able to see. It began to heat the Winthal air just a little with a soft hum that weaved through the maze of falling snowflakes, and I began to smile. I continued to follow the trail of footsteps which ran all the way down the wide opening, between some wonderful, bizarre homes. The best way I can describe them is…if they could talk, they would be hilarious and more often than not, they would not make any sense. Then, before I reached the front doors, I spotted two figures heading my way, but they were too far away to share greetings with, so I swiftly reached for the hanging iron handle of the right-hand door which was icy and freezing, though a little less so where hands had been grabbing, twisting and pulling all evening. I grabbed, twisted and pulled, and entered. I almost immediately caught the eyes of Droog, a dwarf both loved and disliked by many.

"Shut the door, you bastard!" he shouted so the whole world could hear. I laughed and did so. "It's a wee bit chilly out there," he said with a smile.

"It's a wee bit chilly indeed," I replied, mimicking his thick accent. His smile turned into a grin.

"Let me buy ye a drink." I stood surprised for a moment as he got up from his chair and walked to the bar, where a male Rhoon named Tukan was standing. For those who don't know what a Rhoon is, they are beings who have the face and body of a human except they are much larger with dark-blue skin and the males have a black, sometimes grey horn which comes out the top of their foreheads.

"He's a wee bit smashed," explained Panlo, another Dwarf, who was sitting to my right.

"I guessed," I replied.

"Make the most of it," he continued. "He won't be buying anyone any drinks for a while when he realises how generous he's been." I nodded and laughed.

"Here, boy!" Droog exclaimed happily. He held a large tankard of ale high in the air. I made my way over and thanked him gratuitously. After patting me on the back, he pushed me towards a table over by the wall where my friends were sitting. Though it was meant as a friendly shove, the strength behind it almost made me trip and some of my drink fell to the floor. Naturally, my friends began to laugh.

"Hello," I said blushing a little, placing my tankard on the table and stepping over the wood bench.

"Shush your kebab," Keeana, my Rogue friend, replied immediately. I looked at her and saw the corners of her red lips slowly lift in front of her dark, hanging hair. She was staring at a chessboard, which sat on the table in front of her, with great concentration. Her opponent was Senn. He was an Elf, blonde, blue eyed and pale skinned. He looked at me and smiled smugly. Then an evil laugh suddenly came from Keeana's open mouth. "Checkmate, you bastard." Senn's expression turned to shock as he quickly looked down at the board.

"What in this dark, terrible world is this!" he shouted. We all burst out laughing. A little embarrassed, having not meant to shout so loudly, he slumped in his chair and gave Keeana a sad look. "I don't like you when you play games. You start swearing and you get all...rude and...annoying." Her laugh became smaller.

"I'm sorry, Senn. I have no control over it," she said softly. "You're still an ass," he replied. I nodded in agreement. She swiftly looked my way and frowned. "I'll beat you tonight."

"With what?" I replied. She gave me a confused look. "A stick, a belt, a ch—"

"No," she interrupted with a small laugh. "I'll beat you at chess."

"Ah," I said smiling. "I doubt that."

"Don't flirt across the table," Eyla chimed in. She was also an Elf with long silver hair, enchanting grey eyes and fair, almost glowing skin. "It's disturbing," she finished. Taborn suddenly brought out his thin, twisting wand from his long, deep-blue, long sleeved cloak and pointed it at Senn.

"Tickelutenthuthu!" he exclaimed.

"No!" Senn shouted. But before he knew it, a blue spark flew out of Taborn's wand, touched his chest and the blue light spread up and down his body until it was highlighting him from head to toe. A tickling sensation ran up and down his body and he couldn't help but fall into a fit of giggles. We all couldn't help but laugh as he squirmed in his seat, and those around us were quick to join in. The spell only lasted around seven seconds but we all continued to laugh for a little while longer.

"I hate you," Senn finally managed to say. Taborn continued to chuckle, then said, "I'm glad that never isn't funny." Taborn was a Wizard, though he was around the same age as all of us his hair was already a dark-grey colour, as was the small beard that was already growing on his chin.

Lastly, there was Wulan, who was sitting, quietly grinning beside me. He came from a family of Mokes; there were few of these beings in the world even back in these times. They were famous in a way for their incredible reflexes, nimbleness and needless to say, their fast minds. He was small and skinny with grey skin, and he wore a long, pale-brown robe, tied over the top of his clothing. It was decorated with many dark, curving, elegant patterns and it had the appearance of being thick and heavy, and it was quite possibly the warmest garment in the inn, yet when you wore it, you barely felt it on you, it held almost no weight whatsoever. Of course, not every Moke owned such a piece but Wulan was fortunate enough to come from a very interesting family line to say the least.

He was also the only one that could regularly beat me at chess. Chess was a game we were all rather good at. An example of how good would be, if a normal, well-educated human were to challenge one of us, we could beat him one handed while holding a conversation with another fellow, but Wulan could beat him while holding a conversation and drawing a picture at the same time. Though that said, we weren't always defeated by him, on a rare occasion one of us would come out victorious.

"What kept you?" asked Eyla looking my way. "I was minding my own business," I replied straight-faced. "Good lord," added Taborn. "Why are you always so rude, Eyla?"

"Me?" she asked disgustedly.

"Oh, and there you go again. You should have never been born."

"That's a bit extreme, don't you think?" she asked laughing.

"I don't think it is actually. In fact, I'll say it again. You should have never been born." I looked over my shoulder chuckling as the Inn door opened and the two figures I had seen before entered. I saw Droog look and open his mouth to say something, but he quickly closed it again as he realised he didn't recognise the two new faces. I turned back around and looked back at Eyla. "I was just caught up in conversation with my father," I said answering her earlier question.

"Mr Drenak Lethu!" Taborn exclaimed in shock.

"Yes," I replied laughing. Eyla looked to her right, meeting the Wizard's dark-blue eyes, wearing a half amused half-bewildered expression.

"I'm thoroughly enjoying your mood tonight," Keeana chimed in looking around Eyla to Taborn.

"As am I," said Senn and myself simultaneously.

"Children," interrupted Wulan, his back turned to us. "What do we think of these little travellers?" He gestured towards the couple standing at the bar.

"I reckon they be from somewhere different than here," the Wizard said wide-eyed.

"I reckon they be lovers," I added.

"I reckon they be brother and sister," the young Elf man offered.

"Oooo that's a risky one," replied Wulan, raising his eyebrows.

"I reckon they be cousins."

"I reckon they be cousin lovers," I interjected a second time. Taborn and Senn began to laugh. Keeana attempted to give me a disapproving look but failed.

"What species, what race?" asked the Moke smiling.

"I think human," Eyla said with a hint of seriousness in her voice. We all looked at the two quietly for a moment.

"Could be Rogue," Senn added.

"Maybe," the Rogue pondered. "Though they don't look like fighters...I think humans."

"I reckon the wenches be right," Taborn decided. Two fierce looks instantly came his way. "I reckon the two lovely ladies be right," he corrected. "I wonder if they travelled through the wood to get here...we should go on a night time walk," he suggested mysteriously.

"Yes," Keeana said with a smile. "We can go say hi to Hanneth and Tulie," Eyla added. Myself, Senn and Wulan swiftly agreed. "Jolly good," the Wizard said satisfied.

"Though before we go." The Rogue looked my way and gestured towards the chessboard. I smiled and glacially swapped places with Senn. "Right then, dear," I said, setting up my pieces.

"Yes?"

"You look reasonably pleasant tonight," I finished with a small smile.

"Thank you," she replied with a small laugh. "You don't."

"Well, a man can only do his best," I said wearing my best hurt expression. "Yes, that's very true," she sympathised. "I guess if you're born ugly there's not much that can be done." I nodded in reply, the corners of my mouth slowly lifting. "We should really try to have a normal conversation one day," she said laughing.

"I don't think that's necessary."

"No, I don't know why I would ever say that."

I shook my head disappointedly. "Disgusting."

"Shall we begin?" She looked into my eyes and I looked back into hers. They were a deep, dark, lovely, enchanting green. "Let's."

And so, the game began. Our friends continued to hold their own conversations, every now and again looking over to examine the board, while me and Keeana became engrossed in the game and in each other's company.

"You look a little worried there," she said a short while later.

"You look worried," I returned.

"Oh, good one."

"Cut me some slack, woman, I have to concentrate on the game, listen to your babbling and think of good comebacks all at the same time." The Rogue looked shocked for a moment and then unwillingly began to smile.

"Don't call me woman," she said in a playfully disgusted manner.

"Are you not a woman? Ah, no of course, it all makes sense now." She went quiet for moment. I looked up wide-eyed.

"Oh hello, I'm sorry, would you like to say something?" I waited a moment, watching her mind tick and her mouth move a little but hearing nothing.

"Oh dear," I said making a line with my mouth.

"What's going on?" Eyla and Wulan interrupted.

"The chicken seems to have eaten the young woman's tongue."

"Not the chicken, Keeana. I've told you to stay away from it," Wulan said, shaking his head.

"It's too late now," I stated, sounding distraught. "We're going to have to put you down now," I added softly, reaching over to touch Keeana's hand. The laughter she was holding back suddenly burst forth.

"Did you really have nothing?" Eyla asked surprised. Keeana attempted to speak but failed again.

"Oh no," the young Elf lady said with a small laugh. I looked her way and shook my head. "It's a sad thing."

"It really is."

"Right, both of you shut up," the Rogue finally managed. "I'm trying to concentrate." I closed my mouth and silently gestured towards the board.

It wasn't long before Keeana spoke again. "What do you think about the new rumours?"

"The Saven?"

She nodded. "As you're a Senva, maybe you could sense its presence?" she asked unserious.

"Sadly not. Do you think someone actually saw one?"

"Well, the fact they're supposed to be extinct makes me think no."

"Mmmm," I said widening my eyes.

"What do you think strange, ancient species mixed, boy?" she asked.

"You describe me so well. I think that it's…not impossible."

"Apart from the fact that they're extinct."

"Yes," I said smiling. "It would be pretty cool if they did still exist though."

"Very cool," she agreed. "But not so cool if it decided to kill all of us."

"No, but I reckon we have enough fire power to defend ourselves against one."

"That's very true, I think this Inn alone could do a fair bit of damage," she said gesturing to all the different beings that filled the Piper. I nodded in agreement. "We would make a fierce army."

"Indeed we would."

The game continued to proceed accompanied by conversation that quickly went back to consisting of witty back and forth, or what we thought was witty anyway. Senn and Taborn soon joined us at our end of the table as the game was nearing its final stages. They knelt on the floor and watched closely, reacting in over the top ways every now and again and then falling into laughter afterwards.

The game ended with me as victor, and while Keeana gave me the silent treatment, we all leisurely made our way out of the inn and began to wander towards the great Spirit Wood.

"You're so lucky," Keeana said, breaking her silence towards me after only five or so minutes.

"Why is that?" I asked.

"You don't feel the cold," she said, as if it were obvious.

"Well, I do a little."

"Well, I do a little," Taborn mimicked in a high-pitched voice. "If I were you, I would just walk around shirtless, my beautiful dragon scaled body on full show."

"Then you would be stared at constantly, even if I'm just missing a coat on a winter's eve, everyone looks at me like I'm mad."

Taborn shrugged at this. "I wouldn't mind. It would get the ladies' attention."

"Well, you're definitely going to need something like that if you want to acquire a lover because you don't grab one tiny bit of their attention now," Eyla chimed in. The Wizard's expression turned to shock, and he went silent for a moment. "I'm really glad I met you," he began with a fake smile. "You're a joy, a hoot, the bees' knees. The wax to my candle, the water to my flower, the peak to my mountain."

"And you're the crack to my arse," the young Elf woman replied. Laughter spilled out of all of us in that moment, and it filled the cold silence that surrounded us with a great warmth that lasted the rest of the night.

"Thank you for calling my body beautiful by the way," I said looking towards Taborn.

"You're very welcome," he replied with a walking bow.

"Hey," Wulan chimed in. "Do you think Hanneth and Tulie sleep?" Everyone looked thoughtful for a moment.

"I have no idea," I replied surprised. "I've never asked."

"I've never seen them sleep," added Senn. The others were none the wiser. Wulan pouted his lips for a moment. "If they do, I wonder what they dream about. Probably crazy, weird stuff."

"Probably the same stuff Taborn dreams about," Senn said with a smile.

"What do you dream about?" Wulan asked, looking Taborn's way.

"Making love to—"

"No!" Eyla exclaimed. Naturally, Taborn began to chuckle away to himself.

"I dream about a wide variety of stuff," he began. "Though right now, I can't think of any good, non-sacred examples." Wulan suddenly came to a stop and bent down to pick something up. "It's a penny in the snow!" he said chirpily. "How wonderful." He held it up toward the warm yellow, floating ball of light and twisted it around. "You know what my mother used to say…"

"What's that?" Keeana asked, wearing an amused smile.

"She would say, find a penny in the snow…pick it up…and put it in your pocket. Bloody wise woman." I remember chuckling away at this for an oddly long amount of time as we made our way further through Telan. It was a slow, peaceful, wonderful journey, making our way over the wide snowy roads, lit up by large, beautiful Elleth lamps. We passed many sleeping homes and frozen fountains, their centrepieces standing elegant and proud in the forms of Angels, Dolphins, Water Nymphs, Sea Serpents. And there were statues too, great stone structures in the forms of ancient beasts, great wizards, fierce warriors with their sword held high and their foot on the neck of a dragon that he or she had just slain. Of course, not all dragons were considered evil, but those ones obviously were. And there were elves with their bow and arrow pointing towards where the enchanting, deep-violet moon was hiding behind the clouds, and Rogues sneaking around with their intriguing weapons at the ready.

I fully appreciated my hometown on this night. It was a truly beautiful place.

The peace was only broken once on our journey through the large town. After we had walked down the lamp lit hill and through what would have been one of the busiest parts of Telan if it were day, we reached the boarder and that's when we were attacked, sort of.

Three men suddenly jumped out from the shadows, two holding small daggers and the other holding a gun that looked to be a flintlock pistol, commonly used by Pirates. "Ha—" The man was instantly cut off as Wulan lunged towards him, grabbing the gun and leaping into the air. No shot went off as the Moke likely already had hold of the fellow's trigger finger. He swiftly landed behind the man, still holding on to the pistol and as the scum was still desperately trying to keep it in his grasp, Wulan was able to pull him down to the ground for his opponent couldn't help but try and turn and lose his balance.

131

Otherwise, his shoulder and arm would have broken, instead he got away with just a broken finger. A swift, precise kick to the head then sent him unconscious. I was able to see all of this as my man took one punch to the head and instantly fell to the floor, unmoving. It appeared that Keeana took down the other. He lay in the snow, completely still with his own dagger in his right leg. "Idiots," the Rogue spat. "That's twice now!" Taborn complained.

"Well, it is probably our fault for walking around so late," I admitted.

"Mmm," he mumbled. The Rogue crouched down beside her defeated opponent.

"Can you make sure he stays under?" she asked looking towards the Wizard. He nodded, walked over to the body and put his wand to the man's head, mumbling under his breath. A pale-blue light began to wash over the unconscious body as the Rogue took the dagger out of the man's leg, and after cleaning it up in the snow, she lifted the bottom of her black, hooded jacket and began to draw a circle with her finger on the side of her belt which had been handily enchanted by her Wizard friend. After drawing two circles, something began to protrude out of the black leather, and then seconds later, a small scabbard was hanging from the belt. While this was happening, Eyla had knelt down and placed both her hands on top of the man's bleeding wound. An eerie silence fell upon us as ancient Elven magic awoke in Eyla's body and her skin began to glow, a soft, pale, winter glow that grew brighter and brighter until she opened her eyes again and began to clean her hands in the snow, her skin slowly returning to normal. The wound was still mostly there but the bleeding had completely stopped for an invisible barrier covered the wound as if it were a bandage, a very powerful bandage, and in around twelve hours, we all knew that his leg would be back to normal, likely not even a scar would be left. Though that depended on what the man would do with his wound in the meanwhile.

"I don't know why you bother," Keeana said eyeing the man. "Because someone like him isn't going to be able to afford a healer and they probably don't have the resources to clean themselves up," she said simply. The Rogue nodded in reply.

"Are any of the others badly injured?" the Elf asked.

"This one's got a broken finger." Wulan gestured. "But it shouldn't be that bad, it'll just keep him from easily shooting anyone for a while."

"Okay, good," she said staying put. "Well…does everyone still want to go to the wood?"

"Of course," Keeana swiftly replied.

"This is all part of the adventure," Taborn said gesturing around him.

"It was humans who tried to mug us last time too, wasn't it?" Senn asked, as we began to walk again, after taking all the men's few weapons.

"I believe so," I replied.

"They can be a hateful lot, can't they?" he added.

"Well, so can everyone."

"Very true. Everyone needs to relax a bit, be more like us."

"I agree." Eyla dropped back and joined us.

"What are you two jabbering about?"

"How everyone should just relax a little," my friend answered.

"They should…" She went quiet as she thought for a moment.

"Do you reckon we've frightened them into stopping?" Senn asked.

"We're a pretty terrifying bunch," Eyla said wearing a small smile. "Though sadly I doubt it. They're probably not clever enough to stop, though maybe they will eventually. I mean, if they were to manage to avoid getting arrested, in this town, they're more likely to run into gifted fighters than they are not too, so they'll probably get beaten up enough times, so they finally choose another lifestyle. And it's not like they don't have a choice, there's plenty of jobs around here that they could get."

"Indeed," I agreed. Eyla nodded. "Anywho…back to brighter things."

"Does anyone else find Tulie incredibly attractive?" Senn began.

"I personally prefer the male species," Eyla replied. "And I like to be able to touch those I find attractive."

"That wasn't my question."

"Yes, she's very beautiful."

"Wonderful. Athaiel?"

"Very attractive."

"Jolly good. I look forward to seeing her very much."

Eyla let out a small laugh. "How sweet."

"You're sweet," Senn returned in a disgusted manner.

"Why thank you."

"I didn't mean it in a good way."

"Yes, dear."

"Don't look at me."

"Happily." She turned her head and looked on towards Spirit Wood which had just appeared through a gap ahead.

"Elleth," said the Wizard with his wand held high. A string of light began to slowly shoot out of the wand and I watched with a smile on my face as Taborn gracefully moved to one side of us, touched the ground, moved to the other, touched the ground. Then he moved behind us and then in front, doing the same again. "Ela." At his word, no more light came from the wand. He swiftly returned to the middle of the arc where a small ball of light floated in the air as the centre point, where the four curving lines of light met. He touched the ball with his wand and spoke the word, "Ellethal." A soft, warm yellow dome formed around us, acting as both a protective shield from spells and the like, and a source of light. This was just a precaution, it wasn't likely that we would be attacked by any of the spirits but as they couldn't physically touch us, if one were to feel like attacking us it would use spells, and so the dome of light was the perfect defence against them.

The deeper into the Wood we went, the more spirits we saw, their ghostly forms glowing pale colours. Some hovered, their forms the same as us but not made of flesh, just light and cool fire. Some flew fast, darting like small birds, others slowly and gracefully, floating in the air in the forms of larger birds. There were also beautiful Horse, Deer and Stag Spirits, some flying and some almost walking, their hooves hovering ever so slightly above the ground, and of course, we saw a Squirrel Spirit or two along with some rabbits and hares.

I didn't say anything because it was likely just my mind reacting to our earlier encounter with the three men but from the moment we walked into the Wood to when we reached the humungous Hollow Tree that had intrigued us for days a couple of years ago, I felt as if someone or something was watching us, or just me, I didn't know, I couldn't shake the feeling...

The Hollow Tree was our destination as this was where our friends lived. We met them here for the first time when we spent all that time, two years ago, adventuring around and inside the incredible, natural wonder. Hanneth and Tulie found the way we lived to be intriguing and they found the idea rather attractive, so over time, they had made the inside of the tree their home, decorating it using ancient spells that were a delight to see and even more of a delight to watch being cast.

After Taborn had uncast his spell, we entered the trunk through an elegant circular door that was almost impossible to see unless you knew where to look.

Tulie came rushing over, elegantly hovering above the floor. "Hello," she said with what I can only describe as a pure, innocent smile. "We thought we would pop around to see how you were, if that's okay?" I asked.

"Of course," she replied happily. "How very you. Come, take a seat." She ushered us to the middle of the room and swiftly waved her hand while turning a full circle. Chairs, seemingly made of soft white light, began to form around us. We watched quietly in awe as they did. Then we took a seat, still a little warily for they looked as if we would fall right through them.

"That was beautiful," Eyla complimented while I admired the room in the same dreamy state I always did, it was like sitting inside a star lit sky, yet somehow more stunning.

"Thank you," Tulie returned.

"Hello," came another voice. I looked and saw Hanneth floating down the pale, fiery stairwell that spiralled upwards, hugging the inside of the trunk. Stairs were unnecessary for them for they could fly if they wished but they obviously liked them. "How are you all?" she asked smiling.

"We're good," Keeana replied.

"I'm glad."

"How about you two?" the Rogue asked. "We are well. The redecorating is going wonderfully."

"It looks unbelievably beautiful, it always does," Wulan complimented.

"That means a lot to us," she said, visibly very pleased.

"Did you spot any rarities on your way here?" Tulie asked with a hint of excitement in her voice.

"Sadly not," Keeana replied.

"Well, keep your eyes extra peeled on the way back because only a couple of days ago, I spotted a Phoenix Spirit which is a very rare thing indeed. It was…truly enchanting." I saw Senn sit up a little straighter.

"What did it look like?" he asked.

"It looked hot, hot and fiery, made of orange and red flames with magnificent wings, though they weren't large, but they held magnificence, like a king or queen."

"And not too long ago," Hanneth joined. "I saw a Winged Serpent Spirit. They're also quite rare, though not as wonderful or as loved as the Phoenix, but I personally think they're beautiful."

"I love snakes," said the Wizard. "Really?" she asked smiling. He nodded. "There one of my favourite creatures."

"I don't think in all my life I have met someone who has felt that way. Most people fear them."

"I know. Very strange."

"Yes," she said with a small laugh.

"Athaiel, you are an ancestor of the Serpent in a way, aren't you?" Hanneth asked turning my way.

"I guess so, yes."

"That's cool," she said, still not used to using the word cool in such a way.

"It is," I agreed, smiling.

"I can't believe I've never thought about that," the Wizard interjected. "You're so lucky," he added quietly.

"You are," Tulie agreed. "To have a pure Naytha as your mother and to hold the Naytha blood inside of you." I simply replied with a "Thank you," unsure of what to say. "I've forgotten why it is you love Naythas so much?" Taborn asked.

"They have been kind to Spirits throughout history, and to us personally. I have only ever seen one Naytha with a dark heart, a long time ago, before I met Hanneth. I saw him in a forest far from here, I do not know his name and I do not know the purpose behind what he was doing. I flew away as fast as I could as he began to tear apart the trees, the plants, the floor itself. When I returned a few days later, there was nothing left; the entire forest had been destroyed. Before then, I did not realise how much power a Naytha held. I remember looking over the remains to see if there was a clue of some kind, showing why someone would do such a thing, but all there was, was one immense crater that almost reached the same size as the forest before it was destroyed, and it went deeper than I could see, into total darkness. I didn't dare go anywhere near it but from where I was, it seemed there was nothing and no one in it or around it apart from what you would expect. Then I swiftly left that place and never returned. And I'm glad to say that I have never seen that man again and I have never seen another Naytha harm the wild." It was silent for a moment, and there was no doubt that me and my friends' thoughts were of similar things. "Have you heard any stories or rumours that could be related to him since?" I asked.

"In the times soon after the forest was destroyed, there were many rumours but since then, I have heard nothing. And though a part of me wishes for the mystery to be solved, I also hope that it never is and that it died with that terrible man."

"Do you remember the name of the forest?" Senn asked.

"It is now called the Sleeping Forest I believe."

"Do you know why?"

"I may be wrong, but I feel it is not an ancient name or even an old name but not a new one either. I believe many beings have been buried beneath the earth there in maybe the past century or couple of centuries or maybe even few centuries" – she shrugged – "that is why it is called the Sleeping Forest, I think." Senn nodded.

"Would we know any of the places near to the forest? Or was it really, really far away?" the Rogue asked, her curiosity likely getting the best of her.

"It was sort of near Helma actually, the Vast City. Have you ever been?"

"I've only ever heard stories sadly, though it sounds incredible."

"It really is, I would fly up into the sky sometimes and just float there above the city, looking down upon its magnificence."

"I would love to go one day."

"You could all travel there on those vehicles you have, have a look around the Sleeping Forest too, see if you can solve the mystery. I'm sure there's nothing to worry about anymore." We all nodded at this, likely all having already thought of arranging the trip, now being the perfect time as we had the freedom to do so.

"I think we will do exactly that," Keeana said with a small laugh.

"I look forward to hearing all about it."

Ironically, it was likely that the reason behind the forest's name was slowly becoming clear at this very moment in time. Though completely oblivious, we continued to talk, grins on our youthful faces, our minds filled with curiosity and our hearts hungry for mystery.

"I reckon the sword lies deep inside the Volcano of Zendar."

"I reckon it's in Ulath Mountain."

"The caves of the Black Forest."

"Heaven."

"Hell."

"I reckon it's buried with Pheluta," said Taborn seriously.

"Pheluta…" pondered Tulie for a moment. "That's a new one…and a good one," she added, her eyes widening. "That could actually be a possibility."

"Do you think so?" asked Eyla, surprised.

"I mean from everything I have heard about her, it's not a wild guess," Tulie replied.

"I'm glad you agree," said the Wizard smugly. "Whenever I would say it, they would mock me but clearly they're just not as wise as us."

"Clearly, they are not," the Spirit agreed, wearing a smile that made her look like a naughty schoolgirl. We were talking about the MoonSword, a weapon that some believed to be purely myth and legend, others real, and others had lived such a long life that they knew the truth but sadly, those beings were likely also part of Myth and Legend, or so I thought at this point in time. For a little while longer, the topic of conversation stuck around rumours, stories and the likes, sending our imaginations running wild. The six oceans of Leiyal came up, the Elven Bows of Leaf, Spirit, Wind, Healing and Song. These were fun to talk about as no one ever had any idea as to what these bows might actually do, and the guesses were always amusing. Pheluta also came up again and of course the Saven. And then, finally my friends and I realised we had been talking for far too long and so we got up, shared farewells and went on our way.

When the dome was surrounding us once more, we began to walk, more quietly now as we were all feeling tired and to speak would take great effort. So, we journeyed through the maze of tall trees, sleepily admiring our beautiful surroundings until Wulan brought us to a sudden stop. "Look," he said quietly. We all looked in the direction he was pointing. A tiny dragon spirit was slowly flapping towards us, glowing a deep, enchanting purple with hints of pure, dark, dark-black. It came right up to the outside of the dome and eyed us curiously. It stayed for a couple of minutes, watching us and circling us as we stared back at it in awe.

When the rare creature disappeared into the maze of trees, we all began to breathe normally again. "Was that a Twilight Dragon Spirit?" Senn asked before anyone else could.

"Yes, I think it was," said the Moke with a grin.

"That was amazing," added Eyla as we began to walk again. "Are Twilight Dragons usually friendly?"

"They can be, but they can also not be, and from what I've heard you don't want to be near one when it's not being friendly. They're one of the most powerful Dragons out there," I answered.

"Well, I'm glad that one was small and cute then, I was tempted to reach out and cuddle it you know."

"You should have," Taborn interjected plainly.

"It would be nice if you died." Eyla let out a tired laugh.

"Thank you, dear."

"Yes," he replied sleepily.

It became quiet again and stayed that way for the rest of the journey. We left the Wood, wandered past where we were attacked, the bodies were gone and then we walked further through the town, up the lamp lit hill and back to our homes.

I quietly unlocked the front door with a large iron key and entered. After putting the key back in my pocket, I climbed the dark, warm oak, spiral staircase which stood in the middle of the hallway, directly ahead of you as you walk into the house, then across the landing above and into my room. My eyes were well adjusted to the dark by this point in the night so there was no need for me to turn any lights on. Then after throwing my clothes onto the end bedpost which was shaped like a wave in a stormy sea, I got into bed and quickly fell asleep.

Chapter 4
Selhal, the Knight of Death

I woke from a dream feeling more awake than usual. After sitting there for a moment with my head leant against the headboard, I swivelled out of bed. After changing my underwear, I picked up my shirt off the bedpost, smelt it and finding its scent perfectly pleasant, I put it on, then I pulled on my trousers. After, I wandered over to the large, dark mahogany bookcase which covered the entirety of the wall opposite my bed and I searched, climbing up and down the ladder which slid from end to end, this was a feature I was personally very fond of, but I didn't find what I was looking for. So, I swiftly left my room, crossed the landing, popped into the bathroom and then made my way down the spiral staircase and into the library, which was located through a circular, dark wooden door located in the back wall of the hallway. I leapt onto one of the ladders and slid over to my father who held out a hand to stop me from crashing into him. "Hello, son," he said with a deep rumbling voice.

"Hello, Father," I replied, looking into his deep, fiery yellow eyes which were surrounded by the same scales that covered my body, arms and legs and half of my neck oddly, needless to say if you were to look at me while I was naked, I was quite a strange sight, and you should know that a Senva's genitals are not covered with scales, they are the only truly soft skinned part of a Senva. The difference between our scales was that his were red and mine matched my fair skin, which I inherited from my mother, along with my black hair that had the slightest tinge of green that was almost impossible to see, my eyes which were very much green without a hint of any other colour in them, in fact the entirety of my head I inherited from her, also the top half of my neck and my hands and feet.

"Do you know if we have a book about that…ancient fellow, the man who ruled over the dead?" My father was quiet for a moment.

"Selhal?" I shrugged in reply, unable to remember his name.

"I'm sure there'll be a book that talks about him somewhere. Go to the ancient fellows section," he said with an amused smile.

"May I ask why?" he asked looking my way.

"Just curious, I had an interesting dream," I replied mysteriously. "Aaahh, that's not surprising with me and your mother as your parents, you'll probably have vivid dreams every night in a couple of years. They're important things, son."

"I'm aware, Father."

"Are you?"

"Yes, you're obviously getting too old and senile to remember all the times you've told me before."

"I repeat myself because I have a dumb son." We both began to laugh at this.

"Right, ancient fellows," I murmured, moving over to the opposite wall. I quickly found the right section that was actually called Myths? Legends? Truths? Who Knows? And I began scanning over the books. We hadn't gone as far as to put the books in any kind of order so finding what I wanted wasn't exactly an easy task, but it didn't take too long. After scanning the bottom shelves and getting distracted a couple of times by books that talked of some of the topics me and my friends had spoken of the night before, I moved on to higher shelves and then found myself using one of the ladders to climb even higher and there I found, All We Know About Selhal, the Ruler of the Dead. Before I sat down and began to read, I decided I needed something to eat, so I exited the library, the wood panelled floor creaking beneath my feet, walked past the stairs, turned and went through a wide entrance that had no doors. The kitchen was empty for my parents were relaxing in the sitting room as it was the end of the week meaning they didn't have work. I quietly zipped about, warmed some bread and put a couple of eggs on top, just wanting a quick breakfast. Then I ate at a large, round oak table alone, washed up my plate, crossed the hallway, walked through a matching entrance and entered the sitting room.

"What you got there?" asked my mother softly, her voice not breaking the peaceful quiet that lingered in the room, enhanced by the crackle of the fire which sat flickering between two red brick walls. I silently lifted up the black, hard-backed book that was lined and decorated with ice blue and white patterns that were pleasing to the eye and made the book look as if it would be cold to touch. "Naturally," she said with a small laugh.

"I'm thinking about learning dark magic," I said seriously. She gave me a disbelieving look. "I think I'm going to shave off all my hair as well and ink my head completely black." My dad looked up at this and both kept their eyes on my unwavering face. "I'm going to sacrifice chickens in our fire soon so if you could leave before then?" I continued.

"Hey, I got Keeana pregnant." I couldn't help but begin to laugh.

"I'm going to cast a spell on our unborn child, so it comes out looking like a turtle." I continued to laugh while my parents tried their best to stop themselves from doing so, at the same time shaking their heads and looking back down at their books. "Right, if you'd both stop talking now please, I'm trying to concentrate," I finished. I looked down at my book smiling and turned over the front cover. As I began to read, I rocked back and forth in my favourite, beautiful rocking chair with my feet up on the dark, oak table which sat in the middle of the room on top of an old, stunning rug which was decorated with many waving patterns that were pleasing to look at, and feeling warm and comfortable, I easily became entranced in what I was reading and time began to tick by without my knowing.

One of the first things I learnt was that Selhal had many names, most likely made up by folk sharing rumours and telling stories in inns, not afraid to change a thing or two to their liking. Some of the names I liked, others I thought were a bit naff. I'll share a few of them with you.

The Black Sorcerer.
The Cold Knight.
The Soulless Ruler.
The HellBringer.
The HellShaper.
The Knight of Death.
The King of the Dead.
The Broken Prince.
The Fallen Knight.
The Lost Knight of the IceMist Mountain.

I think you get the point. Now what intrigued me about the list of names was how much they varied, and how many times he was called a knight and not a ruler or a king. The last one, the Lost Knight of the IceMist Mountain, that was the one that intrigued me most for the IceMist Mountain was a place. Well, so I had heard, though many believed it to be myth. But in any case, this alone gave me much information. I began to think on it, remembering everything I had heard about the IceMist Mountain. If Selhal was truly from the Mountain that would mean…he was truly ancient, he did not feel the cold, he knew sorcery…but did they practice dark magic? I don't remember the PaleBlooded! That was one of the names they were called by. They were strong without training and fast without trying, they hunted for their meals and got water by melting the ice that always surrounded them. They lived inside the mountain and if they lived on one of the top floors, they would have to climb down many stairs to get to the mountain's foot and go out into the Frozen Forest to hunt and do whatever else they did. Or maybe there was an easier way to get to the Mountain's foot, maybe using a bird of some sort. Maybe there were multiple mountains…these were all the thoughts that were going around my head even though I had barely begun reading, and as I carried on, my thoughts did not lessen, they only grew, slowly filling my head until it could not take any more.

From myths, legends, stories and many, many rumours the writer learnt, though not all the information may have been correct, that Selhal was in fact a PaleBlood, born and raised in the IceMist Mountain or Mountains. Apparently as a child, he was a shy, nice boy who preferred to be left alone. He grew up and became a Knight, a Knight to be reckoned with as all PaleBlood Knights were. By this point in time, he had become much more confident and he also enjoyed the company of others more. As time went on, he became known as one of the greatest Knights of the IceMist Mountain/Mountains. But as he grew in confidence and as he aged, occasionally those around him worried about him for his mind was clearly not always completely well for he had spells of acting in odd, disturbing ways. They hoped that this would not last and the affliction would leave him soon enough. But with time he only got worse until he was told he could no longer be a Knight for he was a danger to all those around him. From this point on, he grew worse and worse until even his own parents were telling him to stay away from them and the people treated him as a prisoner, locking him away and leaving him to his mumblings. The only time he got visitors was when guards would bring him food and drink. Then one day, he vanished, his well-furnished, comfortable room – which he had been imprisoned inside of – untouched except for the before locked door which seemed to be rotting away, dark magic lingering on its wood. No one knows why, how or when his mind started to become infected, maybe it was because of what he saw and experienced as a Knight, maybe he did not have a mind fit to cope. Maybe he encountered a dark being on his many travels and it infiltrated his mind and then his heart. Maybe he was born with the illness. Maybe he was secretly studying the Dark Arts but wasn't strong enough to defend himself against its seductive pull. There was no certain answer.

The people of the IceMist Mountains apparently never saw Selhal again which was lucky for them really, considering who he became. How he attained his powers over the dead is unclear for it is obvious that this part of his life is completely fabricated by the storytellers that fill all the Taverns across the lands, but there are other events recorded that are more likely to be true...

The Battle that Caused the Mountains to Tremble was a battle that Selhal played a role in, a small role for he did not yet hold the title of the Ruler of the Dead. Dark forces teamed up with Orcs and Trolls and attacked Theryndain, the Greatest of the Dwarven Kingdoms. Luckily, for the Dwarfs, the Mountain Wizard along with Lurah, the Mighty Griffin and an army of Mountain Men and Mountain Rogues fought on their side. Though there was much devastation that day, the Dwarves and their allies came out victorious and King Heral lived on and led his people through a very dark period of time and into the light when they grew prosperous once more and the kingdom earnt back the title, the Greatest Dwarven Kingdom.

At a later date, the Elven People of Yel, an extremely rich and extravagant people, found themselves in the Battle of the Shadow Puppets. Selhal himself led an army, an army made of minions that he had created and so they lived to serve him, his wish being their command and their forms having the appearance of shadows, they were named Shadow Puppets. But this attempt to take over Yel was a foolish one for the Elves held in their possession some of the most powerful Elven weapons, apparently including a couple of the Bows that I told you about before. And so, Selhal was forced to retreat. After the Battle, Yel was in a terrible state, it looked as if a long war had been fought on its land. Because of events that followed in the late future Yel never returned to the glorious, luxurious state it was in before the Battle of the Shadow Puppets.

Let us skip ahead now to Selhal's final battles. The BlackEarth War. Selhal held his many titles now and he was feared across all of Leiyal. The War began when he attacked a great city that no longer stands. An army of once dead beings rose from beneath the earth with decayed faces and bodies the colour of ash, and they were reborn with one purpose, to serve Selhal. Selhal and his undead army marched, the dark magic that coated them making all living nature begin to rot at their touch. They brought the city to its knees and Selhal went on to conquer kingdom after kingdom. He gained allies in these days, most of who feared him. Leiyal was a dark planet in those times, hope was slowly decaying with everything else, except for Selhal's hope, his was blossoming, his dreams were coming true, the living would die and dead would rise and they would answer to him and him alone, and one day, every being upon Leiyal's back would be under his rule. He would be free to do whatever he wished and the people would fetch him whatever he wanted. The world would be his completely and nothing and no one could stop him. He would be truly happy.

But one day, these hopes were crushed as a great army filled with mighty warriors – some with names that are still famous now – met him upon the Fields of Ferah and a fierce, devastating battle took place. Heroes were lost that day but Selhal's rule came to an end. Some say he was killed, others say he was banished to live out the rest of his days trapped beneath the earth, unable to move, left to die of thirst and starvation. Apparently, after a few years, many trees were planted in the ground the battle took place upon to make the land beautiful once more and one day, most of what was once the Fields of Ferah became an unnamed forest.

I believe there are books out there that hold more details on these events, if you wish to know more.

Much time had flown by while I was engrossed in the book and when I realised how much time I decided to take a break and let my mind process everything I had read. And because I had woken up mid-morning, it was also now time for lunch. So, I slowly rose from my chair, stretching at the same time, placed the book down on the table in front of me and made my way across the hallway and into the kitchen. "You seemed worryingly engrossed in that book," my mother commented looking away from the lunch she was making on the wooden top. "You're not really practicing dark magic, are you?" she asked unserious.

"No dear," I replied.

She smiled. "Jolly good."

Now, I'm sure many of you will already know this, as this is still commonly the case. Dreams were and are incredibly private things, no one should ask another what they dreamt. The dreamer should decide if they wish to share without any prompting from another. I remind you of this to explain why neither my mother nor father had asked me what I had dreamt. And though I would have told them, the thought of doing so didn't even cross my mind at this point in time.

After making my lunch which again was an easy meal, two Tera sandwiches, for as we all know the ugly bird is delicious in a bluebread embrace, I joined my mother at the table. A pale light spilled into the room through a large, circular window that sat above the sink, lighting us up as we chatted about small things.

"Oh, Mum."

"Yes?" she asked while carrying on to quickly wash up. "We were thinking of driving to Helma, probably tomorrow, would that be all right?"

"I assume we means the usual we?"

"Indeed."

"Go for it. You've never been before, have you?"

"Not that I know of."

"I can't believe we've never taken you there."

"Well, you are terrible parents."

"Mmm...I guess it makes sense that you're a terrible son then."

"I guess it does," I replied with a small laugh.

"What time will you be heading off?" she asked.

"No idea. I'll ask when I see them later."

"Okay, dick."

"Hmm?" I asked.

"Okay, dear."

"Right, that's not what you said though, is it?"

"Isn't it?" I shook my head in reply.

"Well, sometimes life throws a snowball and you just don't expect it."

"You're not making sense now," I said laughing. She smiled and said nothing. "Maryal," I called.

"Don't call me by my name," she protested. "I'm your mother."

"And I'm your great grandmother. Goodbye."

"Goodbye." I heard her chuckle away to herself as I left the room and crossed the hallway once more.

"Father!" I exclaimed over enthusiastically.

"What do you want, boy?" he asked in a low grumble. "Isn't that the question of the century, eh?" Drenak began to laugh and then he just sighed and carried on reading. As I sat down, he looked up at me again. "Have you been outside today?"

"Not yet," I replied.

"You should, go for a fly, it's a fine day." I thought on this for a moment and decided to do exactly that, go for a fly. Not needing anything except less clothes on my back, I swiftly went shirtless and walked to the front door.

Many times, beings who have never met a Senva before but know of us have asked me how it appears I have no wings while I'm wearing clothing. "There's no bump on your back or anything?" they would say. So, for everyone who is wondering, my wings become a part of my back, folding into their own perfect pouches I guess you could say. If you were to look at my naked back, you would see that they take up the entirety of it, top to bottom, side to side, and they do in fact protrude out from my back but an incredibly small amount for they are folded three times over when I'm not using them meaning when they span fully, they are around four times the length of my back, and width wise, they are also folded and when unfolded each one is around twice the width of my whole back plus a little wider I think. They grow as you grow. They are incredibly thin and flexible yet also incredibly strong and I have full control over the entirety of them. Folding them up always felt strange at first but by the age of eighteen, I was used to it. And again, I was an odd sight nude.

Right as I opened the door, my wings ready to lift and stretch wide, I spotted a man dressed in dark armour, a strong raven upon his chest plate. He entered my front garden and walked towards me, helmet under arm, sword sheathed. "Have you come into contact with the woman?" he asked, looking me over, then meeting my eyes and holding them.

"Woman?" I asked. He stared silently into my eyes. For some reason, I started to feel intruded, harassed. *I swear the light around him is getting darker*, I thought.

"Okay," said he. He turned and walked away. I shut the door and entered the living room.

"Whose symbol is the Raven?" I asked my father.

"What?"

"Which king? You know, has the symbol of the Raven."

"Raven King, obviously, you dangus."

"Who's he?"

"Bad man."

"Right, well, I think I just had a pleasant conversation with one of his men?"

"What do you mean?" Drenak asked, looking up from his book for the first time.

"A knight. Just came to the door." My dad got to his feet and began walking to the front door.

"What did he say?" he asked.

"He asked if I had come into contact with the woman?"

"What woman?"

"That's what I said." He opened the front door and walked until he reached the entrance to the front garden. After looking around, he came back inside and shut the door.

"What did the man say after?" he asked.

"He stared at me for a good chunk of time and then said okay. But I swear the light around him darkened." Drenak was quiet for a moment or two.

"Well…as long as you feel fine and he's gone, it doesn't matter. Go on your fly, monkey dick. Don't go looking for trouble." He left me with a pat on the shoulder.

This time, before I had even opened the door, there was a knock. I opened it up and there stood my friends. An amused expression blossomed on all of their faces. "You all right there?" asked Keeana with a smile. "We were thinking of going on a drive," she said gesturing to the vehicles behind them. "But if you're busy?"

"I'll go put my clothes back on," I said laughing and turning back into the house.

After I had dressed myself appropriately and informed my parents on what I was doing, I exited through the arched doorway and walked down the side of the tall and wide house. In the back garden sat three Hovra's, vehicles made mostly of magic combined with a little machinery. I hopped on the back of mine, her name was Ghost, if I would have got her when I was eighteen, I would have likely named her something different but when I was younger, I thought it was a very cool name and now it held her personality and many memories, so it stuck.

As soon as my hands touched the handlebars, the almost silent engine whispered to life. I drove back down the side of the house beneath the canopies of a few healthy green, large-leafed trees that never changed except in the season, Senhu, when they turned a stunning yellow colour. My friends were waiting for me on their smooth, pale-blue and silver, almost spirit, ghost like vehicles, hence the name, and leisurely we began to drive, hovering above the snowy ground, the fresh wind blowing in our faces. We left the secluded spot where my house was located, drove down a wide tree lined path. Some of the trees were naked though still beautiful and others were very much alive and fruitful as they always were in the Winthal season. There were a few clouds slowly flying across the pale-blue sky but there was more blue than white. The Yellow Sun was shining and ahead of me, I could also see one of the Blue Suns, a single blue ray shining down, touching I believe, the Seren Ocean, the light then spreading across the entirety of its body, even to the deepest depths where civilisations live, and ancient things lie. Then when night comes and darkness falls, the ray disappears as if its bed time for the Ocean Dwellers, someone flicks a switch and lights out.

After driving down the long pathway, we made our way past the bizarre homes, the Piper Inn in the distance, but we didn't go down the lamp lined hill. Instead, we carried on over the top of the hill and towards what we and the people called, the Forest in Which it is Fun to Race.

We lined up at the forest's boarder and three, two, one, go. As the forest wasn't a particularly large one, our end destination was the other side. The first one to emerge from beneath the trees canopies and see the clear sky above them would be the winner. Though it wasn't as simple as going in a straight line and dodging a few trees. There was a wide track that had always been there, I believe Boloh Einth was responsible for making it and though I have never met him, I love him for doing so. It curved around trees, squeezed through tight spaces, dived through shallow, small caves and then led back to the surface. It sent you drifting around boulders, up jumps and down sharp ramps. This is why the forest had earnt such a name.

We began side-by-side, all able to fit on the one track. Rude gestures flew back and forth when there was the opportunity but quickly, all opportunity ceased to come, and our expressions went hard with the occasional grin as things got more difficult. I found myself in first place as we zigzagged through trees and made a harsh turn around a large boulder, but a second harsh turn quickly followed and Taborn squeezed through the inside, turning a little better and he inched ahead flashing me a grin, his cloak billowing out dramatically behind him. After slaloming through more trees, we made a long drift and darted left, then we squeezed through a small archway and dove down a sharp ramp into an almost circular cave. Almost instantly, I found myself rising back to the surface. I exited the cave and narrowly missed a rock and then another and another. My mistakes meant everyone overtook me, Wulan making it to second behind Taborn who was still first, Keeana in third, Eyla in fourth and Senn in fifth. I cursed and it's likely my concentration face began to show in all its glory. Another cave fast approached. We darted inside, drifted around a large rock which rose all the way to the roof of the cave and then we rocketed back out the way we came in, curving left down a branching off track. I spotted Taborn going over an approaching jump, he twisted in the air attempting to show off, but it cost him dearly. Because of this, he ended up last, all of us whizzing around him and I imagine he too cursed. A quick, steep dip followed by a short curving S came next and then another jump over the top of a tall boulder, landing on a smooth ramp which sat waiting on the other side. Senn had caught up to second beside Keeana, Eyla close behind. But something obviously went wrong for he ended up behind me. We drifted around to the right, though keeping on going forward and then to the left, a row of rocks creating the perfect opportunity. As we darted past more trees, zigzagging and then bursting forth, I began to catch up with Eyla and she began to catch up with Keeana, but it was too late. With one final jump through a gap in the canopies, the race ended. Wulan first, Keeana second, Eyla third, me fourth, Senn fifth and Taborn came last and he wasn't pleased by the fact. In fact, none of us except for Wulan ended the race pleased.

"Good lord I'm talented!" exclaimed Wulan while he sat on top of MokeyMokaMoka – that was what he had named his Hovra – wearing a smug expression. "If it was longer, I would have overtaken you," said the Rogue.

"I would have overtaken you," corrected Eyla.

"I would have overtaken you," I corrected.

"I would have overtaken all of you," interjected Taborn.

"I would have won," added Senn.

"You shut your face, Senn." The young Elf man looked toward the Rogue surprised.

"Oh bite me," she scowled unable to hide a small, unwanted smile.

"Why is it always me who you take your anger out on?" he moaned. "Athaiel's much better at taking it."

"I like to prey on the weak and laugh when they cry," she replied darkly. I began to laugh. "Don't laugh, you dick," she said meeting my eyes.

"Thank you," Senn murmured. "If I was your dad, I wouldn't love you," I returned.

"If I was your mum, I would leave your dad just so I could get away from you," Eyla added looking at Keeana.

"Why are you on his side?" she complained.

"Sorry, it was just a spur of the moment thing."

While we spoke, there had been someone approaching us, someone riding a kitted out, black horse. This being came closer and closer, seemingly heading straight for us. As it became obvious he was planning on stopping to talk, we turned his way. He eyed our vehicles like they were truly strange to him. He wasn't from around here. He was a knight of Raven King.

"Have any of you seen the man?" He looked from one confused face to another, meeting our eyes. The light around him darkened significantly. "Curse every single one of you," he spat. Then he spun his horse around and went away.

"What a strange fellow," commented Wulan, raising his eyebrows and smiling. We all chuckled.

I dreamt of Selhal again that night, or who I thought was Selhal at the time. But this dream was very different from the last. This one was not just a dream.

Chapter 5
The Dream

Unlike any Spirit, I had encountered before, the Stag's blue and silver fiery form was giving off a heat that kept my front hot on the long journey up the mountain. We first began walking through a dark forest which would have rendered me blind if it were not for the Spirit's gentle light. I followed him closely, trudging through the deep, pristine snow. We walked up a reasonably steep incline, at a good pace, and soon the trees disappeared from above us and snowflakes began to fall upon my face, melting at the touch of my heated skin. We walked further and further, up and up until finally the stag came to a stop. I stepped to his side, aware of a strong female presence, and I looked beyond and saw only darkness and empty air. We were standing on the edge of the mountain's peak and I felt we had reached our destination. The Stag looked my way and met my eyes, then he turned his head and looked towards the stormy sky. With one leap, he began to fly, up towards the sky and as he came near, it was as if the heavens opened, a light shone in the sky and the beautiful Spirit disappeared as he flew through it. The light then vanished, and lightning began to flash accompanied by claps of thunder. I looked out ahead of me and saw a figure, a giant, dark figure wearing a strange sort of crown which curved downwards from the top of his head and macabrely covered all of his face but his eyes, his deep, deep, enchanting blue, almost black eyes that were wholly one colour. Suddenly, I could see the ground at his black, metal armoured feet. Hands, hundreds, thousands of hands were reaching out of the ground, grasping for life. They covered the land for miles. In one sudden moment, the darkness returned, and I was blind to what lay beyond once more. Then returned the light in the sky and what seemed to be an angelic figure, elegantly floated down towards me. The Angel landed by my side and looked at me. I had never felt such peace. Gracefully, she reached out her hand, the beauty of it gently touched my heart and I will never forget it. In her palm lay a small stone filled with many deep, enchanting colours. I held out my hand and placed it on top of hers and the Stone, and the dream faded.

Chapter 6
Nightmare

A small stone floated, amidst nothing but pure darkness. It glowed gently, emanating deep, soft colours. Halt moved his hand towards it, but he couldn't reach it. He couldn't touch it. He tried, and he tried, and he tried again but he couldn't. He felt angry, frustrated, confused, lost, broken, sad, sorrowful. The darkness washed over him, and he woke from his nightmare. He sat up, leaning against the headboard behind him. For a moment, he was still and quiet but then his fists began to clench, his nails digging into his palms. He began to shake. He slammed his hands onto the mattress over and over and over.

Halt woke again in the morning. He opened his eyes and stared for a minute or so at a ray of light that revealed some of the dust which was dancing around the room. Then he swivelled and stood, the floorboards creaking as he did so. After cleaning himself up, he got dressed, then made his way downstairs where Dillie greeted him with a lovely smile. "How was the sleep?"

"Truly terrible," he replied. She frowned. "Oh no. Not because of the accommodation, I promise you."

She smiled and said, "Well, I hope your nights swiftly grow more peaceful."

"Thank you."

"So, what would you like for your breakfast?"

"The largest, most delicious breakfast meal on your menu please." Dillie chuckled at this.

"Very good. Grent!" she called.

"What?" he shouted from somewhere behind the back wall of the bar area.

"Largest, most delicious breakfast meal! For your favourite customer!"

"Very good!" he said. Moments later, loud thumping and creaking sounded as a large male Rhoon made his way down the stairs. "Greetings," he said rather loudly as he appeared.

"Greetings." Halt returned with an amused smile. A clearly agitated, grumpy, venomous looking fellow with dark-green hair and green eyes walked around the Rhoon, bags in hand, muttering something. He took a seat at the end of the bar, as far away from anyone as possible. The Rhoon joined Halt, not noticing the other man. "My name is Hern, short for Hernalma," he said in a jolly manner, holding out his hand. "What is yours?"

"I am Halt."

"It's very good to meet you, Halt."

"And you, Hern" – the Rhoon smiled an honest smile – "you look to me as if you are a traveller. Where is it you are going now?" As Hern asked this, Dillie nervously went to take the venomous man's order. He spoke quick and sharp, clearly not wanting conversation.

"I do not know," answered Halt.

"Ah. Very exciting. I wish I were so brave. I am making my way to the mountains. I wish to make myself proud. Climb as far as I dare." Halt smiled. "I hope you accomplish your goal, Hern."

"Thank you, sir."

"You're very welcome." A darkly dressed red-haired woman appeared at the bottom of the stairs. She silently joined the venomous looking fellow. Hern's eyes had followed her and now he was facing them.

"Hello, what are your names?" he asked. Halt's head dropped. He looked at the counter, finger tapping.

"Be quiet," answered the man. The woman frowned and very quietly said something. "Shut it!" he shouted, grabbing hold of her wrist. He then pulled her off her chair and said, "Go!" She quickly picked up her bags and started walking towards the door. Halt and Hern were already stepping towards the fellow, words on the tip of their tongues. But before they could say anything, the man's hand turned black and with unnatural speed, he touched the Rhoon's skin and then went to touch Halt's but the foul one found Halt's hand around his neck and his feet off the ground. The traveller stared darkly into the wide eyes of his opponent. Then came dizziness, nauseous darkness.

Halt woke moments later on the floor of the inn, his opponent gone. He felt tired and nauseous and had a headache. Hern was still lying completely still, unconscious. He woke up fifteen minutes later – moved from off the floor – when Halt was eating, already feeling better. Unfortunately for the Rhoon, he did not recover so quickly.

Halt had been told by Dillie that he had just dropped to the ground, and the 'horrid green man' as she called him, had sprinted out of the inn. Hopefully, never to return.

The traveller went around the back to see how Hern was doing. He looked pale and was sitting hunched on a chair, his head hovering over a bowl. He decided it was unnecessary to ask how he was feeling. "Why is it you don't look like me?" asked the blue one.

"I do not know," answered Halt. Though he had his theories.

"Well, count yourself lucky. I do not like that man." The common man smiled with a hint of sympathy visible on his face.

"I'm sorry, Hern," he said. "I think you should recover quite quickly though."

"Do you think so?"

"I do." Really, Halt was very unsure. "His touch can't be too venomous if I'm already feeling myself again."

"I hope you're right."

"Anyway, go on your way now, Halt. Leave me to my suffering." He smiled.

"It was a pleasure meeting you," said the traveller with a small bow.

"And you."

Halt made his way to his room. For a very short while, he sat on his bed, thinking. Then he got up and prepared to leave.

After saying farewell to the dwarves who were gifted hosts indeed – they were sad to see him go so soon – he hopped onto Thela, his horse who was ready and waiting and rode off out of the village, onto land he had not travelled across before.

Their progress was swift across the vast, flat land. The wind was cold and fresh, holding the ability to wake up even the sleepiest. *Silence was a heavy presence here. Silence owned this land,* thought Halt. He looked ahead to a line of tall, healthy trees which had been unharmed by the season. He kept his eyes on them as Thela took them closer and closer. *Something powerful is in there.* Suddenly, a Raven flew by him, squawking loudly. The common man cursed and watched as the bird flew at high speeds into the wood.

When he entered, silence was no longer the heaviest presence. Halt could feel the being. Cautiously, he and his partner travelled on. For some reason though this being felt dark, powerful, in charge, Halt didn't feel fearful. The presence lingered on him, but he didn't feel trapped or attacked. He felt like he was being watched but that was all.

An hour later – the feeling still there – the call of a Raven sounded close by. Halt turned his head towards the sound and saw a horse. A dead horse, lying still on the ground. Thela cautiously moved closer then stopped for Halt to get off. The presence of the being was too strong for him to be able to tell whether the horse was dead or not, so he moved closer and knelt beside the beast, laying a hand on its side. It was dead.

"What are you doing?" asked a male, sinister voice. Halt jumped and stood up, unsheathing his sword. He looked around but could see no one.

"You feel compassion towards the beast?" asked the voice.

"Did you kill it?" the traveller questioned, still looking around.

"No, I did not."

"Did it have a rider?"

"A woman with many tricks."

"What did she—"

"Green cloak and dark-silver hair," the being interrupted. "She escaped with painful injuries," he continued. "She killed the beast who attacked her."

"Where is she now?" asked Halt.

"I do not know. You feel," said the voice.

"What?"

"You feel compassion for the beast dead on the ground. You feel worried for a woman. Yet you are a child of darkness. How have you escaped?"

"Escaped what?"

"Darkness."

"I haven't."

"You have blessed me. It has been a blessing to be in your presence."

"Keep on your course. The woman travelled that way, beyond the forest."

Halt suddenly felt ten times lighter. The being had left him. Quickly, he grabbed a bag which lay beside the dead creature and got on his horse, feeling mostly confused by the being and what had just occurred. For some reason, he felt sadness too, loneliness, yearning. But this time, these emotions weren't his...with speed, he travelled on.

Chapter 7
My Dream Like No Other

My vision was blurry at first but then things started to become clear. Thick, long branches stretched above me intertwining with one another. In the gaps, there was blue sky, clear blue sky. Cautiously, I sat up and began to look around. I was sitting on lush green grass; it was the comfiest ground I had ever sat upon. I ran my fingers through the blades. They felt different to any I had felt before. They were thick, healthy, soft blades. All around were thick, again healthy, almost green trunks that grew to tall heights. All of the branches reached into the middle of the circle which the trees created, and they intertwined making a beautiful natural roof. Around me lay my friends and family, all still asleep. My wandering fingers found a flower, a vibrant red flower tinged with violet. Its petals grew outwards and then curved downwards until the ends reached the grass. I looked and saw that there were a few of these around, accompanied by a deeper red flower striped with a vibrant yellow. Movement suddenly caught my eye beyond the circle of trees and I was snapped out of my dreamy state. Through a gap between two of the trunks, I spotted two purple eyes looking at me. "Be at peace," said a soft female voice that carried an accent strange to me. "If I enter, will you attack me?" she asked. She looked into my eyes. Her skin was a deep, dark enchanting purple, she had long dark-blue hair, and dark-green markings made different shapes on the parts of her skin which were bare, them being her hands, her face, her bare feet and the lower parts of her legs for she wore a thin, long, elegant, deep-red cloak of some strange kind. One marking that stuck out particularly was the one in the middle of her forehead. The shape was odd. The top of the marking was a semi-circle. A rectangle grew out of the middle of the bottom of the semi-circle and then the rectangle ended by going inwards, creating a sharp point at the bottom. This endpoint touched the very top of her nose.

"I won't attack if you don't," I said. Cautiously, she stepped through the gap between the trunks, keeping her eyes on me.

"My name is Teela, and you are Athaiel." She spoke softly, and I felt love in her words. I'm not sure how to describe what I mean.

"How do you know who I am?" I asked, both of us still keeping our distance.

"I do not know who you are," she replied, "I know your name, I know your face, I feel your spirit but I do not know you in the way you mean."

"How do you know my name?" I tried.

"Dreams and visions." Unsure of what to say, I stood, silently looking around, thinking, and then I met her eyes once more. "You are in Reignthorl, the Nature Kingdom," Teela informed before I could ask, "and you are standing in Rhu Circle. It is a place to rest, to think, to create, to heal, to dream. It is loved by my people. The name of our kind is Deiyahlu; we are the Deiyahlu people. Your tongue is not our most loved tongue, but we know it. It is not as beautiful as others, but it is a tongue many beings know. It is useful."

The Deiyahlu people's language is a confusing matter. In more ways than one, their letters are different to those of my language and they hold different sounds and when speaking the language, the mouth makes different shapes. The letters themselves are shapelier, each one like a little intricate drawing. They are intriguing and beautiful letters. It would take me a very long while to draw them in the correct way, so when they speak in their tongue I will translate their letters into ours for though they have a very different look and sound, our alphabets are technically almost entirely the same. Though reading my translations, you will not know the true sounds of the letters or see their true shape, though I may draw for you a few examples, you will still be reading their words but their words in our letters if you understand my meaning. I apologise if that is confusing and I apologise that I cannot do better than this.

I nodded. I felt a little more relaxed. "It is beautiful," I said, looking beyond the circle and seeing a lush field, empty except for a few roaming creatures that I could not discern for they were too far away. The field looked simply glorious, filled with the pleasantly strange grass which also lay beneath my bare feet. Where my shoes were, I did not know but I was glad I wasn't wearing them because the grassy ground felt wonderful. "The dreams and visions you have had, are they the reason why I'm here?"

"Yes," she said. "We are sorry for how we brought you here, so far from your home, but we have been treated badly by beings similar or the same as you and your family," she gestured towards the sleeping bodies. "In my dream, I was told that it would have to be done in such a way also or you may not have come, and I think in any of the cases, it was the way it would have been done because it was the safest way. Please forgive us."

"I understand," I said. "If your dreams and visions hold true meaning, then all is forgiven." Teela nodded and bowed.

"Will you sit with me outside the circle and let me tell you some of what I have seen? We will look into the circle as I do and wait for your family to wake." I nodded in reply but before Teela had taken two steps my dad stirred. Teela looked his way, as did I. His eyes opened. He was awake.

"Father," I said looking down at him. He suddenly jumped to his feet and Teela quickly stepped back and took a fighting stance. "Calm down!" I said hurriedly. His eyes found Teela and he leapt towards her, but I grabbed him, put my leg behind his and tripped him so he hit the ground, lying on his back. "Stop!" I tried.

"They attacked us! Do you not remember? They threw some type of gas on me!" he argued.

"I had seen that even our darts would not pierce you," said Teela.

"She has seen me, seen us in visions and dreams and if you just listen to her speak you will feel it. She is telling the truth. I haven't been awake long, and we've talked little but I already feel deeply that she is good and truthful, and I believe she is someone important, someone I need to know, someone that…I don't know. I trust her so trust me and listen to her," said I.

"Get off me then." I stood up and he did too. Teela looked at me and held her eyes on mine for a moment. Her gaze was gentle and meaningful. In that moment, I felt us connect in a way which I cannot explain and for the first time, I realised she was likely around the same age as myself. Then she looked towards my father. "Drenak," she began.

By the time Teela had finished, my father was calm and I could tell he felt something similar to what I did. "I apologise for earlier," he said.

"There is no need," replied Teela, "I understand." My father was quiet for a moment.

"What does Rhu mean?" he asked.

"Heal, healing in your tongue." My father nodded looking around, up and down and beyond Rhu Circle. "And Reignthorl, the name of our Kingdom, it means Nature," she added. Both me and my father nodded, intrigued. It was quiet for a moment. The atmosphere was one of true peace.

"I feel truth in your words, Teela," said Drenak. "But I still know little. Will you be sharing your dreams and visions with Athaiel only or with all of us."

"Athaiel only," replied the young woman. "But then, he may share with you whatever he feels he should."

"Okay," he said. He looked between us thoughtfully. "You are indeed connected in some way…" he pondered quietly. "Though at the moment, I do not know how…" Neither I nor Teela said anything, though I believe that my father spoke the truth. We were connected in some way. We had barely spoken really, yet I felt like I trusted her with my life and I felt I could share my life and all of its secrets and dreams and all with her. I cannot explain the feeling or why I felt it. It was like our spirits were reaching out to one another and intertwining.

I looked down towards my friends and mother. I laughed a little. "It is likely that the things we have used to keep you unconscious affects both of you less than it affects them," said Teela.

"That is probably right," my father said nodding. "Keep us unconscious?" he asked.

"It was a long journey," Teela replied. To my surprise, my father just laughed.

"It must have been for it is sunny and though it is hard to tell I think it is warm here also."

"Yes," said Teela. "It was unpleasant where we found you. We do not like the cold very much."

"Does it get cold here?" I asked.

"It does but not as cold as your home. It can rain and be windy and cold but there is never snow and it never becomes freezing." I nodded, many thoughts going around my head. Teela turned her head and I followed her gaze. A tall, light-grey skinned figure was walking towards us. As he approached, I saw that he was a man, an old man with long silver hair and in his left hand, he held a tall, simple wood staff. At the top of the staff was a stormy wave calved from rosy, healthy wood, and at the bottom of the staff was a leaf, almost heart shaped. The main wood body that ran from wave to leaf was simple and smooth. He also had dark-green markings on his face, hands and feet. The rest of him was covered up by a thin, long white cloak, seemingly the same kind as Teela's. He also wore odd pale-grey trousers, I could not tell their material.

161

"It seems you were right," the old stranger said looking at Teela, as we followed her out of the circle to meet him, my father's scaled, clawed red feet shining a little in the sunlight. Because of his dragon like feet, he never wore shoes.

"We insisted protectors went with her to wait for you all to wake just in case, but she told us that you" – he pointed at me with a wrinkly grey finger – "would wake first and that you would not attack her, and it would be okay. She would not even take a weapon. Eventually, we gave in and said okay for when she speaks with such conviction we have found it means she is right and those who argue against her are wrong." Teela smiled.

"This is Yehfae Tulasmo, the Elder Leader of our people," she informed. "This is Athaiel and this is Drenak his father." Yehfae held out a hand and one after the other me and Drenak shook it.

"We are sorry for the way we brought you here, but we are glad you are now here and there has been no trouble. Teela's wisdom has brought you here and I feel now that the Ghost is confirming many things."

"The Ghost?" asked my father.

"The Ghost is what we call the spirit which flows across all lands and in and around faithful beings and through the homes of those faithful beings. It is particularly heavy on this day. I believe both of you have felt it, not only today but before," he said looking between me and my father.

"I have," said Drenak quietly, seemingly in deep thought. I nodded and met Yehfae's wise, old eyes. "Teela," he said looking her way. "Why don't you walk with Athaiel, show him things and speak together, and I will wait with Drenak for their family to wake." Teela nodded and looked between me and my father to see if this was all right. My father smiled at me and gestured that it was. I smiled back and then turned towards the Elder Leader. "It was a pleasure to meet you."

"The same to you," he replied. Then me and Teela began to walk, a very long line of huge, healthy looking, warm red, warm orange and warm yellow leafed trees far ahead. I didn't know if it was me seeing things, but I thought that the leaves were glowing a little, gentle and warm in the sun.

Slowly, we wandered towards the trees, first in a comfortable, peaceful quiet. The grass was soft beneath my feet, the air smelt lovely and the quiet noises of wind and rustle added goodness to it all. I felt tranquil. I looked up to the blue sky and saw three birds flying up there. Two of them were bright red and as big as eagles. The other was bright yellow and significantly smaller. "What are their names?" I asked. Teela stopped walking and followed my gaze.

"They are Hurils. The yellow one is a child. It will become orange and then red over time."

"And what are their names," I asked pointing to a creature strolling on the ground ahead of us.

"They are called Fenvers," she answered, beginning to walk again. We moved towards the creature until we were right next to it. I stopped cautiously for it looked to be part of the Big Cat family and I knew most of them to be dangerous.

"Do not worry," said she. "They are kind and they don't like meat, so you don't need to worry as long as you are also kind to them, because they can be fierce if they need to be." I stepped closer and slowly put my hand onto its muscular side. Its coat was icy-blue and it had a very large white mane, and upon its chin was a long, pale-grey beard. It didn't look like it belonged in a sunny place. I stroked its warm side and I felt a deep purr run through its body. "Amazing." Teela smiled and said, "I like them very much." She rubbed the Fenver's head goodbye and we began to walk again. The trees ahead looked incredibly dense and were very tall. A faint violet glow that matched the colour of the moon was gently emanating from the shade below the trees. It was an enchanting sight. "Look up as we enter," said Teela with a smile.

We entered, and I did as she said. The other side of the tree was made of violet leaves that glowed gently like the moon. "These are Trees of Sun and Moon," she told me. "In light, they glow with colours of the sun and in darkness they glow with colours of the moon."

"That's awesome."

"Yes, it is. Come, there is much more." I stepped to her side and we walked on. Quickly, the only light that was stopping it from being pitch dark was the glow that came from the nature around. Branches and leaves still grew at very low parts of the trees trunks. The wonderful canopies were so dense that no sunlight pierced through them. There was not a single ray upon the ground. I could hear birds singing in strange ways. Their whistles were long and smooth and almost hypnotic. There was also the gentle sound of running streams and rustling leaves, every now and again, an animal call I did not recognise, and also occasionally voices speaking in a language I did not know. Some people walked by not far away but too far away to share greetings with. I thought of how large this forest might be.

We came to a green path, long grass either side of us, and amongst that grass were flowers, some small and some tall. They all caught my eye but one more so than the others. It stood out for there weren't any others like it that I could see. It was tall, and the petals were large and shaped like miniature trees. The petals were a wonderful mix of pale blue, white and red. They were glowing very softly. I reached out to touch one and it was incredibly soft. I then bent to smell the flower and it held a powerful but pleasant, sweet scent.

We soon came to a stop as the path reached the edge of a circular lake that wasn't small or large. "This is the Delah Water," Teela said after a moment of silent gazing. It was black except for where leaves had fallen and beneath those floating leaves was a dark-blue light gently glowing. Teela crouched down and placed her hand on top of the water. The same dark-blue light appeared beneath and ever so slightly around her hand. I crouched down and did the same. The light came. Slowly, I moved my hand across the lakes surface, lightly touching the water, and the light followed beneath it. "What does Delah mean?" I asked, trying to pronounce it in the way she did.

"It is a word for magic, good magic." I nodded, and all was quiet for a moment. "Let's walk further and go to a place where there is no chance of eavesdroppers. Then I can tell you my dreams and visions. And I can show you more things along the way."

"How long is this forest?" I questioned, as we began to walk again, lit up by fascinating, glowing nature in every direction.

"You will find out soon," she answered. "We will reach the other side shortly and then walk to my home, and there I can tell you what I have seen in peace." I smiled and nodded, excited to see more of this Reignthorl Kingdom.

We came to a stop, still under the canopies of the Trees of Sun and Moon. A small pitch-black monkey with bright-yellow eyes had jumped from a branch and landed on the floor in front of us. He looked our way. "Naya Teela," said the monkey. I stood shocked, staring silently at the creature.

"Naya Bonku," she replied. The monkey met my eyes. "Athaiel, this is Bonku. Bonku this is Athaiel," Teela said. The monkey silently stepped closer, holding his eyes on mine. Not knowing what to say I stayed silent. I had a bad feeling about him.

"Welcome, Athaiel," he said finally, then he quickly leapt into the branches of a tree and disappeared.

"Never trust him," Teela told me after a moment. "He does not have a good or healthy mind. He is a trickster and a liar. His mind is ill."

"I felt it," I said. Teela met my eyes, smiled a gentle, kind smile and nodded. "Sadly, there are others like him here. Not all Malaz," she said with a small laugh.

"Malaz?" I asked.

"Oh, Malaz is his species, the monkey's species. It is a unique and rare species."

"Oh," I replied, nodding.

"I do not understand their minds. It makes no sense for someone to think in those ways. It is strange and wrong, and I don't know how they cannot see that. Surely, their minds are diseased, or they are just missing most of their brains, or maybe dark magic has cursed their hearts. I say all this because it angers me but truthfully, it is probably not their fault. I'm sorry," she said. "I'm Yalala."

"Yalala?" I asked with a smile. "It means when someone is talking a lot and getting lost in their thoughts." She looked at me, asking if I understood.

"I understand," I chuckled. "We call it rambling or babbling. Don't worry, I do it often." Teela smiled and nodded.

"Rambling, babbling," she said quietly to herself. I smiled.

Then we were quiet for a short while as we made our way to the boarder of the Forest of Sun and Moon.

We emerged from beneath the wonderful trees and the sunlight fell upon us once more. We were now standing in a sort of circle, long grass at our feet. People were crossing this circle in all directions. We walked forward and to the right and crossed a simple, lovely, curved wooden bridge which crossed a healthy running stream. We then followed a green path, lush nature on either side of us. We wandered past people, some stopped and Teela introduced me, others smiled and carried on, a couple kept their eyes on the ground, and another two gave me suspicious, unpleasant looks.

After following the path for a short while, we turned right and made our way down a very small hill covered in long, dark grass. At the bottom, the land went flat for only six or so steps and then there was a river and many ropes hanging from the branches of trees above it. Teela took a few steps back and then she ran and jumped, grabbing hold of a rope, swinging and landing on the other side of the river. She looked back and I smiled and did as she did. We took six or so steps forward and then walked up a very small hill, the twin of the one on the other side of the river. "This is HayenNea Tooh," she told me, as we reached the top. I looked upon a spacious wood filled with tall, immensely thick, brown trees. Among the magnificent thick branches were wonderful wooden homes. Some were located in the higher branches, some in the lower, but all were a good distance from the ground. "HayenNea Wood," she said. "HomeTree Wood," she translated.

"This is where you live?" I asked.

"Yes. Do you like it?"

"I do. A lot."

"Good. Come, my home is a little further."

We walked on. Most of the way, I was looking up, admiring the houses. Some had rope ladders dangling down, some of which were the tallest ladders I had ever seen. Others, most, it was clear did not need ladders for the tree's branches could visibly be easily climbed all the way to the houses. A lot were made of dark wood, but some were light and pale, some so pale they were very nearly white. Others were red and rose, both pale and dark, and I also saw a couple of homes that were greenish and blackish. It was intriguing to see all the different kinds of woods I did not know the names of.

We came to a stop beneath a house located a reasonable distance away from any other. It was made of a dark, warm wood, one that looked homely to me. As I followed Teela up the branches, I remembered that I was bare footed, and I was suddenly glad I had tough skin. I imagined Taborn would likely not have made it all the way to the front door of Teela's house without getting at least a scratch or two.

We reached the thick, circular front door quick and easy. I watched as Teela put her forehead and one hand against the wood, then she gently blew on the door and after a second, there was a sound, not like the normal sound which comes from unlocking a door. It was as if a wind blew inside the wood, like it was answering Teela's breath with its own. The door opened, and we entered.

"You will need something to eat and drink," said Teela, as I looked around me. This was the first time since I woke up that I even remembered I needed to eat and drink to keep myself from dying. A great hunger and thirst came over me and I replied swiftly. I followed Teela into what I assumed was the kitchen area. The entire house was open planned, simple and beautiful with wood beams running across the ceiling. All the tops were wood and there was a round wood table with a few wooden chairs around it. There wasn't a lot of furniture, but it didn't feel empty, it just felt spacious and it held a simplicity to it which I personally liked very much. "Deiyahlu people don't spend much time in their homes. The main thing we do in them is sleep. We spend most of our time outside," Teela told me.

"Do you live here alone?" I asked.

"My mother also lives here."

"What's her name?"

"Teetha. Naming your babe here is a very simple thing. If you and your father were Deiyahlu people, then he would have named you something like Lrenak." She smiled.

"That makes it a lot easier."

We took a seat at the round table and both ate off wooden plates and drank from tall, wooden cups. We ate two simple meat sandwiches each. The bread was dark-green. It looked neither appetising nor unappetising. I did not know what kind of meat it was, but it was delicious, as was the bread, and as we were talking about other things I did not think to ask what animal the meat came from.

Once we had finished lunch and the table was clear except for our drinking cups, we quickly stopped talking about little things and our conversation came to Teela's visions and dreams. Or it would have but the dream ended there.

What in all the universe was that all about? I thought to myself.

Chapter 8
The Strange Family

Upon a unique planet named Roebetha, in a vast city called Obneeth, there lived a strange group of beings, their home an immense, old, abandoned cathedral. Leenkal was the name of one of these beings. If a human of earth were to see him and later if they were asked to describe him, they would likely say something like, "A metal, robotic man." In short, this is what he was. In his head was a brain like that of a human's but his figure, though shaped similarly to a man's, was most definitely not pink, soft and hairy. He had no flesh, no bones. He was silver all over, metal all over. An average human engineer – like those who live on planet earth – would be beyond fascinated by him. Luckily, for Leenkal, there was not a single one of these beings upon the planet Roebetha. In fact, he was only a little unique in this part of the universe.

He was standing at one end of the bottom floor of the Cathedral. The end where the massive, circular, Oak and Fer wood, front door stood – the shades of the separate woods were slightly different, but they complimented each other very well, making a beautiful looking door. At the other end stood Arabel, a young woman of nineteen. She had long, dark-brown hair and all her other features matched. Her entire body looked human except for one metal hand. The hand that drew back the string of her enchanting, deep, dark-purple, black tinted and hinted metal bow. Many varying arrows sat inside a metal quiver which hung on her back. The names of the different metals – including the metal of Arabel's hand, the different parts of her large bow and the different parts of her unique arrows and quiver – were Hessh, Daob, Feeh, Lesk, Vah, Gainu, Dashen, Fearmal, Saillask. She wore a Pirate Hat; its colours matched her bow. The rest of her clothing was black except for a dark-grey shirt – beneath her long black coat which reached her black trouser covered ankles – and her also dark-grey boots.

"Ready, slick?" she asked with a smile, bow at the ready.

"I'm ready," Leenkal replied, his voice only the slightest bit metallic. Arabel's face grew serious as she hitched an arrow to the Lesk string and then waited. Leenkal stood silently, ready, staring down the archer with his silver and dark eyes. Suddenly, the arrow was flying towards him at a tremendous speed. Before it could pass the side of his head, just missing him, he caught it in his right hand, immediately dropped it and moved forward. Arrow after arrow came his way as he slowly moved forward. Left, right, left, right, left, right, left, right. He caught every one and dropped them successfully. Then Arabel aimed up and hitched two arrows at the same time. Leenkal followed. He leapt into the air and caught both as they reached either side of him simultaneously. Then he threw both arrows at a target above and behind the archer. They hit bullseye. As Leenkal was falling an approaching arrow burst into a net but before it could embrace him, his hands, in the blink of an eye, disappeared and the end of his arms all of a sudden looked like small cannons of some kind. An incredibly powerful wind shot out of these small cannons and blast the net down to the ground, sending Leenkal higher and a little backward. After an added backflip for a little flourish, he landed on his feet, happy with his performance.

"It seems you have perfected this little dance routine," said Arabel, her voice echoing around the vast cathedral.

"Indeed," replied Leenkal. "Again," he added.

Arabel grunted. "Why?"

"Because that is what I desire."

"I desire your death."

"Look woman—"

"No," she interrupted. There was silence for a moment.

"I'm actually extremely happy to do it again," said she. "I couldn't tell you why I said the words I did."

"Because you're demon faeces." The silver man decided. "Literally disgusting. The worst being. Breast milk." Arabel laughed a little at this.

"Right, hurry up then," she ordered.

Once they had collected all the arrows, Leenkal prepared for the net part of the routine by willing the metal of his body to part a little in many places and suck in air. It took less than a second for him to do this. Now he had enough air to blast away the net like he did before. And so, they began. Then they began again. Then again. But on this fourth time before the two arrows hit the target, located above and behind the archer, they disappeared – Leenkal saw an energy trace as they did. The Metal Man still managed to complete the rest of the routine successfully and as he landed upon his two feet, he called, "Laithy!" in a calm, peaceful manner. The orphan suddenly appeared, aged thirteen. The young boy looked at Leenkal – the being who saved him from truly being an orphan – with wide, colourful eyes that were slowly returning grey, the light of the energy that filled him slowly fading, revealing his also grey skin and funny clothes. He wore bright colours because he liked them. A red and blue leather jacket. He called it the Badass Jacket. He thought it made him look like a Rockstar. There was a plain blue T-shirt underneath said jacket, and then covering his legs were black trousers but of course travelling down, circling each trouser leg were two big white lightning bolts, their end points coming around to the front and touching his bright-yellow electrified shoes. That of course was their name. He didn't like the fact his skin was naturally grey, and his hair was black but his species, his race, named Seez. They were beings with dark features. It was not normal for one of these beings to have such energy inside of them. But fortunately for Laithy, his dark features glowed with colourful energy whenever he wished for them to, so of course this pleased him.

The boy stood in the middle of the walkway looking at Leenkal, one arrow in each hand. "I don't like this new nickname," he complained, talking about the name, Laithy. "It's girly."

"It's cute," corrected Leenkal. "Cute is cool." Laithy made a disgusted sound. His adopted father smiled.

"Hey, Laithy," Arabel called. She had a blunt arrow hitched onto the string of her bow, the string pulled back. The bow pointed almost straight down, the arrow's head very close to the ground. The boy had only just turned around when she let go of the string and the arrow hit the ground and bounced away. She looked at Laithy and shook her head.

"How was I supposed to catch that? I barely knew what you were doing, woman." Leenkal began to laugh. After a shocked moment, Arabel started chuckling too. "You're not old enough to be calling women woman yet," she said. "It's a bad habit of your father's."

"A fantastic habit," Leenkal corrected.

"There are some women who would disagree," she argued.

"Yes, but they're not the kind of women you want to impress," he countered, looking to his adopted son.

"That's true," the archer admitted.

"So, woman is fine?" Laithy asked.

"Woman is fine," agreed Leenkal. The archer made a line with her mouth and nodded reluctantly. Then the boy caught her eye and she raised her eyebrows. He dropped the arrows he was holding and then there was quiet…suddenly, she shot an arrow into the air. Laithy blinked towards it in a flash that fortunately wasn't too bright and in the blink of an eye, he was back on the ground, arrow in hand. His energy trace which followed his blinks started to fade. As did the glow which had brightened around him once more. A sound echoed around the Cathedral. They all looked to the magnificent circular door as it unlocked and swung open. Two tall Lyhnma's – Humanoid Lynx's of modern kind – entered.

"Greetings!" bellowed Almatrak. Altheara – his wife – smiled beside him.

"What have you been doing?" asked Leenkal eyeing Almatrak's armload of junk. The massive, bulky Lyhnma stopped and looked at all the scrap he was carrying. Then silently, he looked up at Leenkal. The Metal Man nodded. "Very dumb question, I apologise."

"What a fool you are, little man," Almatrak agreed. Then his fiery eyes found the mystery to all that was the boy, Laithy, and he raised his whisker eyebrows. Laithy grinned and once the Humanoid Lynx had put down all he was carrying, the boy ran at him as fast as he could without blinking, grabbed his enormous paw – everyone had cleared out of their way by this point – and then the Lynx spun and threw Laithy with great strength towards the immense stained-glass windows on the other side of the Cathedral. "Laithahshu!" Almatrak declared, as Laithy flew. Then before the boy hit the window, he blinked back down to the walkway and began to have a giggle fit. Almatrak began to laugh, deep and strong. The others became infected by Laithy's giggles also. Then Relkaufez – Rel for short – appeared at the bottom of the stone spiral staircase with, Ruler, the capuchin monkey perching on his bare, red scaled shoulder.

Rel was a twenty-year-old Senva, or Dragon Man. He was also once an orphan. Almatrak and Altheara were the ones who became his parents and his heroes. His top half was bare and covered in red scales, including his head, his arms and the back of his clawed hands but not his back for that was filled by his incredibly flexible, thin and strong folded in wings. His ears were pointy, and his eyes were even more fiery then Almatrak's. His legs and genitals were covered by underwear and trousers – a Senva's genitals are the only soft part of their entire body, apart from their eyeballs though few would describe their texture as

171

soft, in fact few would know what an eyeball felt like at all as fortunately the average being did not feel their eyes or others eyes very much. His legs were also covered in red scales, as were the top of his bare, clawed feet. And now, Ruler was an intriguing, mad little capuchin. That is all that needs to be said.

"Why must you gather and speak with such volume?" asked Rel, walking over.

"Wwwwaaaa!" chirped Ruler irritatingly loudly when she spotted Laithy. She pounced towards him and began to chase him around.

"Damn animal, beast bastard," cursed Rel, touching his ear.

"We really need to sort out the level of abuse, sarcasm and general rudeness in this…bizarre little family," Altheara commented, not serious.

"You're eternally damned," replied Rel.

"That one wasn't too far?" the Senva asked, used to being told off for innocently going a step too far with his jokes.

"That one was perfect," Leenkal reassured.

"Aaawweeeeeee," called Ruler from somewhere. The Senva turned and was instantly slapped by a tiny capuchin paw on the end of an unnaturally long stretching, black capuchin arm.

"I will revenge myself," he said, still unsure about where the creature was for her hand and arm had quickly disappeared. Rel looked at Leenkal to see if that half joke was all right. With his expression and gestures, the Metal Man told him it was fine. The Senva nodded, pleased. But when he turned around again, another paw hit his face.

"I'm going back upstairs," he decided. "Don't let the monkey follow me." They all nodded and then moments later, watched as Ruler crept behind him up the stairs. They smiled.

"Did you find anything interesting?" asked Leenkal looking between the Lyhnmas.

"Nothing special," replied Altheara. "But we're going to go back tonight because there'll be a fresh load."

"Are we invited?"

"Of course."

"Jolly good."

"Rel's obviously working on something so I'm sure he'll be happy staying here with Laithy." Leenkal turned around to find the boy trying to fire Arabel's bow which was far too big for him but not too heavy for it was an incredibly light and mobile bow. "Is that all right, Laithy?" he asked.

"What?" the boy replied, too busy concentrating on trying to shoot an arrow at the target.

"Are you all right staying here with Rel when we go to the junkyard tonight?"

"Do I have a choice in the matter?"

"No."

"Well, there's your answer." Leenkal chuckled at this.

"Be careful," added the Silver Man before he turned back around.

"Feel free to have a look" – Altheara gestured at the two piles of scrap on the floor – "while we go put our gear upstairs." Leenkal saluted and Arabel smiled. Almatrak and Altheara returned the gestures. Both the Metal Man and the Archer then crouched down beside a pile as the two Lyhnma's walked towards the bottom of the spiral staircase, Almatrak taking what Laithy called, Cannon Electro off his back.

"You want to come and have a look?" called Leenkal. Laithy turned and in a few seconds, he was crouching beside his adopted father. They all rummaged quietly for a minute or so.

Then suddenly, the curious young boy, with an always ticking brain, looked up at Arabel and asked, "Can you tell us why you ran away from your old family now?" Leenkal looked up at her and raised his invisible eyebrows.

"I can't be bothered," she said.

"Why?" asked Laithy.

"Because it's a long story that takes a lot of effort to tell."

"I'm sorry."

The boy grunted. "Fine."

"One day when I'm feeling energetic maybe," she said smiling.

"You're never energetic," replied the boy. "When you see energetic people, you always say how you don't understand how it's possible to act in such a way."

"It is bizarre," she said looking between Leenkal and Laithy.

"But I'm energetic," the Blinker pointed out.

"Yes, but you're a child. Leenkal agrees with me."

The Metal Man nodded. "Energetic persons are an intriguing oddity." Both he and Arabel smiled. The boy looked between them like they themselves were oddities.

"You make no sense," he decided, talking to his father. "You don't even really get physically tired. You should be more energetic than anyone."

"Well, sometimes life can be confusing."

"What?"

"Sometimes life throws a zebra and you don't quite know why."

"Sometimes," Arabel joined in, "life burns away at the wax of existence, but the nuclear amphibious donkeys don't understand the reasoning behind such malevolence."

"Very nice," Leenkal complimented. Laithy sat looking at them, silent and confused.

"Oh, look at this pretty little thing," declared the Metal Man. He held up a small, slightly rusty metal cube. After blowing and wiping the dust off it, he turned it around in his hands, admiring the markings that covered it. He then discovered that it could be twisted and turned. He expressed his delight by saying, "Ooohh! A puzzle box! How delightful!" Arabel and Laithy chuckled in response and they began to watch and suggest directions as he tried to figure it out. "Definitely left," said Arabel. Leenkal twisted right. "Up this time." Leenkal twisted left. "Now down."

"No, up," Laithy interjected. Leenkal twisted left again.

"You know," began the Silver Man. "A wise man once taught me a trick for unlocking these things."

"He's going to break it open," said Arabel looking at Laithy. He nodded in reply.

"I'm not going to break it open."

"Yes you are." Out of the end of Leenkal's index finger on his right hand grew a very thin, very strong blade like thing that was quite effective when used for picking locks. He then tried to find a seam, a small gap, somewhere to lever. The thing was sealed tight. He sat and thought for a moment. He felt its weight. Surprisingly heavy. He twisted and turned a few more times. Then he decided, "We're going to have to break it."

"Just a corner. Then we can take off a side carefully."

"If you hold it, I'll shoot off a corner," said Arabel.

"You sure you can do that," Leenkal mocked. "I don't think you're good enough honestly. You're like a deceased old grandmother." They looked at each other with straight, unwavering expressions. Then he walked up the walkway, towards the stain-glassed windows. Then up some wide stone steps, past a small eagle statue which once was the perch for a holy book – it was cracked and deformed for a long time but the new, bizarre family that made its home their home restored the statue along with many, many other things – Leenkal stopped at the target and held the box in front of it. Arabel grabbed her bow and hitched one of her arrows onto the string. Then suddenly, the string was pulled back and she was aiming at Leenkal's head. Leenkal jumped and the Archer began to laugh. Once they were both still, she aimed once more, this time at the box. She fired, and the arrow flew, knocking off a corner and sticking into the stone target. Excitedly, Laithy ran up as Leenkal carefully peeled off a side with strong hands. The inside was cushioned, and a single thing sat there. Leenkal took out a strange, small thing. It held deep, enchanting colours. Deep blue, violet, yellow, green, black, purple and deep red like the colour of the moon. It was a beautiful thing.

"Intriguing," said Leenkal with a smile.

"Intriguing indeed," Arabel agreed. The Metal Man crouched down and handed it to his son, who then twirled it around in his hands, entranced by its strange beauty.

"Does it do anything?"

"What an interesting question. I wonder if I know the answer considering I also have only just discovered it," Leenkal replied.

"Don't be an ass. It was mostly rhetorical."

"Good word."

"Thank you."

"We should have a good look at it and get Rel to do some tests on it or something before we decide to keep it. It could be dangerous. Though I don't think it is."

"How mature of you," Arabel commented.

"Yes well, I'm getting old now. And extremely wise. And rather sexy, don't you think?"

"You look like the ass of a baboon," spoke the voice of Almatrak.

"I think that is debatable," replied Leenkal.

"Have a look at this." Laithy placed the object – *which felt and looked a little like a smooth pebble and other things,* thought the boy – in the large brown paw. Almatrak looked at it for a moment.

"Was this hidden in the junk?" he asked.

"In here," Leenkal replied, throwing him the metal box. "Got any ideas about what it might be or do? If anything?"

"It might quite possibly be a ships core. A power, energy core. I'm assuming a ship's. Maybe." A grin grew upon the Lyhnma's face.

"One that looks far greater than our crappy piece of…crap…"

"To the Dome!" he announced.

On the way up, they passed a number of floors and rooms, some big, some small. They picked up Rel from his lab, Ruler too. Altheara joined them also. And soon, they were entering the Dome. The peak of the Cathedral.

"Open ship!" Rel exclaimed, slapping a palm onto its dark-grey body. A dim light shone around the entirety of the shapeless, some might say deformed and ugly ship. Though the family chose the word characterful to describe its beauty. After a moment too long, the glow vanished and the door began to lower.

"If this works, you'll be doing that much faster," said Rel holding the energy core up to the underside of Ship so Ship could see what he was talking about – naturally, the Ship was called Ship – then he walked up the lowered door and into the body onto dark-red, old carpet.

"Combustion," said Rel, greeting the manikin butler dressed in a black suit and bow tie.

The others greeted him also one by one saying, "Combustion," and nodding as they walked past, then following the walkway around until they stood in the centre of the ship. With the help of a couple of tools, the Senva took a dark panel off the centre pillar and then reached in and took out a small, grey cube.

"Hello, turd," said he. Then he placed the new pebble like object inside and went to turn the ships power on. He returned and watched in silence as nothing happened.

"It doesn't seem to work."

"Very observant," commented Arabel.

"Yes," Leenkal agreed. The Dragon Man looked for Laithy and met his eyes. "Energy, child. Zap it," he said. "It may need awakening."

"As they say in Shoola," added Leenkal. No one reacted to this, as they knew the Silver Man was just spouting rubbish.

"What do I do?" asked Laithy as Rel showed him where to stand.

"Just point, make a small ball and shoot," he instructed. "Hopefully, something will happen."

"It is likely that nothing will happen," he added. Laithy then began. He held out his left hand, making a tight fist. Energy swiftly began to surround it and sparks began to dart into the energy core-holding cell. Before the ball could grow too big, he did what he once couldn't and shot the energy forth. When it left his fist, it took the shape of a perfect ball and at a slow pace – he was still working on controlling the speed – it glided into the holding cell and it halted inside, lines of electricity travelling up and down the pillar, seemingly holding it in place – Ruler was chirping with wide, mad, dark eyes – then slowly, the ball began to disappear into the Energy Pebble as Leenkal now called it, and sparks started darting towards the Core from above and below but then disappearing.

"Again," said Rel. Laithy did it again. Then again and again and again and again. The Pebble brightened and brightened gradually and then suddenly, it became so bright they all instinctively looked away. And when they looked back, there was the now bright Energy Core floating in the middle of the Holding Cell, connected to wires of pure electricity packed full of energy and power.

"You are extremely sexy," said Rel, as he stared at it.

"Can we install an AI now?" asked Leenkal like an excited little boy. "We will call it…Swan…nipple. Swannipple," he decided. Then he began to chuckle at himself. "That's brilliant. That was my first go to," he said, looking at them all with a grin.

"It might take some time," said the Senva, "but I'm assuming this thing has more than enough power to support an AI system."

"Very good. Swannipple will be the greatest companion in the entire galaxy. Her name will go down in history." Leenkal turned around and walked off. The others began to chuckle. Then they chuckled some more as they heard him shouting, "What the hell are you doing, Combustion the Manikin Butler. Put your trousers back on! Never do that again! Disgusting!"

Chapter 9
A Couple of Conversations

Luckily, for Rel, he had retractable claws and hands shaped like a human's. This meant he could modify, invent, create, build and test and so on. He loved to do these things and he loved the fact that he had his own lab filled with many brilliant things and some not so brilliant things. He was a being who was harsh on himself when judging his own work. He thought most of what he did was not very brilliant though it was. But his strange family helped him to believe in himself and they helped him to see how brilliant his mind and his work really was. He had learnt much and come far in many ways over the past years. He was happy now. Genuinely happy. And he had his family to thank. He was sitting in the pilot's seat, in the cockpit of Ship, thinking about these things rather soppily when Ruler came and sat in the seat beside him. She seemed to be in her pleasant quiet mood.

After a handful of minutes, the Senva spoke.

"We finally might be able to travel at light speed now monkey." The capuchin looked at him and smiled unnecessarily wide. "You look crazy," said he. Ruler replied by making rude sounding chirps for around four seconds.

"Such an angry little thing."

"Aaaeeoo."

"What does that mean?"

"Aaaeeoo."

"Ah, right."

"Maybe we'll find a weird far away planet that is filled with giant floating dwarfs," he mused. "Or maybe they'll be giant capuchin eating capuchins." The monkey looked at him expressionless.

"I'm still unsure whether you understand what I'm saying or not."

Ruler screeched, slapped him and then ran off mumbling to herself. Rel stayed seated and he began to daydream about the places that they might find. Then after a few minutes, Almatrak entered and sat down beside him. This would have been impossible for the large Lyhnma to do if it were not for the big adjustments they had once made.

"I'm assuming you're all right to stay here with Laithy this evening when we go to the junkyard?"

"Yeah, that's good," replied Rel. "I've got plenty of things I want to do."

"Very good." It was quiet for a few seconds. "So, you want to fly us somewhere tomorrow?" asked Almatrak. A big smile grew upon Rel's face.

"Yes, very much so."

"Do you think the stone is powerful enough for us to travel at light speed?"

"I do," he said, still grinning.

"Well then, you're going to have to take us somewhere far away and weird."

"That's the hope."

"I look forward to it."

"As do I."

The two sat there for a short while longer, musing about where they might end up and what may be waiting for them there…

Chapter 10
The Tall City

Altheara left the Cathedral with some of her family around her. She was a slender cat, flexible and light footed unlike her lover Almatrak. She was equipped with two elegant silver swords, their cross handles an enchanting red colour. They sat sheathed, crossing one another upon her back. She also carried a small pistol sheathed on her side that was the same enchanting red colour. It was a pistol that shot non-lethal, shocking projectiles. Like Almatrak's Electro Cannon, except his weapon shot electricity coated blasts of energy which would knock an opponent off their feet and send them shaking to the ground. Of course, it would not continuously shock them. The shocking would quickly stop for all the members of the family believed that to kill someone was wrong. Killing was an absolute last resort, if they truly had no other choice. So, the shocking would quickly stop, and the being would be rendered unconscious. Almatrak also had two fiery orange pistols – the same kind as Altheara's – sheathed on his sides. Leenkal had his body. Arabel had her bow and arrows.

The walk to the junkyard wasn't a long one. They followed cobbled streets mostly, high walls all around. The city was tall, so tall its nickname was the Tall City. Walls truly were high and there were buildings which reached the clouds, one which stretched into them. On a cloudy day, its top could not be seen. Many strange and wonderful beings had built up this place over many, many years, their talents enabling them to build to such heights with relative ease. There were still so many creative minds living in the city in these days. This was one of the reasons why the junkyard existed and why it was so large and famous. And also why there were often so many scavengers there all day every day. A good number scavenged in the nights too. All of this also meant the place could be dangerous. Sadly, not everybody was pleasant in Obneeth. This is why Leenkal preferred Laithy to stay at home. Especially if it was an evening or night trip to the junkyard.

When they reached the place, they sighed for it was buzzing with activity. A wide variety of folk covered the piles of junk and scrap. The group halted and began to look and decide which area looked best.

"They look like dicks," Leenkal decided, pointing to the right. They all nodded in agreement.

"So do they," Arabel added.

"And them," pointed Leenkal.

"That pile's too busy," Altheara gestured.

"They all also look like dicks," Almatrak commented. They all chuckled.

"What about that crappy, small one?" Leenkal asked.

"I know it's crappy and small but I'm not in the mood for people. And there are very few people…on top of it."

"Did you have a small seizure there?" Arabel chuckled.

"I always forget those bastard words, on top of it," he joked.

"Walk, Butt Dweller," ordered Altheara. He began to walk.

"Greetings!" said Leenkal to the few scavengers of the small, crappy pile. "It is a great honour to be here with you!"

"He's deranged," Altheara explained. Leenkal laughed.

"Deranged enough to fight a sprinting squirrel," he said loudly. Leenkal continued to laugh and found he couldn't stop. Seconds later, Altheara, Arabel and Almatrak were laughing too, trying their best to stop as they attempted to find intriguing looking things amongst the unintriguing things…

Chapter 11
Hide

Alabeya lived on the planet Roebetha. She was a dark skinned, female being aged twenty-two. She had relatively short, vibrant green hair and pale, truly yellow eyes. At the minute, her hair was covered up by a seemingly thin, perfect fitting black helmet which also grew down her neck, then body and then everything else. There were eyeholes in the helmet but nothing else. She was running across roofs, a pack of ninjas behind, chasing after her. In that pack of ninjas was her identical twin sister, Zylune. Alabeya shot her grappling gun at a stonewall ahead. The claw dug into the stone and gripped as if it had a mind of its own. She continued to run until she reached the roofs edge and leapt. The woman – not human woman – hit the wall with her side but it didn't hurt her. At an incredible speed, as if she weighed nothing, the grapple pulled her up as she held the gun's trigger down. Then she double tapped the trigger and instantly the claw let go of the wall and came whizzing up towards her. Alabeya was flying at this point. The grapples pull power had sent her up into the air. She hadn't started dropping yet when the claw was flying towards another wall. It gripped, and she was able to swing towards the building, controlling the grapple so she lowered all the way to the ground as she swung. Then the claw returned, and she sheathed the gun, sprinting onwards. She went smashing through a large, circular wooden door, feeling very little, and found herself inside a cathedral. She never stopped running. This meant all the traps that were set up to catch intruders never succeeded to do their job. She headed for a stairwell and began to climb up and up and up. The next thing she knew was darkness.

Rel speedily took the unconscious body into his lab where Laithy and Ruler were sitting. "There are a bunch of people down there. I think they're chasing this person," he said, able to hear the ninjas even from such a distance away – Senva's have incredible hearing if they wish to have incredible hearing. Drenak does, but to Athaiel's disappointment, he does not. "Blink downstairs and then straight back up. Straight back up. See what they look like."

Laithy did as he was asked. He ran into some that were about to start climbing the staircase. He blinked back. "Their ninjas dressed in black. A silver Senva stands on their pocket bits."

"A silver Senva?"

"Yes."

"Holy shit. Ruler, I'm going to need your help. Laithy hide the body as well as possible. Stay in this room." Rel and Ruler went running out of the room, shutting the door behind them. A ninja was about to come running out of the stairwell, onto the floor their prey was on when a small, stretching black fist came flying towards his head, striking it and sending him tumbling backwards. The ninja behind him managed to dodge the falling body and he stepped onto the floor. Only two had made their way to this floor. The others were searching other areas. A black fist darted at the head of this one too but the ninja caught Ruler's arm and managed to fling the monkey against a wall. Rel blew fire at the one in black who dived out of the way. This had caught him off guard. Relkaufez continued to breathe fire, trapping the ninja in a corner. Then he lunged and went to strike the man in the head. But the one dressed in black ducked and hit Rel in the stomach, smoothly moving out of the corner and twisting around. The ninja let out a small, pained grunt after his fist made contact with the Senva's scales.

"Clearly, you don't know your little silver god's anatomy very well," Rel said, talking about the little silver Senva standing with wings wide on the breast pocket of the ninjas robe. A fast kick came towards Rel's head but he managed to block it with his arm. He blew out flames once more. The one in black span past, feeling heat on his body, and kicked the back of the Senva's head who lurched forward. Ruler sent his arms stretching towards the man's head. His little hands gripped. He lifted off the floor and like an elastic band, he went slinging towards the head, striking it with his knees. The strength of this would have knocked a normal human man immediately out, but the ninja managed to stay conscious. Though he did tumble, almost falling to the ground, Ruler's hands now over his eyes. Rel swiftly reacted and knocked the ninja unconscious with a powerful punch to the head, Ruler letting go at the last second to avoid getting his hands squashed. Rel then turned towards the stairwell and sent fire roaring down the stairs as more ninjas showed their heads. This was when Leenkal and the others arrived home from their outing to the junkyard.

Chapter 12
The Woman

Sail, was the name of the woman with the dark-silver hair and the green cloak. The one who had vanished from Halt's sight. She lay bleeding upon the ground, too hurt to go on. Her eyes were shut. She could hear nothing but the wind. "Maybe this is a blessing," she whispered to herself. Vast green and grey land surrounded her. In one direction, mountains sat far away, watching her with hearts of stone. In all other directions, tall trees stood far away watching her with agitated feet and shaking arms. They could do nothing to help her. She waited silently…peace was coming…no more fear…no more running…nothing…but what about my purpose…I have not left a mark on this world yet…not one that I am happy with…not a significant enough mark…I need…I need…purpose…I need to do something…otherwise everything was for nothing…she tried to move, tried to get to her feet. She struggled and moaned in pain. She succeeded. She was standing. She took a couple of very painful steps and came to a stop. Tears filled her eyes. Sail hunched over and began to cry. The woman sobbed and sobbed…a noise sounded. It was similar to the sound of the wind but different enough to make her look towards it. An immense, white dragon was coming towards her. Terror filled her and she began to run. But the grey-eyed woman didn't make it far at all. She tumbled and hit the ground. Sail just managed to lift her head enough to look at the dragon. Just before it landed, a wave of pure black struck it and wrapped it in a cocoon. The dragon hit the ground and went rolling. Thela galloped bravely towards the fallen lady. Halt's eyes were dark and strong. Suddenly, the dragon broke free and Halt found himself surrounded by the thickest of mists. He couldn't see a thing. He had no choice but to come to a stop. A second later, something hit him hard, sending him flying off his horse. He was truly disorientated now. Completely blind and lost in the mist. Sail could barely breathe. The dragon moved closer to her. She was too weak to do anything. They locked eyes. The beast breathed something that looked like white mist upon her.

"You will live. You will heal." Sail heard these words in her mind. The male dragon had spoken these words in her mind. But then, suddenly came another male voice. Again, it spoke in her head.

It shouted, "Stop! Stop!" Sail looked at the creature and it seemed he had heard it too. The mist that was blinding Halt vanished in an instant, revealing to him the dragon, the woman and the old wizard who he had met before dressed in blue. He rode a noble grey and black spotted steed. "Stop!" the Wizard said again, the word sounding in everyone's head, his mouth not moving, his old wand held tight in his left hand. Halt and Sail met eyes. Sail leapt to her feet with surprising ease. A white spear materialised in her hand. "Stop!" said the wizard once more. "This man is not who you think he is. I have seen you both in a dream. You are running from the same thing. You can help each other. Hear my words. Hear my voice. I am telling you the truth. He came to help you, Sail. He doesn't know who you are."

"What do you mean he came to help me?" she shouted out loud, over the wind which had seemed to have become a little wild and angry.

"He's travelling, running. The same as you. He found your horse. The being who rules that forest told him what had happened to you and which way you went." Therai still spoke into everyone's minds.

"The dark, heavy, terrible presence?" she questioned, a little amused at what she thought was a terrible lie.

"It is good," spoke the dragon, also into everyone's minds, his eyes locked on the wizard.

"What?" asked Sail.

"That being in the forest is good. Not bad. The wizard speaks the truth. I had assumed like you did." His eyes turned on Halt. For a moment, it was silent. "You are like the being. A child of darkness trying to escape," said the creature. Halt stayed silent. "He wishes to help you," the dragon confirmed, turning to look at Sail. Halt and the woman looked into each other's eyes. Sail kept the spear in her hand.

"I saw a raven land on his shoulder! He's one of them!" she argued.

"One of who?" asked Halt.

"One of RavenKing's men!"

"The RavenKing is also who he is running from," the wizard informed.

185

"The RavenKing is the biggest darkness. His biggest darkness. He feels hatred towards him," the beast agreed.

"How do I know you are not all working together?" asked the woman.

"Don't be a fool, woman," replied the creature.

"Have you ever heard those men asking about a man? They ask about a woman and a man!" Halt tried. The woman silently kept her eyes on him. "I am that man! I'm the man they want!"

Chapter 13
Another, Some Might
Say Strange Family

Thui was a humanoid red squirrel who lived upon the planet Leiyal. It was sunny and warm where he lived, which was in a massive wood, named HoiHoi by the beings who lived in it. At the minute, the residents were silent. Silent because unknown beings were spread out across the place, clearly looking for something…all of the creatures of the wood were hiding, watching and wondering. The unknown beings were dark. Raven sat on their chest plates.

"You must be a little warm," Thui whispered to himself, watching one of them. He was hidden away in a hole. Nature around him.

Suddenly, a blur of yellow whizzed past the dark fellow. He span around, shocked and confused. Thui smiled. A blur of white was next. Then a blur of pink. Then a blur of red. Then purple. Thui decided to join in the fun. He bolted and whizzed past the Raven being. The creatures were nowhere to be seen. The man had his sword drawn and was turning silently.

"I wonder how long he'll spin around for," said Thui to a pink humanoid squirrel named Laedy. They were hiding beside each other, peaking through the holes in all the green ahead of them. "He must be warm in that. Really sweaty," she commented.

"That's what I said."

"I wonder what his face looks like."

"I think disgusting. Though you should never judge a ballerina by their attire. Judge them by their spin," he replied, looking at Laedy with big, amused eyes. She grinned and looked at the still turning man.

"A gifted ballerina, I think. The moody look is just for show. No normal dude could spin with such grace."

"My thoughts exactly."

"What are you doing?" called an unknown voice. Thui and Laedy went silent. The man stopped twirling. Another dark fellow was now in their eyesight. He was dressed in the same suit of armour as the other.

"I'm being mocked," he answered. "If you come near me again, I swear I will kill every single one of you!" he shouted, spinning once more.

"He's a little moody," whispered Laedy.

"On his period," Thui replied.

"Do they have periods?"

"Who knows? Don't think so. I think that's just a female type species thing."

"Interesting."

"Interesting."

A white blur rushed past the Raven man. "Curse you!" he cried. The light around him was darkening, Thui was sure of it.

"Calm down," said the other knight. "They probably don't understand a word you're saying. We're a long way from home. Let's get back to the birds and start flying back. It's insanity that the king asked us to travel this far. There's no way either of them would have come here."

"Are you calling the king insane?"

"No." They stood silently looking at each other for a moment and then they set off, staying silent.

"Strange pair," Laedy said, amused. Thui struggled not to laugh. "A really solid friendship I think," he joked.

"Definitely."

Moments later, white fur suddenly filled their vision and they jumped. Laedy squeaked loud enough for the Raven Knights to hear. They turned towards the sound and listened for a few moments. Then moved on as no more sounds followed. Laedy got to her feet – making her around the height of a three, four or five-year-old human boy, depending on the height of that boy – and slapped Hurlay in the face. Hurlay stood completely still for a second and then slapped her back. "Hey," the pink one whispered, annoyed. "I'm not the one who made me jump."

"Well observed," answered the snowy white one – a female humanoid squirrel.

"We decided he would make a very good ballerina," Thui interjected.

"Yes, I do agree very much," said Hurlay.

"What do you think they're looking for?" the red male asked – also standing at around the height of a three, four or five-year-old human boy. This was the common height for these humanoid squirrels. "A bit of joy I think," decided Hurlay. Laedy looked at her, still frowning. Hurlay frowned back. They held their stares. Thui watched with a grin on his face.

"There are more of them around so be careful my minions," Hurlay informed, still holding the stare.

"We are aware," answered Laedy.

"We are aware," mimicked Hurlay.

"We are aware," said Thui.

A bright-yellow squirrel named Frejju suddenly appeared. Everyone turned their eyes on him. Silently, he began to act as if he was melting. He lay still on the floor, face against the ground. A small, green monkey named Bybot came leaping and swinging. He stopped above them and looked down. "What happened to Frejju?" he asked quietly.

"Life, monkey boy," replied Hurlay. She whizzed up the tree and roared quietly in the monkey's face. He didn't budge. "What is wrong with you!" she complained.

"Fear isn't real," he said looking knowingly into the white squirrel's green eyes. "It's all in your head." He tapped his head with a green finger.

"Urgh," she mumbled in a disgusted manner.

Thui, Hurlay and Frejju were related, Brothers and sister. Laedy was a friend. The monkey was also a friend along with the other squirrels who had joined in with making the dark fellow twirl. Thui's mother – Ariah – was a multi-coloured squirrel, the only one – apart from her youngest child – in the entire wood. Her coat of fur held many colours. She and her children were a part of a unique, rare, intriguing family tree.

A portal suddenly materialised in the middle of the group. Everyone jumped back. A couple of seconds later, an old grey-haired wizard stepped through. He ran his wand down the middle of the portal and it disappeared. "Easier to close than to open," he said with a grin. "Now, where is it the travellers stay?"

Chapter 14
The Inconvenient Prophecy

Thui's mother looked out from the doorway of a massive wood cabin which sat on the ground beneath the leaves and branches of thick, very tall, green trees – an invisible barrier protected the cabin from objects that might fall from above. She frowned, trying to make out what she was seeing. Were her children and their friends carrying the body of a man? A wizard maybe?

Indeed they were. Thui and his siblings had been taught to be extra wary of strangers, especially ones like this old wizard in his 'sexy red cloak', as Thui had described it. The reason being, Ariah – Thui's mother – had been hunted a few times in her life. There are ancient prophecies told in a handful of old stories speaking of the multi-coloured Squihu – Squihu being the name of this humanoid squirrel species – And Thui's mother being a multi-coloured Squihu has meant she has unfortunately met beings who have wanted to find out if she is the one that the prophecies speak of. Unfortunately, for her, according to the prophecies the only way to find out is to kill her and absorb her spirit. And according to the stories, her spirit will give you new strength, new knowledge, plus a little something called immortality. Needless to say, it wasn't pleasant, sane beings filled with light who usually wanted to find her.

Chapter 15
The Sleeping Forest

Once a battlefield, then an unnamed forest, then named, the Sleeping Forest. The place lay barren and broken once more. Again, a massive crater filled the space. A hole stretched into darkness searching for true evil. It found it. Beings will give their life for Selhal, the Ruler of the Dead to be whole once more.

Volume 2
Mysteries Beginning to
Intertwine Pictures

Prologue
Unshakable

A Sorceress named Danefal Ehllyf had a dream. First, she saw a tree, then another tree. She knew she had to cast spells upon these trees, but she knew not the reason. Words and markings then began to fill her mind. She knew she had to write these words and draw these markings on paper, and she knew she had to hide this piece of paper near the entrance of a cave, but she knew not the reason why. When she woke, she wrote and drew on an old and beautiful looking piece of tanned paper. She felt the kind of paper was an important detail. Danefal then, with a quick spell dried the ink, rolled the paper up and put it in a segment of a small bag. After this, she did everything else she felt she needed to do. Somehow, the sorceress knew the location of the trees and cave without thinking. She had to travel far upon her bird...

Chapter 1
A Confused Fellow

Thui was carrying an old wizard above him – he had help from his friends and family also of course. They walked in two colourful lines beneath the unconscious, bearded stranger, towards a massive wood cabin which was surrounded by the greenest, lushest of nature. An invisible barrier protected the cabin from objects that might fall from above. "What do I see?" asked Ariah – Thui's mother – when they were close.

"We thought we could eat him later!" exclaimed Frejju – the yellow one – excitedly.

"No, we did not," Hurlay said, shaking her head, then looking at Frejju in disbelief. "Chumbutt, you've got to learn to listen better. And since when have we ever eaten wizards?" Hurlay had snowy white hair. Frejju looked at his sister confused.

"I'm always hearing people say, it's good to try new things. So…if that is the case, then there's nothing you shouldn't be allowed to do."

"That's not right, yellow son," Ariah informed. They all laid the wizard down onto the wooden deck. Frejju looked at Thui. "No wizard tonight then, my brethren."

"Well, it's a good job. I wasn't expecting to eat wizard tonight," the red one replied. Frejju looked at him, a confused expression on his face again.

"What do I see?" the mother asked again. "You see a man who appeared out of a portal and who we are apparently not eating?" asked the yellow one.

"Basically, Mother," began Hurlay, "he appeared out of a portal, SUDDENLY and asked, where do travellers stay? Then we rendered him unconscious. For obvious reasons."

"Did you see those Raven men?" asked Thui, looking at his mother.

"No?" answered Ariah.

"Okay, well there were these darkly dressed knights searching around the place. I think they're heading home now though. So, no worries." The multi-coloured one was silent for a moment.

"Um…" she thought. "Well…I don't really know what to say."

"That's all right," said Frejju with a grin. Silence followed. Everyone began to laugh. The yellow one suddenly stuck out his index finger. A yellow spark flickered. He touched his sister, Hurlay, as his entire body fizzled and popped with yellow and white sparks. A loud pop sounded, and she went flying off the deck, disappearing in the green. A second later, she had rocketed back towards Frejju and sent him flying. Frejju then came whizzing back but Hurlay willed the wind to pick him up and sent him flying above her and over the other side. "That's enough!" Ariah decided, smiling with everyone else. Frejju appeared once more on the deck, a grin on his face. Hurlay gave him a sideways glance and raised one 'eyebrow'.

"So we think this man would like to absorb your spirit mother. Gain immortality and all that good stuff. Though he would miss out on heaven, which would be a bummer," said the yellow one.

"I don't think heaven is where he would go," said Laedy – a pink Squihu friend. Frejju looked at her, confused again. "You know…if he wants to kill your mum and absorb her soul?" she tried.

Frejju nodded in reply. Everyone waited for him to say something. He didn't. Ariah let out an amused sigh. "Ass crap prophecy," said she.

Thui chuckled and asked, "So what do we do?"

"First we take his wand. Then we sit him down in a nice room, in a nice chair and your father can wait for him to wake up. Then they may chat. He may just be a pleasant, magicianous traveller."

"Very good," said Thui. And so, this is what they did.

Follar – Thui, Hurlay and Frejju's father – took a seat in the sitting room. He and the unconscious wizard were the only people in the room. The only people allowed in the room.

Chapter 2
A Calling

Keeana was walking in the Forest in which it is fun to race. This was only the second time she had ever done this in her entire life. She and her friends only ever raced in this forest. But today, this is what she had ended up doing. Keeana had wanted to get away from her family and clear her head. Be alone, breathe and feel at peace. So, she walked in the snow, weaving slowly past trees and gazing at her surroundings…

A noise unlike any the Rogue had heard all morning sounded close by. She turned in the direction and after a moment of looking, she spotted an icy-blue woodpecker, pecking at the wood of a tree. Woodpeckers were uncommon, icy-blue woodpeckers were rare. Keeana began to quietly move closer, admiring it. As she did, a piece of bark – around where the creature had been hitting – fell to the ground. After pecking a few more times, the woodpecker hopped around the tree a little to the right. The Rogue moved so she could keep her eyes on it, still stepping nearer and nearer. She got excitingly close, able to look over the bird and see many of its smaller details before it flew away. She smiled to herself and took a step back. Moments later, her eyes and feet wandered to the place where the bark had fallen off. Her eyes stuck there, and she moved closer. Something strange looking was engraved in the trunk. A strange pattern of some kind. Keeana ran her finger over it. After a few seconds of feeling the pattern – the feeling strange, the lines unable to be felt, something not physical maybe lying on top of the pattern – she noticed it quickly starting to glow. A gentle golden light washed over her and all of a sudden, she had vanished.

Keeana reappeared in a tall, green wood. The green and brown, healthy ground beneath her feet was trembling. Scarily loud cracks and thumps were approaching to her left. She looked and saw a purple-skinned being sprinting towards her, and behind that purple-skinned being was a giant beast with dark-green skin, something like six big grey tusks, and one big eye in the middle of its face.

"Run!" shouted the young Deiyahlu woman named, Teela. Keeana was knocked out of her state of shock when the purple being grabbed her. They both now were running from the reckless, mostly blind, big-footed Rassklar.

The Rogue knew not what to do except to try and follow the tall, fast woman. Fortunately, the purple one seemed to be keeping an eye on Keeana. Making sure she didn't lose her. They dodged and jumped, weaved and ducked. It wasn't long before Teela went darting into the entrance of a cave and Keeana followed. She sprinted in, tripped and went tumbling towards the wall of the cave, her shoulder striking rock, a piece of rock flying off the wall. She then tumbled to the ground, managing to keep any painful moans silent. Teela held out a hand, while one finger from the other hand was over her dark lips, saying, *be silent.* The Rogue got to her feet, not taking the hand. They both then stood there, silently listening. The beast came close and stopped. It thumped around the area for a short amount of time and then it began to thump away. They were silent inside the cave for a little while longer and then Teela looked into Keeana's eyes. "I have seen you before, but I don't know…how or where."

"Where am I?" she replied, hand floating close to the hilt of a sheathed dagger.

"Reignthorl…"

Keeana was silent.

"Are you okay?" asked Teela with a kind smile, looking to the Rogue's shoulder and then to the cave wall. Her eyes went back to Keeana for a moment, then back to the wall. She concentrated on it. Keeana looked. There was something inside a small hole in the wall. *Was that where I struck my shoulder?*

Teela stepped closer to the hole and reached with a finger. She carefully and cautiously took out the object. It was a rolled-up piece of tanned paper. She bent and looked into the hole, then felt around to see if there was anything else. There wasn't. She unrolled the paper, keeping one eye on Keeana. "May I come closer?" asked the Rogue. "To see what it is?"

"If you promise not to murder me, I promise you have no reason to fear me. Reignthorl is my home. Where I spend most of my days."

"I promise," said Keeana with a small smile. "I'm sorry," she continued, not having moved yet. "I really don't know where I am. There was a tree…and a marking. Maybe a spell. I think it brought me here." The purple being concentrated on her face.

"But I have seen you before," she said, "in a dream…maybe. In a dream like…no other dream I have ever had."

Keeana didn't know what to say. Teela could feel her spirit. Keeana could feel something too.

"Come, take a look. If destiny has anything to do with it, um…maybe this will help," said the Deiyahlu woman with an amused, questioning, wondering expression. The pale woman smiled a little and cautiously walked to Teela's side. They both silently looked over the piece of paper for a few seconds. Then the Deiyahlu woman began to read.

I have had a dream. Hope lies in ruins and that hope must be found. The home of the fighters of old is where you must go. The edge of nature is where it sits. The power will be needed. More must be found on the journey. Brains must work. Bodies must work. You must walk on your own two feet and not sit upon the back of a creature. You must only take travelling essentials.

You, Keeana and Teela. You must be equipped. You must be prepared. Show this to no friend or member of family. Talk about this to no friend or member of family. Together it must be done. Prepare now and leave as soon as possible. Be wise, Teela. Be brave, Keeana.

Teela looked at the lines drawn on the left and right sides of the paper. She then turned the paper over. The back was blank. "Fold it," said Keeana. The purple being thought for a moment. Then she understood. She folded the sides of the paper, so they met in the middle of the back. She then rotated the paper around, staring and thinking. Together the markings were drawings of mountains.

"I guess destiny does have something to do with it," said Teela in an absent, quiet manner as she still looked over the paper. She then suddenly realised they were making it harder for themselves by unnecessarily standing in darker lighting. They both moved more into the light and looked over *the letter* – as they would later refer to it – again.

Chapter 3
Thinking Interrupted

The search for Keeana started back in Telan in the late evening.

Keeana's journey began. She felt the unusual feeling of certainty. She had never felt anything quite like it. Teela talked of the Ghost and destiny and a lot of similar stuff. Usually this stuff wasn't the Rogue's 'kind of stuff'. But she…she…she felt a destiny now. She felt it. She felt a purpose, a calling. She knew she needed to do this. She couldn't quite explain it. She didn't quite understand it.

For Teela, this was all quite simple. She too was certain. She also felt what Keeana was feeling, with even more confidence and no doubt at all. And trying to tell all of this to her mother without actually telling her mother what she was doing was another very simple thing. Her mother knew her daughter was a wiser being than her. The old dream with the stone had shown that. And Teela had proved it many times. Her mother was the only person Teela said goodbye to before leaving with Keeana. They obeyed the letter and began the journey as soon as possible.

Evening was a little while away, as they walked through a green and brown, healthy forest. Its name in Keeana's language was, Strolling Trees. The drawings of the mountains on the letter, they had decided meant they needed to head towards the mountains who lined the *edge of nature*. Reignthorl meaning Nature. And, the edge of the Nature Kingdom is where they would find the home of the fighters of old. Teela had not seen this home before. She was sure of that. She didn't know where to look. Keeana had suggested that maybe it was an arena or coliseum where battles would have happened. She had also suggested that it could just be a house where a bunch of fighters had once lived? Who knew…

"Do you know why this forest is called Strolling Trees?" asked Keeana, having stripped off her layers of clothing much time ago. There were some of

Teela's friends' clothes in her bag. Teela's friend being more Keeana's size. Teela had *borrowed* the items of clothing without asking but she knew that was fine. Her friend may not even notice.

"It is called that, I believe…because people stroll here," replied the Deiyahlu woman.

Keeana chuckled a little and nodded her head. "It's a nice place to stroll."

"Yes, it is." It was quiet for a little bit. Keeana suddenly felt doubt and questions creep into her head. She felt as if her faith was being attacked. As quickly as possible, she pushed it away and blocked it out until she forgot about it.

"You're very lucky to have your mother," said Keeana out of the blue.

Teela smiled and said, "Thank you." It was quiet for a few seconds.

"You must be a good daughter," the Rogue continued.

"Why?" asked Teela smiling.

"Well…for your mum to trust you so blindly. I don't know if anyone trusts me like that. Actually maybe some of my friends. I don't know."

"That doesn't mean you shouldn't trust me. You should. I am completely trustworthy I promise," she added quickly.

Teela chuckled. "I do. I feel that I can trust you."

"Okay, good." Keeana watched, as a small, brown monkey leapt from one tree to another. Then another came into easy view. But this one stopped and dropped to the floor. It walked towards them.

"Yes, Bonku?" asked Teela.

"What are you doing?" asked the black monkey. He eyed Keeana with bright-yellow eyes.

"Strolling," replied the purple being.

Keeana was shocked. All the other animals that had past nearby had been making normal animal noises. Could they all also speak her language?

"And who are you?"

"Keeana," answered Keeana.

"A nice name."

"Thank you."

"Has your curiosity been fed?" asked Teela.

"No. Where do you come from?" he asked, his eyes on Keeana.

"Don't answer that," said Teela. "Leave now, Bonku."

"Fine." He left.

Teela stayed still for a little bit, searching her surroundings.

"Don't talk about anything you wouldn't want other beings to know in here," she whispered. They began to walk again.

"I'm assuming he's someone no one trusts?" asked the Rogue quietly.

"For good reason," answered the Deiyahlu woman quietly. "If you ever spot him following us, tell me. He has an ill mind."

The Rogue nodded, then asked, "Do all the animals speak my language?"

"No," said she with a smile, finding Keeana's expression amusing. "Only few of them do around here."

The pale being nodded and smiled. "I like it here," she said, after a couple of seconds of quiet. "It's so nice to be in warm weather again."

They exited the forest and started walking across land which was slightly more open. There were still trees and the like but there was more space between them. Keeana wasn't sure if she was just imagining it but she thought that maybe everything had changed shade ever so slightly. The green was slightly different here than it was in the Strolling Trees. She could see the birds flying above her now and she could see what lay far ahead. It looked as if the land dropped down suddenly.

Later, she found out that indeed it did. She was standing at the top of a very steep rocky slope, looking down. She could see what was likely a river below, not too far away. But before that was a mess of what she would describe as, 'tangled land'.

"This looks weird," she decided, looking to Teela with a small smile. Teela nodded in reply. "I mean it looks like the land just dropped off," she continued. The Rogue nudged a rock with her foot. It easily moved and went rolling down the slope.

"Stay close to each other," said Teela. "Side by side."

Keeana eyed the Deiyahlu woman's bare feet nervously before they both stepped onto the slope. Both of them immediately went sliding. They nearly grabbed each other but didn't. The ground beneath and close to them was sliding down with them. They were picking up pace. Small stones were springing away from them as they slid. Teela dodged bigger rocks with ease but Keeana had more trouble doing so. She managed to hop over one but her landing wasn't smooth. She was off balance now. One of her feet hit another rock. This one didn't budge. Teela tried to grab her but failed. She went twirling and tumbling down the rest of the way…

She woke lying in soft grass, near to a river. She let out a small moan in pain, as she tried to sit up. Teela had already tended to her wounds – she could heal as good as Eyla, the elf could heal – everywhere including her face was scratched up. She felt around her head and felt more than one large bump. Doubt and embarrassment slithered with strength around her head.

"You will be well," said Teela. "Your clothes will be less well."

Keeana managed a smile. "I can't believe I messed up at…the first small challenge."

"Don't be silly," said Teela. "That was unexpected."

Keeana nodded silently. "I wish I had your skin," she said after a moment, eyeing the purple beings undamaged feet.

"It is a benefit." She smiled.

While Keeana rested for a little bit of time, Teela paddled slowly back and forth in the river, clearing and smoothing the riverbed out with her feet. Her doing this revealed something that glinted ever so slightly. She noticed it and bent down. When she tried to pick it up, she realised there was more to it. She cleared the ground around it and saw that it was maybe a handle to something. She pulled. It didn't budge. She pulled harder and still it didn't budge. She pulled harder and twisted, her feet shuffling around. The metal handle twisted and moved upwards. It clicked. Something moved in the corner of her eye. The grass beside the river was moving. The ground was moving. She looked to Keeana. She too had noticed it. The Rogue walked over, limping only a little. They both looked into the hole that had appeared. The metal handle twisted and moved back down. The hole began to close.

"Now…the letter told me to be wise," said Teela with a smile.

"It told me to be brave. And I think the brave thing to do is to go in and have a look around. It did say there would be more. Maybe this is some of that more."

The Deiyahlu woman nodded. "We should definitely go in."

"Very good," said the Rogue chuckling.

Teela went to get a torch from her bag. A torch being one of the many things the Deiyahlu people had discovered in faraway places, over the years, and thought were handy things. She threw it to Keeana and put her bag on her back. Then she grabbed Keeana's bag and gave it to her. "It's probably good for us to keep these close," she said.

"Probably," said the green-eyed young woman, glad she had Teela with her. Otherwise, she would have been straight down there, forgetting about everything she might need to survive.

The dark-blue haired young woman went to twist and pull the handle once more.

They both quickly one after the other disappeared down the hole and started climbing down the wooden ladder.

Keeana climbed below Teela, torch facing down, eyes looking down. A couple of moments passed before the torches light revealed the stone ground below. When they reached the ground, they stepped off the ladder, walked through what could have been a rocky corridor for a number of seconds, then they walked through something that could have possibly been a circular entrance to something. And indeed it was. A single Elleth lamp lit up as they entered, revealing the stonewall ahead. Upon it was an engraving of a horse running. It had riders gear but no rider. In the middle of the room was the wooden wheel of a boat, attached to more wood which seemed to stretch down into the ground. Keeana turned for the torch to reveal more of the room. Other engravings decorated the walls. Teela decided to take the letter out of her bag. She wanted to look over and read it again. Before they could figure anything out, the Elleth lamp turned off and a circular stone fell, filling up the entrance. It was pitch dark except for the torch light. They could hear…movement? Stones moving? Mechanisms working? Keeana unsheathed a sword which Teela had given her before they began the journey. It was straight, light and simple. It was not a long sword, neither was it a short one. Teela too unsheathed a sword. Wholly, deep-violet eyes were watching them now, hidden in darkness. The being could see them clearly. The letter he could see clearly. It intrigued his always buzzing mind. He crept closer and closer. Closer and closer. His feet were circular, their middles so arched that only his nine flat toes – on each foot – touched the ground. He was silent even without the spell he had cast upon himself as a precaution. He watched Teela's hand…Malef leapt. He grabbed the letter successfully. There was a small tear but that was all. After Teela's shouts, Keeana frantically shone the torch around the room. Malef was able to look over and read the letter at an unnaturally fast speed. Then he darted and placed it on Teela's foot. He then left the room. The sounds of movement? Stones moving? Mechanisms working? returned. Then the Elleth lamp lit up again and the stone which had blocked the entrance suddenly dropped beneath the floor. The segment immediately sealed back up. The two young women could hear noises below. Teela had the now dirty, a little beaten looking letter back in her hands. They both swiftly decided it was best to get out of there and get walking again as quickly as possible. They were able to do this with no further trouble.

Back above, as they travelled on at a fast pace, it was quiet for a while…Keeana found herself wondering about the dream Teela had mentioned possibly seeing her in. She didn't ask though. Dreams being the very private, personal things that they were.

Night soon arrived. The breeze was still warm. There was such a pleasant atmosphere beneath the trees of this forest that the two young women began to feel a little peaceful again. Their bellies fed, their legs rested. Their fear and agitation which was keeping them wide-awake had been slowly melting off and now sleepiness was coming closer and closer.

In the midmorning the next day, Teela and Keeana were walking through yet another forest. This one was particularly intriguing with its hot colours. The leaves of the trees were all hot red and yellow, some a mix of red and yellow making them an orange which Keeana found pleasing to the eye. The grass was tinged with red also. The Rogue and the Deiyahlu woman wondered what the reasoning for this was. Out of the warm reddy-brown, tinged trunks of trees grew yellow, orange and red flowers, some of which were such a pale-yellow they were practically white. Some flowers were large, some small. Some had petals dangling down to the floor, others had bodies which grew up and up and up into the canopies. Bees buzzed, squirrels scurried, deer and stag cautiously watched, wild horses occasionally came close though sadly not close enough to touch. Keeana spotted a few red and black bees. They looked a little sinister. There were squirrels with hot yellow and orange coats. They looked a little odd. She saw a gorgeous warm red horse. And a similar coloured stag, looking noble and mighty. She liked this kingdom very much.

"I think I'll move somewhere nearby when I'm older," said the Rogue with a smile. Teela returned the smile and nodded. "I will build you a house."

The Rogue raised her eyebrows and asked, "Have you built a house before?"

"Not completely by myself. But I think I would be able to if I had to. A good, sturdy one."

"Sounds good to me."

"Wonderful. A tree house? Or a house on the ground?"

"Tree. As long as it doesn't fall out of the tree."

"It would never. It would be masterfully built. Our tree houses are built to stay."

Keeana took a swig of water. "I look forward to it."

Meanwhile, as the young ladies chatted, following at a distance was a pitch black bodied, deep-violet eyed, two legged, four armed being whose name was, Malef. He was not enjoying himself. But he couldn't do anything about the power of intrigue and the lure of mystery. He had his theories, his guesses, his questions and answers. Who knew which ones were wrong and which ones right. Some he had confidence in, others less so. The best thing at the moment for him to do was to follow these two young women and see where they took him. Then the puzzle could be solved. Maybe they would lead him to somewhere, something special. He had already searched through their stuff in the night. Sadly, there were no other clues. Just the letter.

Chapter 4
A Brief Chat with
a Stranger

"Hello, sir," said Follar, Thui's father, when the wizard had come too.

"Ugh, Um…what happened? Where am I?"

"You fainted, sir."

"Fainted? Really?"

"Yes, well, my children didn't knock you out," he said with a friendly laugh. "They told me that after you came through that portal of yours you just collapsed."

"Oh…that's strange. But it is possible. It was the biggest jump I have ever done before."

"Jump?"

"Urr, yes. That's what I call it when I travel using portals."

"Ah okay. How are you feeling?"

"A bit of a headache but that's all."

"Very good. So what is your reason for coming here?"

"Oh umm. I. Just. Just wanted to see this part of the world. I never have before. Not really. My curiosity and intrigue brought me here. I am a traveller."

Follar nodded. "Well, we're sorry that we don't have room for you to stay here."

The wizard nodded. "That's okay. I will go searching." Persule – the wizard – felt like this humanoid squirrel did not want him here.

Suddenly, the door to the living room swung open and in came, Wufe, the youngest of the Jerilak family, Thui's youngest brother. Follar's youngest son.

"The others told me I couldn't go in here!" said the young multi-coloured one. "So I proved them wrong!" Suddenly, the young Squihu disappeared.

Thui took him outside. "What are you doing, you…nincompoop," he said quietly.

"You're just jealous you didn't stop me."

"Jealousy's the wrong thing."

"Why?" asked Wufe.

"Because it doesn't make sense in this situation."

"You're not making sense. You stupid bint."

The red Squihu's eyes widened. "Where did you hear that? You can't say that."

"I heard it from Hurlay."

"Right, well don't say it again for a few years."

"Why?"

"Because it's the right thing to do."

"Is it?"

"Yes."

"How do you know?"

"Because I'm…smart."

"Right."

"Good. Are you finished?"

"Finished with what, you silly bint?"

"Man…"

Laedy walked out of the cabin door and spotted Thui and Wufe on the grass ahead. A neither small nor large number of other beings were playing, messing and practicing, all dotted around the place.

"Hello, pinky," said Wufe excitedly with a bow as she came close.

"Hello, little one. How are you doing?" she asked.

"Very good," he replied.

"But did you disobey the rules?" she asked, looking at him with a disappointed expression on her face.

"Yes…" he said quietly, his head dropping.

"Will you be doing that again anytime in the future?"

"No," he answered.

Thui raised his hands in the air in disbelief, looking at Laedy with a look that said, *What the hell?* She then replied with a look that said, *I'm a natural.* Thui shook his head. Wufe then trotted away, distracted by a game some young humanoid creatures were playing. He joined them.

"A delinquent chicken," said Thui.

"You're an old hat," said Laedy.

"In space, there is no such thing as age."

"Huh?"

"I do not know." He sighed heavily. Their eyes both went to the wooden deck as the stranger wizard walked off it and into the wood.

"Let's hope he doesn't return to murder anyone," the red one said happily.

Laedy looked at him and said, "Don't be so dark!" He met her eyes in a sleepy manner.

"Oh I'm so sorry," he moaned. "Oh no. Oh dear. Oh aaaahhhhh…" They stared at each other for a little bit.

"You're a bitchy squirrel," commented Laedy.

"You're a bitchy. I'm a morally perfect."

Frejju, Hurlay and Bybot came outside and joined them. "How does everyone feel about walking?" asked Thui, wanting to go on a walk.

"Never again," answered Frejju shaking his head.

"Yes, fine," answered Hurlay.

"I'm not giddy but it'll do," answered Bybot, the monkey.

"Leadeth thy way," answered Lady, gesturing. And so they all began to walk. Wufe spotted them, whizzed up to them and joined them, leaving the group he was playing with without saying a word.

"Where's my underwear?" he cried.

Frejju looked down at his legs. "Where's my underwear?" he too cried.

"We don't wear underwear, you fool," said Hurlay. Wufe began to laugh a lot.

"Phew," murmured the yellow one.

"Can we go in a cave?" asked Wufe once he had stopped laughing.

"No," replied Hurlay in a very serious way.

"Sure," said Thui.

The multi-coloured one looked to Hurlay.

"Obviously that's fine. I was clearly joking," the white one said.

"It was not clear," commented Frejju slowly, with wide eyes and raised eyebrows.

"Urgh." She waved her hand in exasperation.

"Cave!" the youngest pointed.

"No. I've been in that one a number of times," Hurlay told.

"You're a terrible being."

"I will shave you."

The youngest looked at her with a shocked expression.

"I went into an intriguing one not long ago, not too far away. I will guide us there. May the wind be up our butts," Bybot decided. Wufe began to laugh a lot again.

They entered the cave. Frejju, Wufe and Thui began to glow, on purpose. First, they made their way down quite a steep slope. Then it mostly flattened out and they found themselves curving left. After this, having previously ignored a few entrances, leading off, they reached a dilemma. Three passageways sat around them. "Let's split up," said the youngest.

"I have been down the right one," said the monkey. "I have not fully explored the right one though. I wish to go down the left one."

"Okay," said Thui. "How about me, Wufe and Laedy go down the middle. And you guys may decide amongst yourselves."

"Left," said Bybot.

"What if I wish to go right?" asked the white one.

"What if I wish to go down none of them?" asked Frejju.

Thui, Laedy and Wufe walked through the middle one. The sounds of the others voices slowly died out.

They walked down what most definitely were old, manmade stairs. "Intriguing stuff," commented Thui. The ground then was flat and actually 'rather smooth'. It led them onwards then down. Suddenly, they found themselves standing on the edge of 'a cliff', as Wufe described it. The ceiling was high. More ground lay ahead, beyond the empty darkness that was directly in front of them. Some kind of pulley system sat over there, all alone. Below was black. Running water could be heard.

"It is our duty to get over there," declared Wufe.

"We're not risking you dashing along the walls though," told the red one. "Laedy?" he asked.

"Yes. Easy," she replied. She got on one knee and placed her hands on the edge of *the cliff.* Sunset pink light started to stretch over the drop. It stretched and stretched until it reached the other side. It sat there in place, glimmering enchantingly. Wufe eyed it with wide eyes. It didn't look completely solid. He hopped, skipped and jumped across, making it to the other side and clambering upon the pulley system. Thui was next. Then Laedy.

"Vanish." She demanded with a click of her fingers. The bridge obeyed. They walked on and quickly found themselves entering another circular entrance…

To be continued…